Chronicles of Leight
Book One

Fallen Son

By Evan Kelling

Chapter 1

From the moment you're born, you're always told that there's no such thing as monsters. There's a primal, deep-set fear of what goes bump in the night. We can't help it, and it isn't necessarily an irrational fear either. Our brains are hardwired to fear the dark, or rather, what lies in wait within it. It's a survival instinct that got early man through the darkest of times. Nowadays, that fear doesn't serve us much purpose. You're not going to get randomly mauled by a bear walking down the street at 8 o'clock at night. Unless you're just very, very unlucky. Yet, we still fear the dark. Maybe it's just something left over by evolution. Or as I'd come to learn, there is still something lurking under the cloak of darkness.

Oh, I should probably back up quite a bit there. My name is Tobias Caesar Leight. I am, sorry, *was* your normal sixteen-year-old high school student. I slacked off in class, went bowling with my friends, and spent way too much time on the internet and playing video games. This all started right as the second semester of my junior year began. Welcome to my story. You might want to buckle up.

I found myself waking up a bit earlier than usual. Through the blurry haze of those first waking moments, I turned to look at the clock. 5:58 a.m. I growled contemptuously at the alarm clock. There's nothing like waking up just a few minutes before your alarm is about to go off, especially on a Monday. It's the ultimate insult and the worst way to start the week. Getting up in the morning is probably one of the most mountainous tasks you can put on a teenager. Your body feels like it's made of lead. Of course, if I just lay down, my alarm would blare like a tornado siren and my hearing would never be the same. With the will of a mighty warrior, I heaved the dead weight of my body up into a sitting position and disabled my alarm before it went off. I wiped the gunk out of my eyes and stretched my arms until my body shuddered.

I finally stumbled out of bed and made my way downstairs toward the kitchen. My apartment was fairly small, but it didn't need to accommodate many people. The stairs were directly in front of the front door, and directly adjacent to them was the living room. A couch and a recliner faced a television that was on the wall opposite the stairs. A bookshelf lined the tiny portion of the wall next to the door. Next to the living room was the small kitchen which was just big enough to accommodate the basic appliances, the fridge, stove, sink, and so on.

"Good morning." A voice coming from the small living room said.

To my surprise, my uncle, Bishop, was already awake. He sat in his recliner, sipping on coffee, and reading the paper. Very stereotypical. Bishop was tall, over six feet. He had a permanent five o'clock shadow and had a Mister Fantastic look going on with his hair, black speckled with grey. My uncle was an early riser, he'd probably been up for an hour. He was already fully dressed in a plaid dress shirt and jeans. His eyes were brown, but when he was angry, I swore they turned purple.

"Uh, mornin'." I mumbled, almost incoherently.

"You're up early," Bishop said. "Eager to start back up at school?"

I scoffed in response.

"Mmm, fair." He mumbled before drinking from his mug. "Don't forget, you've got training today as well."

"Yeah, yeah I know." I groaned. I glanced over at my duffel bag, which was stuffed with martial arts equipment, including my gi and gloves. The bag had plenty of wear and tear after years of use, and some of the seams were starting to come apart.

"But remember, school and homework are a priority. If I find out your grades are slipping, I'm pulling you out of your martial arts." Bishop flipped a page in his newspaper. "Make sure to take out Scout before you leave."

At the mention of his name, my dog, Scout, poked his head from behind the recliner. Scout was a German Shepherd whom we had adopted a couple of years ago as a puppy. Now he stood a little past my knees. Scout usually spent his time lounging around or going on walks with Bishop, among other doggy things, but I swear, there was something about the way he looked at you. It's like he was trying to say something with a glance.

"Yeah, I'll go ahead and do it right now. I got time." I nodded. "Scout, come on."

Scout sneezed and then rose to his feet, coming to my heel. I walked with him out of the apartment towards the frost-spotted grass outside. It was pretty cold. My apartment was located in the suburbs surrounding Seattle, and in January, you'd be lucky to break 50 degrees. My thin pajama pants and T-shirt didn't do much to keep me warm either. I rubbed my arms and blew warm breath into my hands in an attempt to keep warm. Lucky for me, Scout wasn't one to take his time. He took care of his business and trotted over towards me.

Scout walked at my heel as we made our way back to the apartment and out of the cold. The grass was laced with frost and made a satisfying crunching noise as we walked. The cold had definitely woken me up fully, and I could feel my body getting jittery as it tried to stay warm. That's when I noticed that the crunching of Scout's paws on the frosty grass seemed to stop. Puzzled, I stopped in place and turned around to look behind me. Scout had stopped a few feet away from where I was. His head was low, and his eyes were locked onto a cluster of bushes and trees. Scout let out a low growl, something that would be barely audible to humans. Now that was strange, Scout rarely growled. At least, not in an aggressive way. I followed his line of sight to the greenery. There was a spot where the greenery seemed to be displaced, as if something was standing within the hedges and bushes, but for the life of me I couldn't actually see anything. But the longer I stared at the spot, the more I got this weird, disturbing feeling in the back of my mind. I could feel goosebumps beginning to lace my skin, and I started to feel sick.

I didn't want to stay out long enough to find out whatever was hiding in there. Probably some big cat or something. "Scout!" I snapped and slapped my thigh to catch his attention.

With reluctance, the dog made his way over to me. He never took his eyes off of the spot. I nearly had to drag him by his collar to get him inside. I let him inside and took one last look over my shoulder towards the bushes. Whatever had given me that weird feeling, it was gone now. Maybe I had gotten more paranoid without those last two minutes of sleep. That was definitely what it was.

Scout trotted over back to his spot near Bishop's recliner and laid down, poking his head up and sniffing towards my uncle. Bishop absent-mindedly put his hand on the dog's head and scratched behind his ears. Bishop mumbled something but I couldn't make it out. I suppose it wasn't important enough for me to hear. It didn't matter, I had to get ready for school.

I went through my morning ritual like always. I showered for about fifteen minutes or so, listening to music as I did. I always felt so much better after a shower. Saying I felt clean was not only obvious, but an understatement. I never knew how to explain it. After running shampoo through my brown hair, I finished showering and brushing my teeth, then returned to my room to get dressed. Most of my clothes consisted of jeans and T-shirts with various pop culture icons on them. Everything from video games to TV shows to movies. Today, I decided on a T-shirt with the Thundercats logo and a pair of weathered jeans, secured with a seatbelt belt with symbols representing the Justice League members around my waist. I pulled my pair of Converse on and tied them tight. Standing up, I grabbed my backpack from the corner of my room and made my way back downstairs.

"Alright Uncle Bishop, I'm outta here for the day." I said, waving to him from the door.

"Okay, Tobias." He smiled, setting his newspaper down. "Stay safe, and keep warm."

I grabbed my sweater from the back of the front door and slipped into it as quickly as possible. With that, I made my way out into the cold.

I arrived at King's View High School with ten minutes to spare. The school was fairly typical of what you would expect. It was made up of several large buildings, the largest of which stood front and center on the block. Brick stairs led up to the main building with glass doors, large text with the school's name, and two flags waving on poles at the base of the small set of stairs, one being the American flag and the other being the Washington state flag.

Among the scattered teens trying to keep warm were two of my friends, a short girl standing on the second step to stand evenly with a large, brawny guy. Her name was Claire Williams, she was a junior like me. She wore a big, baggy gray sweater with the Seattle University logo on it, and a pair of black skinny jeans. Her golden locks were up in a messy bun. Her glasses were slightly fogged from her breath, and they sat upon a small, cute nose that was dotted with faded freckles. Beside her was my best friend Jacob Lewis, he was a pretty large guy, almost like the Juggernaut had a baby. His skin was the color of bronze and he had dark, curly hair to match. He had small, alert eyes and a big honker of a nose that the unwise would tease him about. He was built like a tree, and it made me happy to know he was a gentle giant. I'd hate to see him angry.

"Toby!" Claire ran over and hugged me, nearly pulling me down to the ground in the process. "How was your Christmas break?"

"Pretty typical," I shrugged. "Just me, my uncle, and the dog, as usual."

Jacob bumped fists with me. "Missed you during the break, man. Hey, did you do the project for English?"

"Uh, yeah, definitely." I scratched my head.

"You didn't do it, did you?" Claire asked, calling my bluff immediately.

"Well, I started it." I sighed.

"What am I going to do with you, Toby?" Claire shook her head with her hands on her hips.

"Don't worry, you can use mine as a reference. English isn't until fifth period, anyways." Jacob reached into his bag and handed me a folder.

I took it and tucked it into my own bag. "Appreciate it, I'll get it back to you in time."

The first bell rang, echoing throughout the block. With my friends by my side, we headed into the second half of our junior year. Little did I know it would hardly be a normal semester, or rest of my life, for that matter.

My first class was History. As a message to all high schools, never put History or Math as someone's first period. We, as teenagers, are simply not capable of committing ourselves to these subjects before noon. I was gonna use the time to finish my English project, but I ended up dozing off, almost immediately.

I don't usually have vivid dreams, but I suppose there's a first time for everything. My vision was blurry but slowly came into focus. I found myself in a dark, concrete room. Besides five candles in the center of the room, there was no light. Not even a window or a lamp. That's when I noticed the five candles dotted the points of a star drawn in some sort of red substance. Paint, I think? But judging by the smell, I had a feeling it wasn't. The air was thick with a metallic scent that made me scrunch my nose. The five points of the star breached a circle that closed around the center of the star, etched with strange symbols that honestly looked like the scribbling of a child. What the hell kind of dream did I come up with for myself? I wasn't really one to watch horror movies or anything like that, so this was even more strange. As the thought passed through my mind, the strange markings in the circle erupted into a fiery light as disembodied voices began chanting in a language I didn't recognize. The candles flared with flames too intense for any candle to produce, and the floor within the circle seemed to swirl and distort. The chanting began to grow louder and more intense.

That's when a new voice rose up above the rest. It came from the swirling center of the circle. It started off as a growl, but then it spoke. "Let...me...out!" The voice was deep and gravelly, and it had a distorted echo to it. A clawed hand erupted from the swirling mess and gripped the solid ground. The arm was far too skinny and had way too many joints to be human. The skin was charred and burned like it had been set on fire. The fingers themselves were much too large for the hand attached and the claws dug into the concrete floor like it was made of paper. "You! Let. Me. OUT!" A white light flashed as a snapping sound erupted in my ears.

I shot up from sleep with so much force my desk shook as my knees jolted in surprise. My history teacher stood in front of me, her ruler pressed firmly against my desk, as if she'd just smacked it. She was an ancient woman, old enough that I wouldn't be surprised if she was in one of the later chapters of my history book. She adjusted her large-framed glasses and looked at me with disdain. "Mr. Leight, I know the Boston Tea Party isn't the most engaging subject, but I would appreciate it if you didn't disrupt my class with your rumbling snores."

Several chuckles erupted from around me as I wiped away some drool that had dried on my cheek. "Uh, I'm sorry, Mrs. O'Neill."

I shook my head, trying to shake away the image of my dream. Though, no matter how hard I tried, the image seemed to be burned into the back of my mind. What had that been about? Even in my wildest dreams, as scarce as they were, had never been so bizarre, so disturbing. Dwelling on it would get me nowhere though, and eventually I just tried to let it fade to obscurity, as hard as that was.

My day proceeded as normal, from that point. I went through the motions of my next couple of classes, and after fourth period, I got to go to lunch. I wasn't super big on eating during the day. I usually ate before school, and then after. Eating food when I was at school tended to make me a bit lethargic and sleepy, so I would only have a couple snacks throughout the day. I found a spot in the lunchroom that would accommodate myself and my friends and got comfortable, unwrapping a granola bar. I munched on it, absentmindedly, while I waited for my friends to arrive. Jacob was the first to make his way over to me. He held a lunch tray with a foil-wrapped burger that had probably been frozen for months, along with a baggy of apple slices, and an orange juice.

"You know, you should really start eating during the day." Jacob commented as he squeezed onto the bench. He set his tray down and opened his apple slices up. He crunched into a slice, and then looked over at me. "You done with your English project yet?"

"Oh, yeah. Thanks again." I pulled his homework out of my bag and handed it over. He set it aside, focusing on his apple slices. "Hey, have you ever had any weird dreams?"

"I mean, yeah sure." Jacob gestured with his half-eaten apple slice thoughtfully. "Like showing up to school in my underwear, or that I'm Donald Trump. Stuff like that, right?"

I chose not to acknowledge the absurdity I'd just heard and shook my head. "I was thinking more along the lines of, extremely spooky. Demonic cult-type stuff."

Jacob stopped mid-chew and gave me a look. The kind that precedes putting someone in a straitjacket. "Uh, no. Can't say I have. Why, did you have a dream like that?"

I took another bite of my granola bar. "Yeah, I dozed off in history. It was really strange. There were some strange symbols painted on the floor, like something out of the occult. And there was a voice asking me, no, demanding that I let it out."

Jacob let out a nervous chuckle. "Dude, you need to lay off the scary movies. Halloween was like three months ago." He'd finished his apple slices and had unwrapped his burger.

I chewed on my granola bar thoughtfully. Jacob knew I wasn't one to watch horror movies, if I could avoid it. I was a wimp when it came to that type of stuff. "Yeah, I guess so."

"Hey guys!" Claire's voice called over to us. She approached us with a brown paper bag in hand and sat down next to me. She began unpacking the sack, and it was full of typical lunch items, a sandwich, some chips, fruit snacks, and a Capri Sun. "How's your guys' first day going?" Her voice was full of life and cheer, she had a way of lighting up the room just by walking in the door.

"Well, Tobias here is officially going crazy." Jacob laughed. "He's having dreams about demons and the occult."

I kicked Jacob in the shin, though not very hard. I'd learned from experience, Jacob might as well have been made of steel, which lends itself well to my Juggernaut analogy.

Plus, it wasn't really meant to hurt him, of course. "Probably just too much sugar before bed or something. I tore through one of those extra big bags of M&M's before bed last night." I laughed.

Claire clicked her teeth. "You and sugar, I swear." She rolled her eyes playfully. "Hey, you guys wanna catch a movie or something after school?"

"I'd be down." Jacob said through a mouthful of microwaved meat.

"I can't," I said. "I have martial arts almost right after school. I don't have time for anything in between."

"Oh yeah, our very own Bruce Lee, over here." Jacob chuckled.

"I wouldn't go that far. I'm not that talented." I shrugged.

"Well, we wouldn't want to distract you from becoming a badass," Claire said. "Who knows, maybe you can save me from a mugger or something, someday." She winked, I did my best not to blush, but hey, when a girl as beautiful as her winks at you like that, the response is just automatic.

After lunch, I was preparing to head to my next class, when Mrs. O'Neill stopped me in the hall. "Tobias, where have you been? The whole class has been looking for you." She lectured.

I gave her a puzzled look. "Uh, at lunch?"

Mrs. O'Neill gave me an exasperated look and shook her head. "Did you really forget about the field trip today?"

Field trip? It wasn't ringing a bell.

"Uh, no." I said, very intelligently.

She touched a hand to her forehead lightly. "The field trip to the Burke Museum of Natural History? To see the new exhibit of old artifacts found in Europe?"

Something in my brain clicked and I slapped my forehead with my palm. "Right, I'd completely forgotten. Sorry, Mrs. O'Neill, it's been a weird day."

Mrs. O'Neill made a tsk tsk sound at me and shook her head. "Well come along, everyone has been waiting for you." She turned on the spot and began walking down the hall.

Well, at least I was free from classes for the day. I jogged for a moment to catch up and we made our way to the bus drop-off.

Chapter 2

I hate school buses. They're cramped and musty. They smell of teenagers who don't know how to properly apply deodorant. And why the hell don't they have seatbelts? I don't care what the science says, I'd take a seatbelt over super compact seats any day of the week.

And I don't know what it is about teenagers and school buses, but they just don't know how to just chill out and relax. Everyone turns into spazzy, vulgar cartoon characters as soon as they set foot on the bus.

Yikes. I'm starting to sound old.

The Burke Museum of Natural History is a large rectangular building near the University of Washington. It was a very large yet understated building with large windows on each side. Mrs. O'Neill herded us out of the bus and in front of the museum's entrance.

Students chattered excitedly, surely at the thought of learning about priceless fossils and artifacts. Mrs. O'Neill shushed us all with notable effort. It was surprising she didn't go crazy trying to shut us all up every day, let alone outside of school.

I took a deep breath and then at the top of my lungs yelled. "Shut up!"

That caught everyone's attention. There were a few more murmurs but they'd gotten the message. Mrs. O'Neill gave me a disciplinary look but gave me a nod that was most definitely a show of thanks.

"Alright, now students. We're here for the new European artifacts and mythology exhibit." Mrs. O'Neill explained. "We'll be passing through several other exhibits. But I must stress this point; Don't. Touch. Anything. Understood?"

There was a murmur of affirmative answers, but one look around showed me a few devious looks on my fellow students' faces. I rolled my eyes. We made our way through the museum, and I did my best to subtly coast back and forth around the group of students to keep them away from the more expensive-looking exhibits. It worked out in my favor because I was genuinely interested in what the museum had to show off.

There was a pretty awesome saber tooth tiger skeleton. It was mostly educated guesses of bones with a few genuine articles thrown in for authenticity. You'd be pretty hard-pressed to find an entire skeleton fully preserved. It was posed as if it were about to strike down with one of its claws.

As we made our way toward the back of the museum the exhibits slowly turned into stuff you might see at a renaissance fair. At the entrance to the exhibit were two fully assembled suits of armor. One was a set of chainmail and leathers with a bucket helmet with two slits for eyes and holes for breathing. On the cloth chest piece was the symbol of a standing bear.

The other set of armor was something more typical when you thought of a knight. Armored plating head to toe, a visor that you could open up to see better. Under it was more chainmail where the wearer would need more flexibility. It was pretty cool looking, I had to say.

Mrs. O'Neill told us the history and purpose behind various artifacts as we passed by them. There were old sets of clothes, tapestries, and tools the old Europeans used in their day to day lives. Most of it was mundane junk that didn't actually hold much significance. In the back of the exhibit was their centerpiece, a boulder about three feet tall that sat on a pedestal. Embedded in the stone about halfway in was a shining iron sword with an ornate jewel-encrusted hilt.

"And the finale of our visit today, the legend of King Arthur." Mrs. O'Neill said dramatically. She waggled her fingers for added effect. No one seemed to be impressed.

"King Arthur was a legendary king of Britain who defended the kingdom from some of the most dangerous enemies the nation had known in its early days, or so the legends say. His most famous weapon against his enemies was the legendary sword of Excalibur. With it, he was said to cleave mountains and split bodies of water in half. When all else failed, he would take the field against his enemies. But it was not the only weapon he had to defend Britain."

Mrs. O'Neill ushered us past the sword in the stone to several pedestals grouped together with several cups, each radically different from the last. At the center was an overly large goblet with glass sides and gems and jewels lining every inch of the golden base. Surrounding it were several other more modest cups. A clay bowl that didn't exactly seem like a cup. A simple wine glass that was tall and thin. A much wider but still modest chalice made of wood.

"The Holy Grail, a mysterious artifact of unknown origin. There are many stories about where it came from. Some say it was created by the fairies of Old Britain. Others say human wizards crafted it. And even fewer believe it to be the same cup that Jesus Christ drank from during the Last Supper. It's believed to have amazing powers to heal and strengthen any who drinks from it. It was this cup that King Arthur drank from to give him the power to wield Excalibur."

"What a bunch of nonsense." A dark-skinned student muttered.

Mrs. O'Neill gave him a critical look.

"But that's all just legend, right?" A goth girl with short hair said.

Mrs. O'Neill centered herself and nodded. "Of course, while the legend of King Arthur was an integral part of Britain's history, there simply is not enough historical evidence to suggest King Arthur actually existed."

Students murmured their carefully constructed opinions to themselves. Mrs. O'Neill continued to walk us around the exhibit, spouting more exposition and information about the history of Western Europe. After we'd made a couple laps around the exhibit, it was time to go.

We made our way back to the bus, and by the time it had reached the school, the last bell had already rung. Students were already beginning to rush out of the front entrance. There was nothing left for me to do at school, so I exited the bus and walked down the street.

I made my way home, taking the usual route through the neighborhood surrounding the school towards my apartment complex. As I walked, I felt that sick, disturbing feeling from this morning. I could feel it tickling at the back of my head. I took a few more steps and then stopped. With a swift motion, I turned on my heel, putting my left foot about a step back, and put my fists up, level with my head. My fists were positioned on either side of my head, acting as a tunnel around my vision, while guarding either side of my head.

No one was there. Just me and the melting snow. "Great, first the bad dreams, and now I'm getting paranoid." I shook my head. "If this keeps up, I'm going to end up like one of those tragic-yet-badass characters you see in anime and video games." I took a moment to consider. "And now I'm talking to myself. My descent into madness is worse than I thought." I chuckled nervously.

I made a quick stop at my apartment to drop off my school stuff and grab my training bag, a red and black duffel bag filled to the brim with my various equipment. Bishop and Scout were nowhere to be found. Bishop worked from home, so if he wasn't here, he was more than likely running errands or just walking the dog. Scout pretty much went everywhere with him. I never understood how he could take that dog just about anywhere and no one seemed to notice. I didn't think anything of his absence, hoisting my bag onto my shoulder, and locking the door behind me.

Chapter 3

My martial arts school, or "dojo" I guess, was based in the local YMCA. It was a large gym complex, with a quarter of the main hall being lined with exercise equipment. The adjacent quarter was home to a sectioned off basketball court. With the remaining half being dominated by an artificial soccer field, complete with fake grass and dirt particles, for true immersion. Surrounding the main gym area were several rooms sectioned off for various classes. Spin class, yoga, jazz Pilates, the list went on. Then there was my martial arts class.

The discipline we practiced was called Kajukenbo. It's a mixed martial art developed in the less fortunate neighborhoods of Hawaii. To put it simply, five martial arts masters came together in the late '40s to develop a martial art specifically designed to be functional in the real world, or the streets, I guess you could say. These masters put together the best aspects of Karate, Judo, Jiu Jitsu, Kenpo, and Kung Fu, and created a truly brutal art. I'd been practicing since I was eight years old, and through that practice, I've achieved the rank of brown belt, which was a rank and a half under black. I say rank and a half, because Brown Belts who are close to ranking up to black belt are awarded with a red stripe on their belt, signaling their experience and potential to move up to black.

Given my rank, I often assist in warming up and teaching the class, so I tried to arrive a little early. Before proceeding to the room where class was held, I headed to the locker rooms to change. I found myself in a corner of the room to quickly change out of my normal clothes and into my gi. I stripped and put on the free moving, but heavy pants of my uniform. I put on a maroon shirt with a white logo, a clover of sorts with some other details, on the left pec, and a larger version on the back. I shrugged into the gi top, which was weighted for training purposes, and tied the strings to secure it, crossing one side over the other. I put my belt over my shoulders for convenience and put my regular clothes into my duffel bag. I splashed some water on my face at a nearby sink and walked back towards the classroom. Some of the usual early arrivals showed up, many accompanied by parents, some of which even trained with their younger kids.

The room was lined with mirrors on two of the walls, with large cabinets lining another, and the fourth wall had windows that viewers from the gym side could look in through. In the far corner of the room, where the two mirror walls met, stood my instructor, Sigung Carlos. He wasn't a big guy at all, at least a foot shorter than me. He was of Hispanic descent, with a short goatee and clean-cut black hair. Sure, he was small, but he was pure muscle. I didn't know anyone who'd want to pick a fight with him. He wore a gi like mine but weathered by time and experience. A black belt with red lining hung around his neck. Upon seeing me, he inclined his head in greeting, and I walked over.

"Tobias!" He said, a hint of cheer in his voice. He offered his hand, holding it out in front of his chest.

"Sir, good to see you!" I gripped his hand, and we pulled each other into a firm embrace, like how a couple of guys would. He'd seen me grow up over the last nine years or so. He was a sort of father figure, I suppose.

"Lead the warm-up today, and then we're going straight into sparring." He spoke.

"Sounds good." I glanced at the clock. It was just about time to get the class started. I cleared my throat and projected my voice. "Alright, let's go! Line up!"

The class, filled with people from ages five to fifty-five all lined up, higher ranks and older students in the back two rows. Being the second highest ranked, besides Sigung, I stood in front of the class, next to him. There were probably around twenty-five people in attendance today. Good sized class.

We bowed in, putting our belts on. The more experienced students put on their belts with practiced motions, while the newer students struggled a bit. The proper knot was a bit odd, so you couldn't blame the newer students. I helped a couple of students put on their belts. We rose, bowed again, and then everyone's attention was on me for the warm-up.

Then training began. I ran the class through the usual warm-up, starting with alternating jumping jacks and burpees. We did knee raises, ran laps, and other exercises to get the blood pumping. After sufficiently getting them moving, we winded down a bit by stretching out our legs, arms, and backs. After a brief water break, Sigung and I split the class into two groups for sparring. I primarily took the younger kids and lower ranks, while my instructor took the older folks and higher ranks. We didn't discriminate here, boys fought girls, men fought women, tall fought short, and so on. You never knew who you might have to fight in the real world, and we did our best to train the students for any possibility.

Finally, after countless matchups, it was finally my turn to put the gloves on and go a few rounds. Sigung Carlos paired me with a lower rank guy in his mid-30s, named Ricardo. For his rank he was pretty talented, but my obstacle was his size. He had a few inches on me and a good fifty pounds. I took up my fighting stance, as did he, and the fight began.

He was a patient guy; he didn't need to rush in with the first move. Ricardo knew I would have to attack first. I had to make every move count; I was too small to let myself take too many hits from him. I shuffled forward, feinting with a double jab. He blocked it from hitting him in the nose and went in for a right cross, but I was expecting that. I lunged to the right, leaving him twisted and compromised. I sunk a right hook into his ribs, and I heard an audible grunt. I used the force from my twisted body to unleash a left hook, the tension and momentum enhancing my second strike, and I caught him right in the gut. I didn't want to get greedy though, and I pushed off him, jumping back and forcing him further off balance. He stumbled but managed to right himself.

He couldn't let my attack go unchecked though, and he moved in to strike. I lunged to his right again, but he had expected that. It was my go-to move, being right-handed and all, and he swung his arm towards my temple. I should've been ready for it, but I let my guard down. My head rocked and vision flashed with white as his fist hit my temple. I was able to keep my footing, but I was stunned long enough for him to get a front kick into my groin. I gasped at the pain, as any man would. I don't care who you are, it doesn't matter how tough you are, or how big and bad you are, if you get kicked in the family jewels, it's gonna stop you.

He went for a left punch towards my chest, but I deflected it with a block, moving outwards from my body, and leaving his body exposed for an attack. I hit him with two punches in the chest and kneed him in the groin, then leaned into a third punch that sent him stumbling onto his backside.

"Break!" Sigung called, and we ceased the fight.

I offered my hand to Ricardo, and he accepted it. I helped hoist him to his feet, and we bowed to each other, then

Sigung. I had a few more rounds with a couple of the higher ranks, but soon, it was time to go home. Class was wrapped up, and the students dispersed. I said my goodbyes to Sigung Carlos and a couple friends from class and left the classroom. I was too exhausted to change out of my uniform, so I just threw my gi top into my duffel bag and began the walk home.

The sun had just set by the time I left, and the temperature had dropped significantly. The cold felt good against my bruises and scratches. I walked slowly past the suburbs surrounding the YMCA, and soon found myself on the main streets again, passing by various grocery stores, fast food places, and other smaller shops. It took me a moment, but I soon realized that the streets were oddly empty. Sure, there was the occasional car, but not nearly as many as there should be. Where were all the people getting off of work? The teens going out to eat and to the movies and stuff? Even weirder, the streetlights seemed to be strangely dim.

"Aww man, did I just walk into a Stephen King movie?" I said, hoping the joke would calm my nerves. No sooner had the words gotten out of my mouth, that that sick, disturbing feeling hit me again with full force. The streetlights in my immediate vicinity went out, sparking in protest as their lights blew out. All of them, except one. In the cone of light, stood a large man in a trench coat. When I say large, I mean huge. He was well over seven feet tall and was built like an SUV.

Trying not to freak out, I managed to force words out. "Dude, I so don't want anything you're selling."

"Tobias Leight, you will surrender yourself and come with me." The huge man growled. I mean literally growled. His voice came out rough and distorted.

Okay, I was officially freaking out now. I took a nervous step back. "You couldn't afford me, man." I choked out. "Listen, you don't want to do this. I don't want to hurt you."

The man laughed. It was a gross, disturbing sound. "You hurt me? You barely understand what you are, or what's happening here."

"What the hell is that supposed to mean?" I asked, my voice cracking. I set down my duffel bag and prepared for a fight. This guy wasn't a mugger, that was for sure. That sick feeling boring its way into me told me this guy wasn't normal. I felt myself get jumpy with adrenaline. There was no avoiding this fight. I was sore, but far from unable to fight.

Then he took off his coat. And I realized he wasn't a man. I didn't know what it was. As soon as he took the coat off, I was hit by the stench of rotting meat, so grotesque that it literally made me stumble back. Its body was covered in rippling, raw, rotting muscle. It had a severe hunchback, its head nearly being in the center of its body. Its arms were about as thick as my body was wide, and its knuckles dragged along the ground as it took its first slow step. Its lower legs were reptilian, covered in obsidian scales. Long claws dug into the concrete with each step. It had a long whip-like tail that flicked around as if it had a mind of its own. It had sharp, mismatched teeth of many different sizes and shapes. Its eyes were completely black, except for glowing red beads in their center. Its bestial head was framed by curling ram horns. All I could think to call it was a monster.

No amount of martial arts training could prepare you for something like that. I stood in my fighting stance, but every fiber of my being was shaking in terror. I could barely stand, my legs felt like jelly. My hands felt clammy, and it was hard to keep them in solid fists. The lumbering beast took a step forward, and I nearly fell on my ass.

"Don't get any closer, Igor!" I yelled, my voice cracking. Very cool, I know. I was up there with the great action heroes, James Bond, Captain America, John Wick, Tobias Leight. They'll remember my squeaky voice for generations.

"Tobias Caesar Leight," the creature growled as it took another step forward. "You will come with me. And you will reveal the catalyst to my masters so we can return the Blinding One to this world."

Catalyst? Blinding One? Of all that mumbo jumbo, the scariest thing it had uttered was my full name. My uncle Bishop had this weird rule about never giving my full name to anyone, it wasn't even on my school paperwork. But this thing knew me. "The Blinding One? Is that one of those new age rock stars I keep hearing about? Sorry dude, but I'm not into buying tickets for some indie rock concert." No amount of not-so-witty banter would keep me alive. I was just hoping someone, anyone, would show up and save me from this nightmare. Where was everyone? No people or police were in sight. There was so much wrong with this situation.

The creature no longer seemed interested in entertaining my small talk. And it charged. Holy crap, it came right at me. As undeniable as an oncoming train. It moved way faster than it had any right to. Each lumbering leap shattered the concrete at its feet. But as fast as it was, I was still faster. On pure reflex alone, I rolled out of the way to its right as its enormous fist hit the concrete, sending shards of rock in all directions like a hand grenade had just gone off. Small shards of concrete scratched at my arms and cheek, but it wasn't enough to disable me. Again, on pure reflex and instinct, I threw a punch towards where it's ribs should be. That was a mistake. It was like punching a brick wall and I heard my hand crack against its body and a wave of pure putridness overwhelmed my senses. It dislodged its fist from the crater it had created and swung its arm back around towards me.

I didn't even have a chance to react. It's arm hit home, barreling into my side and sending me flying across the ground for about ten feet or so. I'm not sure, I wasn't exactly counting the inches. I felt a fiery pain erupt in my chest. Well, there goes a rib or two. Dozens of scratches zigzagged across my skin from my stint as a Donkey Kong barrel across the ground.

This had to be a nightmare. I was going to wake up at any time now. I tried to stand but everything in my body protested that attempt. The beast swaggered over slowly. It was like a lion playing with its food. It knew it had won. Whatever it had planned for me would come to pass, and there wasn't a damn thing I could do about it. The monster stood over me, what I assumed was a triumphant smile spread across its misshapen face.

"Time to sleep, boy." It raised its arm to knock me on the head. Who was gonna tell this thing it'd probably kill me in one swing to my noggin? Not me, apparently. I was too stunned and in too much pain to utter anything intelligible.

Through the haze, I could hear heavy footsteps sprinting towards us. Fantastic, he had friends. As if my situation wasn't hopeless enough.

And then something sent this beast sailing through the air and into a nearby convenience store, probably scaring the pants off some poor teenager working the counter. The monster crashed into shelves and scattered chips and candy everywhere. The sound of wrenching metal screeched into the night and the lights in the place started flickering, it had probably crashed into some important electrical wiring on its way in.

"What the-?" I managed to sputter out.

Standing over me was a large man. A rival monster wanting to steal the kill perhaps? No, I knew this person. He was huge, for his age, with large arms and broad shoulders. He was wearing a black hoodie that seemed stretched to the brink by his hulking body. It was the baby Juggernaut. It was Jacob freaking Lewis. What the hell was he doing here? And how the hell did he send that thing flying?

He glanced over his shoulder at me, keeping the convenience store in his peripheral vision. A flicker of motion made him glance back. It was just the convenience store clerk running for his life out of the store. Jacob looked back at me. "Can you stand?" He asked me. Something was different about his voice. It had a strange property to it, like the sound of grating stone.

I couldn't find the words, or maybe I was still too out of it to even begin forming words. My head drifted lazily and my vision was blurring in and out of focus. Out of the corner of my eye, I could see something hurtling towards us. I wanted to warn Jacob of the incoming danger, but my mouth still couldn't make words.

Then without any sign of effort, Jacob focused his attention on the incoming object and caught the convenience store counter like it was a softball, one-handed and everything. He threw it off to the side just in time to see the monster charging at full speed. Jacob braced himself and the two locked hands as they collided. Jacob skidded back a foot or two but sunk his legs into a sturdy base and stared down the monster. Their strength caused their arms to shake against each other involuntarily.

"Foolish guardian," The creature spat. "You have no business here! The boy is my prey!"

The monster used its grip to sweep Jacob off his feet and fling him into a nearby lamppost. Jacob fell to the ground, momentarily dazed, and I swear I saw cracks forming in his skin. The lamppost had been noticeably bent and looked like it was ready to fall over.

"*Tellus!*" Jacob shouted the strange word, and his fist seemed to glow with a strange light. He punched the ground hard enough that it should've broken his hand, and several chunks of concrete, asphalt, and rock erupted from the ground and hung in the air.

That...was something you didn't see every day. With a flick of his wrist, Jacob sent the chunks of stone flying at the creature. They exploded into a million pieces against the monster's body. It let out a roar of shock and pain as it stumbled back.

While the creature was off balance, Jacob did a twisting motion with his hand and yelled "*Descendat deorsum!*" His voice thrummed as he spoke, and I felt a shift in the air. The ground under the creature suddenly liquified and it sunk down up to its neck. It didn't matter how much the creature struggled, it could not escape. Jacob smashed his open palms together and shouted, "*Contundito!*"

The quicksand that had swallowed the creature suddenly surged with movement and I heard an agonizing scream as black blood erupted from the quicksand. In a moment, the ground had returned to its normal solid state. Jacob clasped his hands in a praying gesture, and let out a deep breath. The air around him seemed to relax.

My vision got blurrier. My limbs seemed to grow heavier and less responsive. I was awake just long enough to see Jacob turn to me and answer a call on his phone.

"Bishop, I've got him."

Chapter 4

A bright light startled me as it tried to burn through my eyelids. My body ached and my head felt like someone was driving a stake through it with a hammer. I slowly managed to force my eyes open. My vision was blurry and shaky. I could see a familiar figure at the edge of my vision. The figure moved towards me when he saw me waking up. His voice echoed, coming out distorted and unintelligible.

"Tobias!" Bishop's voice brought me back to reality. My vision focused sharply and suddenly, almost disorienting me.

"Uncle Bishop," My voice came out slurred and thick. "Where am I? What the hell happened?" Then the memories came flooding back to me. The monster in the street, Jacob showing up, the fight, and the ground consuming the creature.

"Wait, where's Jake? How did he make those rocks fly? What the hell was that thing he fought? How did he even fight it?" The questions came out like a machine gun, firing off one after the other.

"Slow down, Tobias." Bishop held his hand up. "You were banged up pretty bad. The doctors are still working on healing your injuries."

The way he phrased that seemed weird to me. I wasn't sure how to explain it. He said it as if my broken ribs, broken hand, and possible concussion were something that could be healed within a matter of minutes. I turned my attention away from my uncle and took a gander at my surroundings. We seemed to be in a forest. I'm not sure how that didn't register until now. I was laying on a typical hospital bed, but leaves and vines seemed to be coming out of the bed, fading into the frame and mattress the closer they got. There was a strange prismatic ball of light, like a miniature sun, floating above us, illuminating the immediate area around us. The forest itself was something out of a fantasy movie. The trees towered high into the sky, though I could not see it. Light peeked through the dense leaves, causing the light to cascade into beautiful sheets. The trees were covered in green moss and vines that seemed to glow faintly. A vine near my bed seemed to morph into a IV that went into my arm. A golden liquid, literally golden, flowed into my veins.

"What is this stuff? Where the hell are we?" I asked Bishop, my hand already motioning to touch the IV to investigate and potentially pull it out.

Bishop put his hand on mine, stopping me. "It's helping with the healing process. Don't touch it. I'll explain everything in a moment." His face was twisted with concern. He looked like he was searching for the right words. "Once Jake is here, we'll explain everything."

The mention of Jacob brought memories flooding back of the fight. My mind was racing with a million questions but not enough words to ask them.

It didn't take much longer for Jacob to arrive. A column of blue light opened up near some wooden steps. It was a door of some kind. The door swung open and the blue light seemed to fade. The door was only visible from the outside, impossible to see from this strange forest hospital. Jacob walked out of the space-bending door, emerging from a pristine white hallway. He swung the white paneled door back and it sealed shut and disappeared, as if it were never there. He was wearing a plain black T-shirt and grey sweatpants. While he was a big guy and I didn't doubt his physical capabilities, I still couldn't picture him as someone who could take on a hulking monstrosity. If I hadn't seen it for myself, I wouldn't have believed it.

"Hey man, glad to see you're on the mend." Jacob said. He definitely seemed nervous. Uncomfortable, really.

"How are you holding up, Jacob?" Bishop asked, with a disturbing level of familiarity. Sure, Bishop and Jacob had met quite a few times, but it's not like they knew each other as anything more than their relation to me. What was I missing here?

"The demon certainly packed quite a punch and it'd been awhile since I was in a fight, but it was nothing I couldn't handle." Jacob rolled his shoulder, as if working out a kink. "Nothing more than a moderate workout, by the end of it."

"Hello?" I said expectantly, my irritation and confusion clearly showing on my face and in my tone of voice. "Can someone give me some damn answers already? You said that thing was a demon? What the hell does that mean? And how could you fight it? Why are you and my uncle speaking like you've known each other for years?" The questions came out in a frenzy, before I could even think to ask them.

Bishop and Jacob exchanged a look, and then my uncle let out a deep sigh. I saw sadness and regret in his eyes.

"Tobias, I'm not entirely sure where to begin." Bishop said, strain in his voice.

"Try the beginning." My voice lashed at him. It came out harsher than I meant it to.

"Very well, there's no way to put this lightly." Bishop nodded his head, as if coming to terms with what he was about to tell me. "You know all those tales of wizards, fairies, and demons I would tell you about as a kid?"

I nodded, urging him to continue. Though my eyebrow was raised skeptically.

"It's real. All of it." Bishop said. "Yesterday, you were stalked by a demon who had intended to kill or kidnap you."

I was stunned. I wanted to laugh in his face and tell him he was absolutely wasted if he thought this story of his was gonna fly. Clearly I had suffered some delusional episode as a result of being a stressed out, hormonal teenager.

"No, I'm not lying." He said, beating me to it.

I let out a nervous chuckle. "Okay, for sake of argument, let's say you're not completely full of it right now. Why would this 'demon' want me? I'm nobody special."

"Tobias, what do you remember of your parents?" He asked me, his voice becoming very serious.

That question seemed out of left field. What did my parents have to do with this? Truth be told, I didn't remember much of my parents. I was very young when they passed, maybe five years old. The only figment of a memory I could bring to light was the thought of my mother's smile. The memory filled me with warmth and comfort, and it made me feel safe. I brought myself out of that line of thought before I got distracted. "Nothing really, they died in a fire before I even started kindergarten."

"Yes, and what did I tell you was the cause of that fire?" Bishop asked me.

"Some freak electrical short?" I tried to recall. It had been ages since I asked about it. I didn't like to remember it.

"Yes. But that was far from the truth." Bishop said. "Yes, there was a fire. But it was no electrical accident." He paused dramatically, the nerve of this guy. "Your parents were murdered. They were murdered because of their heritage, who they were. Your parents were wizards, Tobias. And they passed that onto you."

What was he talking about? My parents were wizards? Like from Harry Potter? Or the Sorcerer's Apprentice? He had to be joking. If he was right, that made me a wizard too. I looked over at Jacob. Is that how he fought that monster? Because he was a wizard too?

"I think you've been hitting the scotch a bit too much, uncle." I said, though I didn't sound too confident.

"If this was just a drunken rant, could I do this? *Igni!*" Bishop said, right before his hand burst into flames.

I recoiled in shock, damn near falling off of the bed. The flames flowed along his hand as if it were a log in a fire pit. They licked along his fingers, flowing like a flag in the wind. "How did you-?"

He clenched his flaming hand into a fist, snuffing out the fire. "Because I am also a wizard, nephew." Bishop said.

Holy crap. How do you even react to something like that? That your entire bloodline has magic running through their veins. It was certainly a hard sell. I took a deep breath.

"Even still, how do you know that I'm a wizard too?" I asked.

"You come from an extremely strong bloodline. One where nearly every member of the family has some level of a magical aura." Bishop explained. "Your parents had you tested when you were very young and confirmed the existence of a notably potent magical aura surrounding you."

All things considered, I suppose it made sense. My uncle wouldn't lie to me about something like this, especially when it was apparent he was a wizard. The pieces seemed to fall into place. There was only one more question burning in my mind. I looked at Jacob.

"So how do you fit into all of this?" I asked him. "You're a wizard too?"

Jacob, who had remained silent until now, moved closer to the bed, standing beside my uncle. "Not exactly. I am what is called a golem . We were popularized by Jewish wizards, especially around World War Two." He flexed his arms, and they took on a grainy, stone-like texture to them. "Nowadays, golems are used to seek out and protect potential wizards."

A flash of anger washed over me. "So you aren't even really my friend?" I spat. "You were just 'keeping an eye' on me?"

"It's not like that, Tobias." Jacob shook his head. "Of course I'm your friend. This doesn't change anything we've been through together, not in the slightest." He had a pained expression on his face.

What I had said hurt him. A dark part of me didn't care. Say what you will, but he had deceived me. I rolled over, turning my back to him and my uncle. Bishop let out a heavy sigh.

"Jacob, would you give us a moment?" Bishop asked in a hushed tone.

"Uh, yeah. I'll be outside if you need anything." Jacob said, I could hear the pain in his voice. He retreated to the wooden stairs and the door of light appeared once more. He left with a satisfying slam of the magical door.

"Tobias," Bishop began. "You cannot blame Jacob."

"The hell I can't!" I snapped back at him. "He lied to me. He pretended to be my friend. All the while he was just trying to keep an eye on me and find out if I was some sort of magician." I waved my hands mystically around my head for emphasis.

"Wizard." Bishop corrected, raising a finger. "Magicians do stage magic. We, wizards, do real magic."

"I really don't care right now." I growled.

"Give Jacob a chance. He has spoken highly of you, enthusiastically so." Bishop said. "I've never seen a golem so fascinated with a prospective wizard before. He truly cares for you, Tobias. Don't let your anger get in the way of a solid friendship."

He paused for a second to let me mull it over. There was so much going through my head right now. Magic, golems, demons, what was next? Elves?

"Oh, here comes your nurse." Bishop turned to someone emerging from the forest.

My jaw dropped to my chest. Think of the most beautiful Victoria's Secret model you've ever seen. The long, gorgeous hair, the chiseled, sensual curves, and the most elegant femininity and grace. The kind of woman that men kill their best friends for, commit crimes for, and even start wars for.

The woman who approached from the forest depths made them all look like garbage. Besides her indescribable beauty, the first thing I noticed was that she was tall, at least seven feet, to be exact. She had long, blonde hair that reached down to her waist, and it seemed to flow in the air as if she were underwater. A crown of bleached wood traced her hairline, coming up in two horn-like pointed branches. She wore a mint green dress that flowed along the ground flawlessly, avoiding snags that any other woman would have struggled with. The dress fit tightly around her torso, accentuating her hips and chest. Her eyes were the color of amber and I swear they stared into my soul.

Bishop put his hand to my chin and closed my mouth for me. "Down, boy." He said sternly, though I could hear the amusement in his voice. "Tobias, I would like you to meet the elven noble, Sylf."

"Wait elven, as in?" I began to say.

"Yes, as in elves. Sylf is one of the highest nobles of the Ljósálfar Court." Bishop answered me.

"Tobias Leight," She walked to my bedside. "I have heard much about you from your uncle. It is an honor to meet you."

My mouth didn't want to cooperate with the words I tried to spit out. "Yes, uh, meeting you is the uh…"

Sylf smiled. "Don't worry, child. Your reaction is typical of a human your age."

"Sylf works with us as our expert healing consultant." Bishop explained. "Healing sickness and injuries is one of the Ljósálfar's specialties. Though it's at it's best when we're on their home turf."

"Their home turf?" I asked.

"Yes, what you see around you is one of the deepest forests of Alfheim, one of the nine realms of Yggdrasil." Sylf explained.

"Yggdrasil, like Odin and Thor? That Yggdrasil?" I asked. "Norse mythology is real?"

"Along with many other pantheons and worlds." Bishop confirmed. "However, there is a time and place to educate on such matters." He rose to leave.

"For now, you need rest, young Tobias." Sylf seemed to glide along the ground towards me. "I came to begin the next phase of your healing."

"Wait! But I have so many-!" A million questions fought to burst forth, but Sylf placed a gentle, slender hand on my forehead.

"Sleep." She said quietly. I felt myself begin to drift off almost instantly. My vision blurred and seemed to spiral as I fell into unconsciousness.

Chapter 5

Have you ever been put to a sleep by an elf's mystical powers? Best sleep I've ever gotten. ZzzQuil eat your heart out. When I awoke, I was in a different room, I was no longer in the Alfheim infirmary. Man, that still felt weird to think about. Now, I was in what looked like a small dormitory. It was not made of trees and glowing vines, but exactly what you might expect a college dorm to look like. Navy colored carpet, plain milk-colored walls, and two sets of bunk beds that were pressed against the walls. Otherwise, there was nothing remarkable or magical about the room. I sat up on the lower bunk of the bed, rolling my shoulders and twisting my neck, trying to shake off the sleep. I was no longer in my old tattered clothes or whatever scrubs I had been wearing in the infirmary. Now, I was wearing a plain white shirt, jeans, and white socks. They were clearly kept on hand for situations like mine, because they were only an approximate fit. The jeans were a little too tight in all the wrong places and the shirt was a size too big.

All things considered, I felt pretty great. Whatever Sylf had done for me, my wounds and broken bones were as good as new. Clearly the Bright Elves had way better healthcare than I did. Did my insurance cover Bright Elf medical care? I put that query under "Ridiculous Questions for Later." The list was starting to get a little long. There was a knock on the door, and shortly after, it opened.

A girl not much older than me entered the room. Her hair was bright red, cut short on the sides, shaved down with zig zags trimmed into the remaining fuzz, and done up so that her bangs hung over the right side of her face. Her eyes were the color of the summer sky, and she had dark makeup around them so that they seemed even bluer than they already were. She had a tattoo of a serpent around her neck, it curved around to bite on its own tail, the Ouroboros, I believe. She wore a short sleeved black T-shirt with a My Chemical Romance logo on the front, angled slightly. The shirt had many holes cut into it, and it was cropped to reveal her midriff. Her arms were covered in more tattoos of varying imagery. Her black skinny jeans also had many stylish rips and tears, they were ruffled slightly where they met her combat boots. The kind of girl your mom would be put off of if you brought her home, at first glance.

The girl looked me up and down, chewing on her lip. She didn't seem impressed. "So, you're Bishop's nephew?"

"Uh, that's me." I said. Yep, that's me. Master of words. "And who might you be?"

"Kat." She said bluntly. "Come on, it's time to meet with the bearded geezers." Kat made a motion for me to follow her.

"Wait!" I stood up. "Can someone stop for a second and just let me figure this out?'

Kat rolled her eyes. "Look, kid, I really don't care how confused you are. Nor do I care that you're Bishop's brat, I'm just doing what I'm told so I can go home. Now come on, they aren't the most patient people in the world."

"Well, aren't you pleasant?" I sighed. She walked out of the room and I followed.

We emerged into the pristine white halls I had seen from the infirmary. People from all walks of life were scarcely scattered across the halls. They all looked at me like they expected me to do a flip or something. Or maybe they were staring at Kat's mid-2000s goth look. Who was I to say? We walked down the halls, taking multiple turns, many of which I thought should have crossed over each other, but the layout of the various halls were always different. I could see myself getting lost in this place very easily, but Kat seemed to navigate the contradictory halls with ease, as if she'd done it a million times.

After what seemed like an eternity of walking, we found ourselves at an obnoxiously large door, decorated with gold trim in various vague floral designs. It definitely seemed like the door you'd go through to find a bunch of grumpy old wizards. I was still convinced I was on some sort of elaborate acid trip or something. Kat stopped right before the door and motioned for me to continue.

"How exactly do you expect me to open this big ass door?" I asked. "It's got to weigh like a bajillion pounds."

"The door responds to the innate magical aura of wizards." Kat explained, exasperated. She spoke as if it were to be obvious that the magic door would magically open to my magic touch. "Just approach it, and if your Uncle's not full of it, the door should open for you."

"Oh yeah, like the grocery store." I said seriously. Kat didn't seem amused, did she even get the joke?

I shrugged. The door magically opening for me would probably be the most normal thing I'd seen today. Wait, how long has it been since that demon showed up? Not the point right now. I did as Kat suggested, and approached the door.

As soon as I took one step past Kat, the golden trim began to glow. The room rumbled as the door began to creak open, the sound of dragging stone filled my ears. It opened upon a large gathering hall, like something you'd see in a government building where all the important government folks meet up. The walls were lined with marble columns and support beams. The ceiling was covered by a classical painting, depicting several wizards in flowing robes, wielding various elements against a cloud of darkness that seemed to oppose them.

Desks lined descending steps that led to a large raised desk where several individuals sat, each wearing robes that took inspiration from various cultures from all over the world. The desk ascended to higher levels until it reached the center, which stood notably higher above the rest.

The man sitting at the top level was an ancient man of African descent. He wore dark green robes over a maroon dress shirt, complete with a black tie. I guess wizards didn't have the greatest fashion sense. He wore his hair in long, gray dreadlocks that draped themselves down his neck and over his shoulders. His hands were steepled in front of him, and he sat slouched, very relaxed. I'm guessing he was the grand poobah. I was so taken in by the room and the wizards at the high bench, that I didn't even notice Bishop and Jacob standing before them, apparently waiting for my arrival. I felt myself pacing in place, gripping my hands into fists over and over. I was nervous. Hey, you would be too if you had to walk into a room with a bunch of people all waiting on you. Especially when those people were apparently wizards who probably had decades of experience and knowledge at their fingertips.

I took one nervous step forward, my legs felt like lead. Then another step. Then another. Eventually, I made my way down to the floor, standing next to Bishop and Jacob. Jacob still looked a little defeated. My anger towards him had subsided, and was replaced by guilt and sympathy for him. Bishop was right. Jacob had done no wrong by me. I wasn't angry at him, but the situation I had been thrown into headfirst.

"Tobias, how are you feeling?" Bishop asked, putting a hand on my shoulder.

"Well, I'm not dead." I shrugged.

"That's good to hear." Bishop smiled slightly. He turned me towards the large bench, looking up at the various wizards, his arm over my shoulders. "Tobias, allow me to introduce you to the Elders of the Mystic Order."

In total there were nine of them and they all seemed to originate from different parts of the world. But it was the man with dreadlocks who spoke first.

"It is nice to finally meet you, Tobias Leight." He spoke with a light German accent, as if it had been a long time since he'd lived in Germany. "I am High Elder Roland Braun of the Mystic Order. I suppose you could say I'm the man in charge around here." He gave me a friendly smile. The skin around his eyes crinkled, you could tell he smiled a lot. "I wish to welcome you to our humble abode."

"Humble's not the word I would use." I said before I could even think about it. Oops. Foot meet mouth. Bishop squeezed my shoulder hard. Clearly I had not said the right thing.

"I suppose not." Braun laughed. I'm pretty sure he could see the sudden panic on my face, because he spoke reassuringly. He waved his hand dismissively, shooing away any tension I might've conjured up. "Fear not, Tobias, I'm not the stern school principal or anything like that. I simply want to get these things sorted out." He leaned forward in his chair, laying his hands flat on his desk. "Do you know why you're here, Tobias?"

"Umm, because a demon-monster-man tried to pulverize me?" I guessed.

"Well, yes." Braun could not help but let out a chuckle. "As your uncle has explained, you come from an ancient line of wizards. Your innate magical ability makes you a very tempting target for the less-than-favorable parties in play."

I was quick to figure out that less-than-favorable parties was smart wizard speak for "bad guys." But who knows, I could be totally wrong.

Braun continued to speak. "Your arrival here was inevitable, though we were hoping to wait until your eighteenth birthday. However, circumstances have forced our hand and you've been exposed to our world. Now that you're aware of it, it's important that your training as a wizard begins so you are capable of facing the threats our world has to offer, should it come to that."

"I'm going to be trained to do magic?" I asked, skepticism coating my words. "So is this Hogwarts? Where's the Sorting Hat?"

Braun let out a chuckle. "No, of course not. While you are considered an apprentice wizard, the Mystic Order itself is not a school, more like a government body. But yes, you will be trained how to use and control your magic. Effective immediately."

"I've already been given the go ahead to start your training." Bishop stepped forward. "Is there anything else, High Elder?" My uncle asked, looking up at the bench where Braun sat.

"I know you have many questions, Tobias." Braun said, his voice sounding reassuring. "Answers will come with time and experience. For now, your training begins."

And that was that. There was no fanfare, no fireworks, or trumpets. I was officially a wizard, or an apprentice, I supposed. Bishop and Jacob flanked me as we walked out, back towards the grand door I had entered through. But as we walked away, I felt a tickling sensation on the back of my neck, like someone was breathing against it, ever so slightly. I turned back towards the elevated judge's benches and looked up. My suspicions had been right, that tickling feeling meant someone had been watching me. I did my best to approximate where the feeling had come from, and sure enough, a very plain looking man with short red hair was staring directly at me, leaning his face against one finger while another tapped his cheek. I'm pretty sure it's hard to make that look sinister, but he managed it just fine.

My first day in magic school and I was already making friends.

Jacob and Bishop led me down another spotless hallway. What I assumed were other wizards passed us by as I did.

They didn't exactly scream wizard to me, in terms of appearance or demeanor. A lot of them just looked like regular people that you might pass by on the street. Everyone seemed to come from a different background. There was one grizzly looking gentleman who looked more at home on a large farm. Another woman with dark skin and a shaved head walked by without even noting our existence. There was a pale man wearing ragged robes who was absolutely covered in complicated tattoos.

I turned my attention back to Jacob in front of me. "So like, have you always been a uh…"

"A golem?" Jacob turned his head to look at me from the corner of his eye. There was an amused twinkle in his eye that told me he'd probably been expecting the question. "Yes, I've been a golem ever since I was born. Though I guess that's not the right word for it. Made, I was made."

"You said golems were a Jewish thing, right?" I asked. "To fight the Nazis or something?"

Jacob barked out a laugh. "Well yes, but the original creation of golems dates back much farther than the forties. The originals were much simpler in mind and cruder in appearance. We used to be just giant hulking living statues of clay who had no sense of agency besides what their masters told them to do. But magic has come a long way since the tenth century, now we can think for ourselves and live amongst humans. The basic idea is still there, we're created from clay and infused with magic. Finally, a ritual takes place.

What's known as a Shem, or a Name of God, is written on a piece of paper and sealed into our foreheads."

Jacob placed one large finger on the center of his forehead. "Right here. It gives us life, our sense of purpose, our very being. In ancient times, we protected and served the Jewish people. Now we're created and serve the larger wizarding community."

I raised my eyebrows. It was an interesting piece of mythology I hadn't heard before. Even still, it was a bit strange hearing it spoken as fact rather than fiction. But I'd almost been killed by a giant demon, so the idea of clay guardians wasn't totally out there, I suppose.

"So, everyone I've met so far has said that I'm a wizard too. That it runs in the family." I said. "And don't get me wrong, it's cool. Super cool, in fact. But why is everyone so insistent that I train, that I learn magic, that I become a full-fledged wizard."

Jacob looked at Bishop, who hadn't really paid attention to the conversation until now.

Bishop cleared his throat and spoke without turning to face us. "Wizards come into their power, one way or another. The training makes the difference between someone who uses and controls their magic, and someone who is used and controlled by it. You have a lot of potential, Tobias, and I mean, a lot. To be blunt with you, if you aren't trained, you could end up becoming one of the very things the Mystic Order works to destroy. A rogue wizard. A warlock."

A chill ran down my spine just then. That didn't sound good, not at all. If years of reading epic fantasy and playing Dungeons and Dragons had taught me, becoming a warlock was a less than favorable career path. Dealing with and being consumed by dark forces did not sound fun to me.

"Well, okay then." I gulped. "Training sounds good to me."

Bishop nodded. "Good, because it begins now."

Jacob and my uncle took me to a basketball court where a tennis ball launcher was set up under one of the nets. It was kinda weird seeing something so normal and mundane in magic land.

"Alright then Tobias, we're going to start with the most basic magic that everyone learns." Bishop explained. "The ability to conjure wind."

"Oh yeah, just the basics, right?" I said, sarcastically. "I'm a regular Avatar Aang over here."

"You joke, but air is by far the easiest of the elements to summon and control." Jacob said. "Even golems like myself, who are best at earth magic, can easily call up a gale of wind." Jacob took a deep breath and then threw out his open palm, his voice echoing *"Ruach!"*

Even from a distance away, I could feel the force of the winds that rushed from his open palm. The tennis ball machine was hit with an audible thunk sound and went flying across the court towards the bleachers. It crashed and crunched under the pressure, no longer resembling its original shape.

"See?" Jacob looked at me with an obvious look.

"More importantly than any amount of magical talent, is the belief that you can call the wind." Bishop said. "If you don't believe it, it won't happen."

"So the magic word for wind is ru-ruach?" I asked. I struggled to pronounce the word. It was Hebrew, I think.

"There's no such thing as universal magic words." Bishop shook his head. "Sure, you can also use ruach, but it can be any word related to the spell you're about to cast. Hell, it doesn't even need to be a real word. It can be gibberish, so long as the intent and the relation are there."

I mulled over that, thinking of what words I would rely on. "Okay, anything else?"

"To reach for your magic, try imagining a large fishing net wrangling in a school of fish." Bishop explained, mimicking pulling in a bunch of imaginary fish. "The power is there, within you, and all around you. Let it respond to your call."

"Okay." I said, dragging out the word skeptically.

Jacob walked over to a nearby storage closet and pulled out a standing punching bag, the kind that has water or sand filling their bases so they could stand on their own. He carried it effortlessly, like it was a load of groceries or something. He set it down where the tennis ball launcher had been, and then stood back off to the side with Bishop.

"Now, give it a try." Bishop said, gesturing towards the punching bag.

I took in a deep breath, bouncing on the balls of my feet like I would right before I loosened up for a sparring match. Then I took a fighting stance, without my hands raised in fists. I held my hands near my stomach, miming as if I were holding a ball, shaping it in my mind. I focused on what I wanted to happen. I imagined the wind gathering between my hands from all around me, preparing for release. Bishop was right, I could feel something there. Not with my normal senses, but some sort of sixth sense, I guess. The subtle tension in the air. No, not tension, almost like a sort of pressure. One more deep breath.

"*Kaze!*" I thrust my palm out forward. To my surprise, something lashed out from my hand and rushed towards the punching bag. The sound of rushing wind filled the court, I felt it pull at me as it rushed away from my body and towards the punching bag. Wind. I had called up wind! The wind ripped and roared towards the punching bag, and sure enough, the punching bag rocked back from the notable force, but after a few seconds of teetering back and forth, it settled back into its normal position. It hadn't been a hurricane or anything, but I'd made the bag move.

I looked down at my hands, stunned. Sure, I had seen plenty of magic and an encounter with a demon to solidify this new reality for me, but actually performing magic myself was a different story. My hands tingled with electric sensation, as if I had built up static electricity by rubbing my socks on the carpet.

Bishop grunted, a small smile forming on his face. "Well done, Tobias. Definitely needs some work, but a good start." He tilted his head toward the punching bag. "Again."

We practiced the wind spell for about half an hour or so, each time the spell seemed to get a little stronger and a little more focused. The punching bag rocked further back with each attempt. It was the last attempt when the punching bag was rocking so far back it went horizontal, parallel to the hardwood floor. But it was at this point that I started to feel myself get winded — no pun intended. My head started to swim, and I wobbled precariously where I stood. Jacob jogged over to my side and kept me from falling.

"Alright don't you think that's enough for today, Bishop?." Jacob said.

Bishop nodded. "You've made extraordinary progress, Tobias." Bishop smiled. "Let's call it a day and get you home. You need a hot meal and some rest."

Home. Would it be weird if I said I had completely forgotten about any prospect of home? I had been so enveloped in this new world that I had completely forgotten about my regular life. As wonderful as this place was, home sounded really nice. School. Coffee. Claire.

Claire, I'd completely forgotten about her. She'd probably be worried sick. What would I tell her? Maybe Jacob could give me some advice on living a split high school life.

Jacob and Bishop walked me out of the basketball court and back into the labyrinth of hallways. The hallways were definitely going to be something I'd have to get used to if I wanted any chance of finding my way around here.

As we walked, we passed by a huddle of robed figures. I couldn't see their faces but I heard them muttering amongst themselves. Their voices were hushed but urgent. I could only catch fragments of what they were saying.

"...been stolen." One voice said.

"Is it happening...?" Another asked.

Yet another chimed in, "...Grail must be recovered. Find the thief..."

I wanted to listen more but Jacob wrapped a huge arm over my shoulders and pulled me in tight. "Come on buddy, don't fall behind. These hallways can get confusing if you're not paying attention."

I smiled but I found myself frowning in thought. They seemed awfully worried about something. Seems like something pretty important had been stolen. It had happened fairly recently too, from the sound of it. Maybe I was just thinking too much into it, but could it really be just a coincidence that it happened around the same time that I've been roped into all of this?

I shook it off. Of course it was a coincidence. The universe doesn't line things up like that so perfectly. Life isn't a movie, after all. I mean, really, who'd want to see a movie about my life anyways?

Tobias Leight: Loser Teenager, it'll sell all of five tickets for sure. Now the sequel, Tobias Leight: Loser Teenage Wizard-in-Training, that'll be a hit. Where was I going with this again?

Eventually, we found ourselves in a large hall with what looked like hundreds of plain doors, all evenly spaced out along the walls, and eventually leading to a second level with even more doors. People, I presumed wizards, bustled about, going in and out of doors, walking past us in both directions.

"Woah, uh, that's a lot of doors." I said lamely.

"You're full of great insight, bud." Jacob laughed at me. "This is the United States Portal Nexus. All of these doors lead to cities across the country, including Seattle."

"Huh, so I just walk through one of these doors and I could be in Los Angeles, or New York?" I asked, just to be sure I understood.

"Precisely." Bishop interjected. "But it's not something to abuse. Best to just stick to the Seattle door." He nodded his head to a door on our immediate right. It was the third on the right. On a plaque, in big glowing letters, it read SEATTLE, WA.

Without another word, we approached the Seattle door. Bishop gave the knob a twist, and then pushed the door open. Bright light blinded me momentarily as the door swung open. I could feel Jacob or Bishop gently nudge me and I walked forward. In an instant, we were no longer in the white hallways of the Mystic Order. We had returned to Seattle. More specifically, Pike Placc, a fish market and a sort of underground mini-mall. Even more specifically, we had emerged from the Market Theater Gum Wall.

The Gum Wall is covered, and I mean covered, in used chewing gum left by tourists. It started in the early 90s when patrons of the Market Theater would stick their gum to the wall, and then stick coins in the gum. Don't ask me why, I don't know. But the traditions stuck, and the wall is now polka-dotted with countless colors of gum. It was cool, in an incredibly disgusting sort of way. And apparently it also hid one of the portals to the Mystic Order's headquarters. Judging by the light, it was around midday, which meant plenty of tourists were gawking at the sickly landmark.

Several feelings and sensations washed over me as I passed through the gateway. For one, all sense of up and down left my body for a second, and I had to struggle to keep myself upright. I held onto the Gum Wall briefly before I recoiled in disgust. I looked from the glowing gate to the pathway around us, a bit confused. Sure, demons were one thing, but magical gateways were another matter entirely.

I hooked a thumb behind me towards the door we'd just come out of. "So, uh, how's that work?"

"Do you want the actual technical explanation or the second grade version?" Jacob asked.

I scowled and let out a breath. "Second grade, please."

Bishop chimed in then. "There exists a realm parallel to our own where most magic and magical creatures originate from. It has many names, Fairyland, Hades, the Realm Inbetween, Wonderland, and so on. The most common name for it among wizards is The World Yonder. It's composed of many realms, domains, and territories. The Mystic Order's main base of operations exists in a mostly empty pocket within The World Yonder."

"And since it exists outside of typical time and space, the Mystic Order is able to create mostly permanent links between it and locations in the mortal world. There's pretty much a door for every major city in the world." Jacob explained.

"So I can walk through this door here, in Seattle, walk a few feet, and find myself in Cairo?" I asked, trying to grasp the information.

"Pretty much." Jacob nodded.

I raised my eyebrows at that. That was a certifiably bonkers idea, and they'd explained it so matter of factly, as if it were no big deal. "That seems like a pretty dangerous system to have access to, isn't it?"

"Oh, absolutely." Bishop confirmed. "The creation of portals from one place to another is a closely monitored practice. Otherwise it'd be a whole mess, and we'd have mortals accidentally falling into portals left and right."

I looked around us as the door seemed to close itself, disappearing and blending into the rest of thc wall. The tourists and passerby walked right by us without even giving us or the fading portal a second glance. "How come they don't notice us?"

"The portal is protected by a long term veil of sorts. It's nothing too fancy, it just convinces people not to pay this particular area too much attention." Bishop explained. "That being said, we shouldn't leave the door open or stick around too long. Magic will only keep them distracted for so long."

"I'll call us an Uber." Jacob said. There was something so mundane about calling an Uber after everything I'd experienced today. Jacob pulled out his phone and got lost in the process.

"How long were we gone?" I asked my uncle.

"A little less than forty-eight hours or so." Bishop said. "Don't worry, I already called in your absence from school. Sick grandma." A devious smile spread across his face.

I let out a laugh. This was something. Magic, demons, elves. What a crazy new world I lived in.

Chapter 6

The idea of going back to high school seemed incredibly mundane and well, normal. Dividing fractions or trying to figure out why an author made the curtains blue was nothing in comparison to the world of magic I had been exposed to. I stood in front of the school steps, my feet felt stuck to the ground. There was a new level of intimidation with high school now. I was even more of an outcast than I was before.

Sure, I was never bullied or beat up or anything like that, but I was far from popular. Of course no one knew I was a wizard now, or what I had experienced. But Bishop felt the need to have some extra eyes on me at all times. Scout, my German Shepherd, was sitting patiently beside me. He wore a heavy-looking red vest that said "SERVICE ANIMAL. DO NOT PET." Scout looked quite proud of his vest, looking up at me with a doggy grin while his tail wagged furiously.

I'm not sure why Bishop wanted Scout by my side at all times now. He was a dog. What was he gonna do against another demon, pee on him? Either way, Scout was happy to be here and I always enjoyed his company.

"Come on, Scout." I tugged lightly on his leash and began walking up the school steps.

No one seemed to pay much attention to Scout, even though he was wearing a bright red vest that practically screamed for him to be noticed. Plus, he was a cute dog. That alone should warrant at least a little bit of attention. I wondered if Bishop had placed a spell of some kind on Scout to make him invisible or something. But the other students made an effort to give him a wide berth, so that didn't seem exactly right.

"So I'm guessing there's no chance you're gonna improve my chances with girls, is there?" I asked him.

Scout sneezed. He was full of wisdom, truly.

The first bell rang, and I made my way to History. Last time I had been in this class I'd had my demonic dream, which I probably should talk to Bishop about sometime. It seemed a hell of a lot more relevant now. My list of questions for later continued to expand.

Scout and I strolled over to my desk and he curled up next to it, as far out of the way as he could manage. Other kids walked past my desk and seemed to effortlessly avoid him without actually noticing the dog laying there. Was my dog a wizard too? Could dogs even be wizards? I was going to need to start writing these questions down.

The bell rang again, signaling that first period had officially begun. Everyone got to their seats, just as the teacher arrived. In retrospect, I should've known something was off about the woman who entered. She wasn't Mrs. O'Neill for starters. The woman was much younger, but her skin seemed tight against her body. She had very pronounced cheekbones and a large nose. Her eyes were a muddy brown color and her hair was a dull black color. It was pulled into a bun on top of her head, but many hairs frizzed out around her head, giving her a very weird look. She wore a woman's business suit, complete with a pencil skirt, pantyhose, and cheap high heels.

Students were talking quietly amongst themselves, casting sideways glances at the woman. Her voice came out like a whip, savage and precise. "Quiet! To your seats, brats!"

The handful of students who hadn't settled in their seats scrambled to their desks with a sense of panicked urgency. Yikes, I've never seen any teacher get a bunch of rebellious teenagers in line so effortlessly. One snap of her vocal whip and they were cowering.

"I am Ms. Serpiente, your substitute teacher for today." Her voice came out with a breathy quality to it. I wasn't sure how to explain it.

Scout perked up and stared daggers at her. I could feel him vibrating against my desk, a nearly inaudible growl. But I was sure that's what it was. I rubbed my foot against his back lightly, trying to sooth him. He ceased growling, but refused to take his eyes off of her.

If she had noticed Scout or his sudden alertness to her, she didn't let on. She simply continued speaking. "Now, please take out your textbooks and turn to page three-hundred and ninety-four." Ms. Serpiente said with an audible hiss. We did as she said, many of the students bringing out the wrong book in the midst of their fear of the substitute teacher.

One student raised his hand. She turned her head to the girl raising her hand. "What? I did not open the floor for questions!" Ms. Serpiente growled.

The girl put her hand down and spoke nervously. "Well, I was just wonder where Mrs. O'Neill was today?"

Ms. Serpiente spoke between clenched teeth. "Your teacher has found herself indisposed. That's all that matters." She turned her head and locked eyes with me. That's when I felt it. I felt sick, as if a sudden wave of nausea had washed over me. The last time that happened...

The demon.

Oh crap.

That's why Scout had suddenly become so alert. Whoever, or whatever, Ms. Serpiente was, she wasn't human. Which meant I was in trouble. Panic began to set in. Crap, crap, crap. Two monster attacks in the same week. Just my luck, right? I took a deep breath. Just remain calm. Jacob was at school today, right? All I had to do was send him a text or call him as soon as I could. But wait, I hadn't seen him when I was walking up to school today. He always hangs out in front of the school before the first bell. Doubt started to set in, but I tried to reassure myself. Surely Ms. Monster Face over here wouldn't try anything in front of all the other students, right?

Class proceeded as normally as it could. Ms. Serpiente threw a book at a student and emotionally scarred another. But that's high school, right? Oh, who am I kidding? Then the moment I was dreading came to pass, the bell rang. Class was over. I moved to get up and be the first out, but apparently everyone else had the same idea. Desks groaned and skidded along the ground as students practically jumped out of their seats to escape the tension-ridden classroom. I was practically trapped in my desk, and Scout even had to curl up completely under my desk to avoid being stepped on.

Eventually I had an opening and I scooted out of my desk and made my way to the door, Scout close on my heels. But I was too slow. Ms. Serpiente swooped over to the door just as the last student was leaving and slammed the door shut. I'm pretty sure she clipped the back of a kid's shoe on their way out. I heard the hardy click of the door's deadbolt lock.

"And just where are you off to in such a hurry, Mr. Leight?" Ms. Serpiente hissed. Literally hissed, like a snake or an alligator.

"My dad was Mr. Leight." I said with shaky sarcasm. Okay, so it wasn't my best quip. Sue me.

"Quick-witted." She purred, sarcastically.. "I like that in a young wizard. Too bad you won't live through the day." Then she swung at me, whipping her arm out in a backhanded strike towards my head.

Thank God for quick reflexes, it probably saved my life. I dropped Scout's leash and lifted my right arm in a defensive gesture to protect my face. Our arms met and it went completely numb for a moment from the impact. I stumbled to the side, crossing up my legs and leaving me unbalanced. I managed to right myself, but I was facing away from her. Before I had the chance to turn around, she struck my back with an open palm and I went stumbling into the wall, completely out of control.

Scout snarled and jumped at her, going for her throat. Woah. Scout would barely jog with me, and yet he was leaping into the air to take her head off. Ms. Serpiente was far too quick for the German Shepherd though. Scout let out a yelp as the substitute teacher from hell grabbed him by the throat, and then proceeded to fling him to the other side of the room. Scout hit a corkboard on the wall that had various flyers on it. He fell to the ground, and the corkboard fell onto him with a heavy thump.

"Scout!" I yelled. "Stay away from my dog!" For a moment, fear was absent from my body. I fully righted myself and then ran straight at Serpiente. I was going to kick this chick's teeth in, and then some.

Then, in an instant, Ms. Serpiente was gone. Well, not gone. She changed. Her clothes melted away, and her legs merged together into a serpent's tail, covered in onyx scales. Her skin became the color of chalk, making her resemble old Greek statues, no clothes and all. Her body looked like it was sculpted to perfection. If I wasn't terrified out of my mind, I'd say she was stupidly attractive. Her hair was free of the bun it had been in, and now fell perfectly around her chest. Her arms were spotted with patches of scales and her fingers ended in two-inch claws. Her eyes had become slitted and bright yellow, glowing with an eerie light. The creature's mouth had stretched farther across her face, but it was still not large enough to accommodate her huge, numerous razor sharp teeth. Two large fangs unfolded themselves as she opened her mouth and stretched, before folding back in as she closed her mouth.

She let out a roaring hiss and then swung her long serpentine tail at me. I tried to sidestep, but I underestimated her reach. Her tail connected on the tail-end of her swing, no pun intended. I fell into a desk, the edge of the table jabbing into my ribs uncomfortably. She readied to strike, much how an actual snake would, curling up its body and building tension. Then she lunged at me. Before I was able to react, she was on top of me, pinning my arms down with her claws. Her long, bladed nails cut into my wrists in the process.

Serpiente's mouth opened wider than I would've thought possible, her fangs poised to strike. Her gaping maw looked like a bottomless void, and her fangs dripped with a sickly green substance. The drops landed on the ground near my head, and began to steam and sizzle.

"Yeesh lady, you need a Tic-Tac, or twelve." I strained against her grip but it was no use. There was no way in hell I was going to physically overpower this snake lady.

Wait a freaking second. What was I doing? I could do MAGIC now. I was no longer prey, like I had been with my encounter against the demon. I was far more capable now. I flexed my open palm, aiming at her mouth to the best of my ability. I reached for the power. The magic in the air feeling like a silent tension. I pulled at it with my mind, and it bent to my will. The magic gathered in my palm and soon enough, it was primed for magical badassery.

"*Kaze!*" I bellowed, my voice echoing in the room. Wind erupted from my palm and raced directly into Serpiente's gaping maw.

She let out an inaudible gasp, as she choked on the air I had forced down her throat. Serpiente couldn't help but recoil from the gale I had called up, slithering back and away from me. I scrambled to my feet, and immediately readied another magical attack.

"*Kaze!*" I called. Wind rushed from my outstretched hand once more and flung her into the whiteboard, cracks streaking across the surface. She slumped to the floor, clearly dazed from the attack.

She hadn't been expecting it, and that was my advantage. I immediately prepared to call up another blast of wind, hoping I could use it to knock her out long enough for me to escape. I reached for the magic, just as I had before. I molded it into the wind spell that so far had served me faithfully. Then, I went to unleash it. Dizziness and nausea immediately enveloped me. The magical energies I had gathered simply evaporated. I collapsed to a knee, holding onto a desk to stop myself from completely falling over.

What happened? Why was I suddenly so weak and tired? I could still feel the magic around me, but I couldn't draw it in and use it. My legs felt like they were made of lead.

Serpiente let out a breathy laugh as she stood up straight, her hair bobbing slightly. She shuddered, arching her back with sheer pleasure. The thrill of the hunt seemed to excite her. The snake woman returned to a less erotic posture and faced me with a victorious smirk.

"Foolish mageling," Serpiente cackled. "I will admit, your magical strikes were incredibly powerful, but you are far from the skill and finesse of a true wizard."

Serpiente slithered towards me, effortlessly pushing the desks aside as she circled me. She looked at me like I look at a steak, or a stack of brand new comics.

Serpiente made a tsk-tsk sound. It sounded strange coming from her reptilian mouth. "You've drained your reserves. An understandable mistake for a novice, but a fatally foolish one as well."

I looked up at her, tired defiance in my eyes. Of course, I should've known. In video games, you usually have a magic meter. I guess it's safe to say my MP had reached zero.

"Now, where was I?" Serpiente's voice was full of excitement as she closed in on the kill, or capture, whatever. I hardly cared in the moment. She raised her needle-point claws into the air, poised to strike.

The sound of nails clicking against the tile could be heard for a brief moment, before a canine snarl ripped through the air, and suddenly, Scout was latched onto the monster's wrist. Serpiente roared in anger and pain, flicking her arm and sending Scout flying. But this time, Scout didn't hit the wall helplessly. He hit the wall on his feet, bouncing back off the wall and flying back at Serpiente. Scout leapt past Serpiente, slashing her with his fangs on the way. Scout landed on the far side of the room, skidding across the tile, but he was ready for a fight.

Then, just as quickly as Serpiente had become a monster, he too, changed. Scout's hair faded away as he grew, both in size and muscle. He let out pained, angry snarls as his body grew and shifted. His forelegs looked like a bodybuilder's, rippling with muscle. His front paws morphed into monstrous hands, causing his stance to shift to something more akin to a bulldog, wide and sturdy. His jaw widened and filled with even more sharp teeth. His skin was the color of coal, and his eyes burned like the hottest of embers. Flames erupted along his spine, giving off far more heat than the modest fire should have.

Monster Scout let out a distorted howl before charging at Serpiente. She hissed in a panic and attempted to dodge. But as big as he was, Scout was incredibly fast. He clamped down on her arm and slammed her into the wall. Well, through the wall. Wood and metal screeched in protest as Scout barreled through the wall and the lockers on the other side. I could hear panicked screams as the two monsters rampaged into the hallway. But one scream rang out above the rest, and I recognized it. Claire Williams. I managed to stand and was able to see her through the dust and debris, pinned under a section of lockers. Scout and Serpiente fought only a few feet away. One wrong move and one of them would crush my friend under the lockers.

I fought against the exhaustion, managing to stand and stumble over to where Claire was pinned, being careful not to put any weight on the lockers that she was trapped under.

"Tobias?" Claire said in between frightened sobs. "What the hell is going on?" She whimpered as she tried to slip out from under the lockers.

"My dog got in a fight with the substitute history teacher. Any other questions?" I explained, as if it were completely obvious. "Come on, we gotta get you out of here." I grabbed the lockers and braced myself to lift. As soon as I tried to lift it, my vision swam and I almost fell over.

I stifled a curse. Maybe if I had been at full strength, I'd have been able to lift the lockers enough for Claire to slip out. A loud crash filled the hall as Serpiente pinned Scout to the wall. Even for a supernatural snake monster, she had a surprising amount of strength. Scout snapped his jaws at her arm, but she was just out of his reach. At this rate, she was gonna kill him.

Anger surged up within me. To hell with the exhaustion, or the aches and pains. It all faded away as I stood up. "Get the hell away from my dog!" I roared, anger pouring out of me with notable tangibility. "*Kaze maximus!*"

A hurricane filled the hallway, rushing through me and directly for Serpiente. It hit her like a missile. She cried out in agony as the winds hit her directly in the side of her stomach. That much wind hitting one point was a deadly force of nature. It ripped her in half, almost perfectly where her beautiful woman half met the deadly snake half. Her dismembered body flew down the hallway before rolling to a stop as the winds died down. Scout managed to collect himself and closed the distance to the brutalized snake woman. He landed on her torso half and wrapped his jaws around Serpiente's head.

Serpiente screamed in a language I didn't recognize. Her voice was weak but full of fury. She stared directly into my eyes as she cursed at me, but Scout had evidently heard enough, and closed his jaws around her head. Blood erupted into every direction. It sizzled and smoked, melting holes into the floor and walls.

"Holy crap..." I said under my breath. I swayed dangerously, but Scout the super dog was by my side in an instant to support me. I looked at my demonic beast of a dog, doing my best to speak. "Scout, Claire needs our help. Can you lift the lockers?"

Scout looked at me sideways, making eye contact. There was intelligence in the look. He nodded deliberately. He carefully walked forward, making sure I could keep up, until we were in position near the lockers.

Claire's face was full of fear. She did whatever she could to put distance between her and Scout, though it wasn't as though she could move much. I suppose he did look pretty scary, but in the moment, he looked like a god damn angel to me.

"Claire," I said breathlessly. "He's not going to hurt you. If it wasn't for him, we'd both be dead."

Scout gave me a moment to sit myself down so he could work uninhibited. Claire's voice was full of panic. "Oh God, Tobias. Oh God. Please."

"Don't worry." I said, putting my hand over my eyes to alleviate some of the nausea. "I promise, I'll explain everything."

Scout wrapped his massive jaws around the side of the section of lockers. He braced himself, and then began to lift carefully. It didn't take much, Claire only needed a little bit of room to slide out from under the lockers. Once she was clear, Scout simply opened his mouth and let the lockers hit the ground with a metallic crash.

I could tell Claire wanted to run away, but my body spun back and forth. I could feel my vision fading and my mind got more foggy. Instead of running, the small girl stumbled over to me across the debris. I felt myself fall into her arms, and as my vision blurred in and out of focus, I could see two tall figures approaching from down the hall.

Chapter 7

Needless to say, school had been cancelled for the day. The faculty had come up with some story about a gas leak or something. There was no mention of the snake lady or giant dog busting a hole in the wall or destroying a classroom. It was amazing what people would do to deny reality that slapped them right in the face.

Bishop, Jacob, and I took turns explaining the basics to Claire. She was surprisingly receptive to this new reality. I don't think she could have denied it if she wanted to, she had a front row seat after all. I sipped on some orange juice and nibbled at a cookie. Apparently, the remedy for rejuvenating one's magical stamina was the same as donating blood. Bishop mentioned something about simple pleasures being very important to one's soul. I'm not sure I bought it, but I never turned down orange juice. It is the most superior juice after all.

We had returned to my apartment while everyone else at the school was figuring out what the hell happened. Claire lay in the recliner, her legs propped up while Bishop ran his hands over Claire's legs with a white magical aura surrounding them.

"I'm not an expert in healing, but this should definitely help you along." Bishop said, his face contorted in deep concentration.

We hadn't talked about the nitty gritty details of what had happened yet, only enough for Claire to get a basic idea. It was driving me a little crazy, and the deliciousness of my orange juice could only distract me for so long. Scout the monster dog had returned to being Scout the normal dog. While I sat stretched out on the couch, he laid against it as close to me as he could. Looking at him, you wouldn't have thought he was actually a monster in disguise.

"So are we actually going to talk about what the hell happened?" I asked as I sipped the rest of my orange juice. "What was that thing and why did it attack me? And since when has Scout been an undercover super dog? Not to mention, when I was fighting her, I was only able to throw out a couple of wind blasts before I felt tired, like I'd just run a marathon."

"Well first of all, you have to be careful with how much magic you perform at a time. Think of it like working out, do too much at once and you're going to wear yourself out quicker." Bishop said. "As for Scout, when I brought him home two years ago obviously I didn't actually bring him home from the shelter. He was the spoils of a mission to the Underworld."

"The Underworld? You mean Hell?" I asked.

"Oh no, two very different places." Bishop said, shaking his head. "A lesson for another time, though. Scout is a hellhound, ironically enough, since he isn't from Hell."

Scout lifted his head, as if listening intently. He stared directly at Bishop as he spoke.

"Hellhounds have many different purposes. Omens of death, guardians, and gatekeepers being their most well-known jobs." Bishop explained, still intently focused on healing Claire's leg. "Scout here is the infamous runt of the litter. He's much smaller than most hellhounds, and thus, was abandoned by his pack. I saw an opportunity, and so I brought him back with me. After laying a disguise enchantment upon him, I brought him home to us, and he's been the family dog ever since, his true power laying dormant for whenever he'd need to use it to protect us."

Scout's mouth opened into a doggy grin and he wagged his tail happily, soft impact noises could be heard as his tail hit the couch.

"So he's our family guardian, then." I patted him on the head.

"In a sense, yes. Guarding comes very naturally to hellhounds, anyways." Bishop smiled. The glow around his hands faded away, and he flashed a fatherly smile up at Claire. "Well, I've done all I can. Just take it easy for a couple of days and you'll be right as rain."

"Not sure how I'm supposed to take it easy after watching Medusa and a literal hellhound duke it out in the hallways." Claire said.

Her voice was still a little shaky. Hell, I couldn't blame her. In some ways, her world had been rocked harder than mine. It's not every day that you see literal monsters wrecking your school and dropping lockers on you.

"Ah yes, the nagini. Very strange to not only have one show up, but a malevolent one at that." Bishop scratched his scruff thoughtfully.

"Nagini? Like the snake from Harry Potter?" Claire asked.

"Ah yes, the pet snake of Lord Voldemort." Bishop laughed, he seemed to find it very amusing. "No, a nagini is a female naga. A type of river spirit originating from Hindu mythology." He put up air quotes to emphasize the last word. "They are typically seen as peaceful, benevolent entities, but there are the rare few who are far more vicious. Evil, in fact."

"This is the second time Tobias has been attacked within the week." Jacob said, finally speaking up. "Maybe we should consider moving him to the Mystic Order's headquarters. He's being hunted. We can't protect him as effectively here."

"Hmm, perhaps." Bishop pondered.

"No." I snapped at once. "I'm not going on house arrest just because of a couple of monster attacks."

"I'm not sure I entirely understand all of this, but maybe Jake and Bishop are right, Tobias." Claire said, her face was full of concern.

"Listen to your friends, Tobias." Bishop warned. He spoke in a very stern tone, the kind that usually preceded me getting grounded. I was very familiar with it, to say the least.

"No. Something stinks, and I don't think hiding me away is going to fix anything." I said. "Too many things are happening at once for it all to be sheer coincidence."

"What do you mean?" Jacob asked, lifting a skeptical eyebrow. He leaned against the wall farthest from me, arms crossed.

"Remember that weird dream I told you about a few days ago? I've never had dreams like that." I explained. I could feel my brain putting together the puzzle pieces.

"Yeah, it's what prompted me to keep an eye on you for the rest of the night." Jacob nodded.

"Okay, so I have that dream about some demonic monstrosity demanding I let him out. Then, later that day, I'm attacked by an actual demon, and I'm pretty sure it had been stalking me since that morning."

Claire's brow was furrowed in concentration. "So what, you think you had some kind of vision in a dream?"

"No, it felt too real to be some sort of hint or vision of the future." I shook my head. "I think someone, no, something reached out to me. Using my dreams as a sort of channel for communication. Am I on the right track?" I looked towards Bishop for confirmation.

Bishop nodded. "Jacob did tell me about that dream you had. I was hoping it was nothing, but that was far too optimistic."

I looked back and forth between Bishop and Jacob. "These two monster attacks and that strange dream are already weird enough. But there's something I overheard at the Mystic Order headquarters that's been scratching at the back of my mind."

I took a dramatic pause, giving someone the opportunity to speak up. No one did, so I just felt a little awkward. So much for the wizardly aura of mystery and suspense.

"When we were on our way out of the headquarters, I overheard someone mention that something had been stolen." I said. "Know anything about that?"

Bishop crossed his arms, tilting his head in deep thought. Jacob stared off into space, as if he was going through his mental records like a filing cabinet. Bishop was the first to speak up, shaking his head.

"Doesn't sound familiar, and I'd be one of the first outside of the High Elders to know." Bishop said.

"And I definitely wouldn't know if Bishop didn't. It's outside my pay grade." Jacob added.

"You get paid?" I asked.

"Nope. Messed up, right?" Jacob held out his arms and laughed.

"Not now, Jacob." Bishop said sternly. "I agree with Tobias though. There's too much happening at once for it to all be coincidence. Monster attacks don't happen that often, let alone in broad daylight in a high school."

"So if you don't know, but seemingly random wizards within the Mystic Order, what does that mean?" I asked.

"I'm not sure yet. We don't have enough information." Bishop shook his head. "If we're to get answers, I'll need to head back to the Mystic Order."

"Let me come with you then!" I demanded. "I can help you flush out whatever it is going on here. We'll go right up to the High Elder's council room and bust their door down."

"No." Bishop's voice came out sharp. "For one, we can't just go all cowboy, guns-a-blazing up to the High Elders. Secondly, you're not coming with me. It's far too dangerous. Plus, you have school to worry about."

Jacob raised an eyebrow and looked towards me, eager for my reaction.

"No way in hell am I getting benched on this, Bishop." I shook my head, my voice tinged with anger and annoyance. "I'm already involved. These monsters are gunning for me, and if we're right about it having to do with whatever was stolen, then I sure as hell have a right to get in on this."

"You don't have enough training yet." Bishop retorted.

"Are you kidding me?" I almost laughed in disbelief. "I've been up against two of these freaks already! I had that nagini on the ropes! The only way I'm going to continue to learn and get better is with experience!"

"It's not exactly like he'll be on his own, Bishop." Jacob noted. "With you, me, and Scout with him at all times, he'd be safer coming with us than if he was laying low at school." Jacob didn't comment on how if it wasn't for Scout that Nagini would've had me dead to rights. But he did know I'd find myself involved with or without their help.

Bishop let out a heavy sigh. I could tell he didn't want me involved in the slightest. After a few minutes that felt like an eternity, he threw his hands up in surrender. "Fine, I'd rather bring you in on my terms than having you go in alone half-cocked."

"Yes!" I pumped my fist excitedly. "You won't regret this, uncle."

"In the meantime, get some rest." Bishop said. "Tomorrow, I'm pushing your training up. If we want you to be ready for anything, we're going to have to put in a lot of extra work."

"I'm ready, Bishop. You'll see!" I smiled.

"For now, take a breather and get Claire home safe." Bishop said. He clapped his hands and stood up, turning to Jacob. "Jacob, come with me. We have things to discuss."

While Bishop and Jacob walked out, I helped Claire up. I was careful to make sure she didn't put too much weight on her bad leg. Bishop had been able to repair most of the damage but it was still tender and sore.

I didn't have my license yet, so we had to walk back to Claire's place. Luckily she didn't live very far from my apartment. I offered to help support her weight, but Claire was strong-minded, and insisted on walking herself. If she wasn't so small, I would've compared her to She-Ra. Beautiful, strong, and smart. That was Claire. Even bruised and shaken, she stood on her own. Nevertheless, I kept an eye on her as we walked.

"So what's it like being a super cool wizard? When do you get your pointy hat?" Claire asked me as we walked through the cool Seattle night.

"Not sure, but you'll be the first to know." An image invaded my mind of me wearing a grey cloak with matching pointy wizard hat. I imagined a beard to complete the Gandalf look and I couldn't help but laugh at the image. "This week has had its fair share of exciting moments. But it's definitely not all fun and games."

"Oh, yeah I bet." She said quietly. "Fun and games or not, I just want to say..." She trailed off, and looked away. It was hard to see in the dark but I could tell she was blushing.

"What?" I asked, puzzled.

"Seeing you come through the classroom wall with your giant dog from hell and blasting that snake chick with wind, it was pretty cool." Claire pulled back a stray hair.

I felt my stomach do a flip as she pulled back that stray hair. It was such a simple gesture, but damn it made her look so beautiful. The kind of beauty that she would never notice. That girl-next-door level of beauty and grace. I made a motion to grab her hand and take it in mine. I'm not sure where it came from, I'd never really seen her that way before. Maybe all the craziness that had happened in the last few days had given me a new perspective. Maybe it was just teenage hormones or whatever. But nerves got the best of me, and I pulled my hand away before she noticed.

We continued walking in comfortable silence. People always assume you need to constantly talk with your friends and family when you're together, but that's not true. When you're truly close with someone, like really close, sometimes you just need each other's presence to be happy. Don't take those simple pleasures for granted.

After a brief walk, we'd arrived in the white picket fence neighborhood that Claire lived in. It was the embodiment of suburbia. Colorful, cookie cutter houses that lined the streets with fenced in yards, wrap around porches, and the occasional barking dog. Nothing against my tiny apartment with Bishop and Scout, but this is the kind of life I'd always envisioned and wanted. Claire got to live in her classic suburban neighborhood with loving parents and sister, I couldn't help but be a little jealous.

As a wizard, would I ever get to achieve that life? A wife, a few kids, and a family dog? A normal job I hated and beers with the boys at the hole-in-the-wall bar across town? I wanted to throw parties for the Super Bowl and Halloween, not blast monsters with my magic powers, as cool as it was. But who knows, Bishop managed a relatively normal life. Maybe I could have it too.

"Well, this is my stop." Claire waved a hand to her house. It was a large and adorable house, one of the few in the neighborhood with three stories, though it wasn't as wide as other houses. It had the wrap-around porch with a porch swing and a bench surrounding a table. Her mom loved to tend to their garden, and in the summer, there would be a beautiful rose bush by the porch stairs.

"Alright, get some rest, kid." I smiled, teasing her.

She playfully punched me in the arm. She didn't hit me hard, but I was sore from my fight earlier, and it hurt more than she meant it to. I did my best to hold back the wince of pain and she pretended not to notice.

"Will I see you tomorrow?" Claire asked me. She knew the answer, and a hint of sadness tinted her voice.

"Not sure, I don't know what Bishop has planned." I shrugged. "But I will let you know." I let a smile stretch across my face.

"Maybe, after all this has settled down, we could go get coffee, or go to Pike's Place." Claire suggested.

I felt myself become nervous. My hands felt sweaty and I wanted to fidget like a madman. "Uh, yeah." I stammered. "I would like that."

She giggled. It was like music to my ears, and it made me even more nervous. "Okay, it's a date."

Claire gave me a bear hug, her strength surprising for her size. Like I said, She-Ra. After a moment longer than necessary, she let go and smiled up at me. Then she turned around and made her way inside.

Wow, where had those nerves come from? My legs felt like jelly and my hands were clammy. My stomach was full of butterflies, fluttering like crazy and making me feel like I was going to fly away. I'd never seen Claire that way before. We had always been good friends, but that was it. Maybe I had a new perspective on life? My world had become a whole lot more dangerous lately. Life was short, might as well enjoy what time you have and who you have to spend it with.

Chapter 8

The following day, I found myself back at the Mystic Order's training gym with Bishop. He'd pulled me out of school for the day to help me catch up on my training.

Oh, and to throw fire balls at me.

A flaming comet the size of a bowling ball came hurtling at me and I barely had time to dodge it. "Son of a-!" I squealed, my voice cracking.

"Come on Tobias!" Bishop barked out a laugh. "I wouldn't actually hit you."

"You got pretty damn close!" I growled in response.

"Fire is one of the most basic yet versatile tools a wizard has at his disposal. It can be used to fight, keep you warm in the cold, and light the way through the darkness. And to harass our nephews, of course."

"Ha ha." I said dryly.

"Okay, now you give it a try." Bishop invited. "Fire is a direct mirror of our emotions. When calm, it can be controlled, aimed, focused. But when your emotions are out of control, well, I'm sure you've heard of the Chicago fires."

I looked at him doubtfully. "You're kidding, right?"

He didn't answer me, choosing to move on. "Let your emotions be your channel for your fire spells. And when you've got it all gathered up, say your incantation."

Bishop turned to a nearby target dummy, about six feet to my left. He took a deep breath, and then punched his fist forward. "*Igni!*"

A column of flame erupted from his fist like a flamethrower, roaring across the gym and consuming the dummy like it was kindling.

I nodded, rolling my shoulders and jumping a couple times to loosen myself up. Then I took a fighting stance, reminiscent of what I was taught in my martial arts classes. I took a deep, slow breath. Then with an effort of will, I thrust my palm out, stepping forward as I did.

"*Hinote!*" I roared.

Several sparks erupted from my palm, but nothing more than that. No fire ball. No flamethrower. Nothing.

Bishop looked at me critically. "Again." He said simply.

I repeated the ritual before thrusting my palm out again. "*Hinote!*" Nothing but sparks again, though they fizzled out much faster than the first time.

We kept at it for almost an hour, each time the result dwindled even more. I was growing more and more frustrated, which Bishop said should actually cause the flames to erupt more, but still nothing. I kicked a nearby training dummy and sent it toppling over.

"Hey, calm down." Bishop placed a firm hand on my shoulder. "It's not common, but fire isn't for everyone. You're still pretty good at summoning wind, that'll do you some good."

"Yeah but who doesn't want to throw fire balls around?" I groaned. "You do it and it's freaking awesome." I crossed my arms, frustrated with myself. How embarrassing, I couldn't even perform one of the more basic spells. I felt like a joke.

"Don't be too hard on yourself." Bishop said reassuringly. "Here, let's try something else."

He stretched his arms out before resting them by his side again. "If you can manage this spell, I think you'll find it pretty useful."

"What is it?" I asked. I didn't seem very enthusiastic, and that's because I wasn't. I couldn't even throw fire balls around. I'd be stuck as the guy who could help you get your kite in the air at this rate.

"*Durcir!*" Bishop flexed and I felt the energy in the air suddenly rush towards him. His skin took on a metallic sheen and he seemed more rigid than before.

"You oiled yourself up?" I asked. "No offense uncle, but I don't see why I'd use the oily skin spell." I scoffed at him.

"Watch and learn, my young pupil." Bishop said. Even his voice had a different feel to it. Like it was going through a filter. It had more of an echo to it.

He approached another training dummy, this one made of stone. He took a simple fighting stance, reared back with one arm, and punched the dummy as hard as he could.

It shattered into a million pieces. The sound of it echoing around the room. I had to cover my ears, it was so loud.

"Woah, how the hell did you do that?" I asked him, completely amazed.

"Hardening spell, something I came up with." He explained. "Turns your body into something like metal. It makes you more durable, and a bit stronger." An invisible release of power washed over him, from head to toe. As it did, his body seemed to return to normal. But it was so seamless that I had trouble keeping track of the change.

"Now you try." Bishop said. "Don't worry about the fire spell, any doubt in your mind could ruin the spell. Just focus on what you're doing now."

"Alright then." I sighed. I took a deep breath and resumed my fighting stance. I concentrated, focusing my dwindling power on this next spell. I seeped my will into the incantation and shouted. "*Duro!*" I felt my body tense up. I felt stiff, but strong.

"Amazing Tobias!" My uncle barked out, laughing in excitement. He directed me toward a nearby stone dummy. "Now hit it!"

Using my martial arts expertise to guide me, I stepped forward and thrust out my arm forward, just like I'd been trained. I punched the dummy right in its false face. It exploded into thousands of shards of stone, flying in every direction.

"Yes!" I cheered gleefully. I couldn't help myself, it came out before I could even think about it. While I'd failed with the fire spell, the hardening spell had come so naturally. Paired with my martial arts training, the hardening spell was an incredibly useful, and dangerous tool.

We repeated the exercise for another hour or so. I would let the spell dissipate before calling it up again to shatter more stone dummies. I tried different punches, kicks, and other strikes, all to similar effect. The hardening spell enhanced my martial arts training to a dangerous degree. With it, I'd become a force to be reckoned with. Bishop even threw a few fireballs at me, and while the heat itself was uncomfortable, the flames didn't actually burn me.

After a few more rounds of practicing the spell, I walked over to the bleachers and sat down, letting the spell fade. Bishop sat down next to me, clapping a hand against my back. "You're progressing very well, Tobias. For the most part, you've got a natural talent for the art."

I smiled, but it quickly turned into a frown. "Except for that damn fire spell."

"I told you, don't beat yourself up over it." Bishop reassured me. "Everyone has their specialties, and everyone comes into their magic in their own time. Fire just isn't your thing right now."

I looked up at him and nodded. It didn't really make sense that I was beating myself up over not being able to make fire, when I could still summon hurricane winds with a flick of the wrist.

"Come on, let's head home and get some grub." Bishop stood up and offered me his hand. "How's pizza sound?"

I smiled. "Better than anything you'd cook."

The next few days have been pretty quiet. I went to school, though the hallway I destroyed was closed off, so a lot of the classes had to be redistributed. Claire and I ended up in the same history class. Lucky for me, it proceeded without incident. No attacks from Skeletor or Shredder to ruin my day. In fact, all of my classes went as they should.

Although I would've preferred a monster attack instead of the English project I had to do by next Wednesday. Before I knew it, school was over and I was free to go. Claire caught up to me as I walked down the front steps.

"Tobias, where are you off to?" Claire's voice chimed above the crowd of teenagers.

I stopped for her and smiled. "No real plans today. I was probably just going to head home."

"Wanna go to Pike Place with me?" She asked. She had her arms behind her back, leaning forward slightly and giving me her best smile. "I have to pick up a few things."

What could I do? I was a sucker. "Well you'd be twisting my arm, but alright."

Our school was a short bus ride from the bustling city on the coast where Pike Place was located. We stopped at the top level first, which was dominated mostly by the fish market. I couldn't stand the smell of fish, but Claire just loved seafood. So, I sucked it up and put up with the smell.

Like I said, I was a sucker.

It was her night to make dinner, and she made seafood every chance she could. I often had dinner with her family, but I actively avoided those nights. We spent an hour working our way through the many stands and shops. Claire was careful to closely inspect each and every potential purchase.

After the fifth fish stand, I had to walk away before I ejected the frozen burrito I'd had for lunch. I took three deep breaths, before righting myself. Seriously, I hate fish. I happened to look up and glance across the street.

I saw... something. I wasn't sure how to describe it. It was like a shadow, but no one was there to cast it. It just stood in the middle of the sidewalk, passerby completely ignoring it. The only evidence that they noticed it at all was how they seemed to unconsciously avoid it, stepping to the side just in time so they wouldn't touch it. Unlike everything else I'd seen so far, it didn't make me feel sick, or even scared. All I could feel from it was pure malice. The thing was full of hate and anger.

I had to find out what this thing was before it could get the jump on me. Or hurt any of the people around us. With purpose, I crossed the street. Moving quickly, but not running. I didn't want to catch anyone's attention or give any indication to the thing that I had noticed it. Unless it had already noticed me. There was that possibility to consider. I was across the street now and I turned in its direction, picking up the pace. I couldn't have been more than twenty yards away from it.

Fifteen yards.

Ten.

Five.

I was so close now I could start to make out features. It was still a shadow, but I swear I thought I could make out humanoid features. A head, ears, eyes, a nose. Only a few more steps.

A random passerby crossed my field of vision, cutting off my view of the shadow. I squirmed to get past them and lock onto the shadow again. But by the time I'd gotten past them, the shadow was gone.

I muttered a curse. That shadow thing had given me the slip, whatever it was. It made me nervous to think that some spook was watching me. Was I being hunted?

My phone vibrating against my leg freed me from the trance of thought I'd fallen into. I pulled it out and glanced on the screen. Claire was calling. Her caller ID picture was a picture of us using that dog ear filter on Snapchat. I answered.

"Yello!" I said as if I hadn't just been pursuing some shadow monster.

"Tobias, where'd you go?" Claire asked.

Oops. I guess I did kind of just ditch her suddenly. "Oh, sorry. I thought I saw a friend and so I ran across the street. Everything okay?"

"Yep!" She said happily. "I just got the last of my groceries. Ready to head to my place?"

"Yeah, sure." I said, only partially gritting my teeth at the thought of seafood for dinner.

We returned to Claire's house. She lived not too far from my apartment, in the suburbs surrounding Seattle. Her home's interior was something out of a Disney Channel sitcom. The front door led into a short hallway next to a set of stairs that went up into the ceiling, cut off from the first floor. There was a small table immediately to the left of the door. Several pairs of shoes were organized neatly under it, and directly above it was a key rack mounted on the wall. There were a few knick knacks on the table itself, along with bills and junk mail. The hallway itself was decorated with family photos. One showed a much younger Claire running away from her mom on the beach. She was maybe seven or so in the photo. They both had laughing smiles plastered on their faces. Another photo was more professionally taken, it showed the family posing together, all wearing similar shades of lavender. They looked happy. I felt a pang of jealousy intrude in my thoughts.

I didn't have any solid memories of my parents, and no pictures to speak of. The pictures had been destroyed in the fire that killed them. Bishop had said that fire wasn't an accident. Who killed them, and why? It had been in the back of mind since Bishop mentioned it back in the elven infirmary.

"You okay, Toby?" Claire asked.

Her voice brought me back to reality. "Oh, yeah. Sorry." I apologized sheepishly.

She shook her head. "Don't be sorry. I just worry when you get all spacey."

"Don't worry about me." I laughed it off. "Come on, let's join up with your family."

Dinner went without incident. Claire's parents have become well accustomed to my aversion to seafood and had already prepared a box of cheap mac and cheese. I put up no protest, I was known to tear into mac and cheese, usually killing an entire pot of it by myself. Even the cheap stuff. Claire's mom went the extra mile for me, adding various odds and ends to the mix to turn the cheap noodles and cheese powder into something Gordon Ramsay might find somewhat impressive.

Claire's dad was a healthy fifty-six years old and was the kind of guy who looked intimidating but he was a big softy. He'd gone bald years ago and had developed a big pot belly from six too many beers. Her mother was quite a bit younger. I never asked exactly how old she was, out of courtesy, but I'd have to say she was in her early forties. She had blonde hair, complimented with the handful of grey hairs that come with age. She didn't care for them but I personally thought they didn't look too bad.

Mr. Williams often talked to me about sports. He was just the kind of guy that assumed all boys were into sports. I knew just enough to keep a conversation going with him. Claire had politely told him time and time again that I cared more for Spider-Man comics and Nintendo games than talking about the latest Mariners game. Mrs. Williams was well educated in my interests, and was often guilty of buying me the latest comics and game releases for Christmas and my birthday. She treated me like the son she never had. I wasn't big on asking for gifts like that, but she always insisted.

After dinner, I helped Mrs. Williams with all of the dishes and putting leftovers away. I'd spent enough time here that I knew where everything went and what was stored in what. I didn't like to eat and run, so I went to the living room. They kept a bunch of board games in a drawer under the entertainment center and pulled out some discount version of Monopoly. I'm not particularly good at the game, but I'm very competitive about it anyways. Bishop says I get it from my dad, but hell if I know.

We played the game for maybe a couple hours, with Mrs. Williams slowly but surely dominating the board. Her competitiveness rivaled my own, but she was actually competent at the game.

"Boo-yah!" She cheered as she forced her husband into bankruptcy. Claire had been the first to fall, but she had given me all her properties and money so I would have a fighting chance, but it was ultimately a losing battle.

I uttered a PG curse. Even with the combined resources, Mrs. Williams still dominated almost three-fourths of the board. I had the railroads and a few high-taxing properties, but for every time she landed on one of mine, I landed on her's three times.

Eventually the inevitable happened and I threw in the towel.

"'Twas a valiant attempt, but you could not stop the inevitable." Mrs. Williams said dramatically.

"Yeah yeah," I muttered in defeat.

Mr. Williams took a big sip of beer and laughed. "Hey, you made it farther than either of us did."

Claire laughed. "Don't lump me in with you. You somehow lost on the third turn."

We all laughed at that. Claire's family felt like my own. Like I said, when I was here, I was treated like family. Like Olive Garden, but with less breadsticks.

But like all other good things, this too, would come to an end.

Chapter 9

It was time for me to get home. I said my goodbyes to Mr. and Mrs. Williams and began walking towards the front door, with Claire a step or two behind me. I reached for the doorknob, and before I had even touched it, I felt a spark of energy hit my fingertips. Any other day I would have mistook it for static electricity. But experience had taught me otherwise.

The pinprick of energy tickled at my magical senses. It gave me a sickly feeling, making me almost nauseous. The telltale sign of a magical predator. And then the feeling went from a small warning to an all-out red alert.

I felt my instincts practically scream "DANGER!"

What the hell? It was like my Spider-Senses were going off. I stared at the door for one more eternal second. My eyes suddenly widened in realization.

Everything seemed to slow down. I pivoted on the spot and tackled Claire back down the hall. The door exploded into a million pieces, several scraping against my back and shredding into the paint on the wall. The remaining big pieces bounced down the hall and against the walls. Claire and I hit the hardwood floor hard, I heard a loud gasp escape her as the wind was knocked out of her. I spun up on one knee, facing the door, holding my hand out ready to cast a spell.

My breath caught in my throat. I could feel my body shaking in shock and fear. Standing in the doorway was the hulking demon who had tried to kill me almost a week ago. Perfectly alive and intact. I never really appreciated just how big the bastard was. It had to hunch to see through the shattered door frame. And even then, it would never have a hope to fit through without taking out a foot of brick and drywall on each side.

"Tobias Caesar Leight..." The beast growled. "You and I have unfinished business."

"You're looking pretty good for a dead guy, King Koopa." I shot back.

It chuckled. "Your puny golem friend isn't here to protect you this time."

"Don't need him to. *Kaze!*" I roared. My voice echoed as the magic moved through me.

Sixty mile per hour winds rushed from around me and barreled towards the beast down the hall. It struck the demon with an audible boom of impact.

And then slipped harmlessly off of it.

The demon let out a hearty laugh. "Silly mortal child." It shouldered the wall and burst right through, slipping into the house. "It takes more than a slight breeze to do me in."

Well, crap. The demon lumbered closer to us and I was preparing to send another blast of wind at him. But I didn't get the chance. Something like a small roar assaulted my senses and a small impact hit the demon. And then another. And another. The demon didn't seem to notice, besides jolting slightly at the impact. I looked up at the stairs, where Mr. Williams stood with a pistol trained on the demon. Son of a bitch. I didn't know Mr. Williams even owned a gun, let alone how to use one.

He'd done everything right. Three shots straight to the chest would have put anyone else down. But judging by the demon's smug look and it's overall verticality, I'd say it wasn't going to have the intended effect. The demon blurred and had crashed straight into the stairs, sending wood shrapnel flying everywhere, and it grabbed Mr. Williams, wrapping its giant hand around his torso.

"Put me down!" Mr. Williams screamed in terror. "Tobias, Claire, get out of here! Run!"

I heard a sickening crunch as the demon squeezed and crushed Mr. Williams' ribs. He screamed in pain, firing off two more shots wildly and completely missing the demon.

"Daddy!" Claire screamed through the tears running down her face. She moved to rush over and try to help, but I stopped her.

"Where's your mom?" I asked her.

"In the backyard, drinking her tea." She said. "Sound doesn't carry well in this house so she probably hasn't caught on yet."

"Good, get her and run, Hop the fence, break it down, whatever you have to do but get out of here!" I ordered.

"But what about-?" Claire started.

"I'll get your dad. But for now you have to go! I can't save him and protect you at the same time!" I barked. She looked from me to the demon and back again, paralyzed as the terror set in. "GO!" I screamed at her.

That got her moving. Claire rushed out the hall towards the backyard. Two Williams safe, one to go. Let's make it three for three. "*Duro!*"

I felt my skin tighten up as my entire body hardened like rock. The demon was still distracted with Mr. Williams and it gave me an opening. I lunged forward and dug my fist into the demon's side.

Literally dug it in.

My fist pierced the demon's putrid hide and blood that seemed a bit too dark in color erupted from around my arm. The demon roared in pain, dropping Mr. Williams on the ruined stairs. He grunted in pain, but he was a fighter. Claire's father slowly began to drag himself up the remainder of the stairs. He didn't make it far though. I'm not sure if it was the pain or the shock, but I saw him drift off and pass out just before the top of the stairs.

The demon was hurt, but it was far from defeated. It twisted its torso and brought down its fists on my back. Without the hardening spell, I'd be saying bye-bye to my spine. I still felt the impact and it sent vibrations through my entire body, but I was still in one piece. I pulled my fist out of the beast's side only to deliver another blow straight into its gut. I ripped through its thick skin again, plunging my fist into its stomach. Blood spewed from both wounds and it definitely seemed to have an effect. The demon seemed more lethargic and pale, but it wouldn't quit. The beast grabbed me by the neck of my shirt and flung me through the wall and into the kitchen.

I crashed into the sink and a pipe must've burst because water erupted from the sink. My clothes were quickly drenched and stuck to my body. I felt dizzy and my vision was a little blurry.

"Is that all you got, big boy?" I mocked. "Pinkie Pie could hit harder than that."

I don't know if the demon understood the reference, but it was insulted anyway. It slammed its fists on the ground like a pissed off gorilla and charged towards me. But I'd done the damage I needed. I took aim and let out an angry "*Kaze!*"

A rush of wind hit the demon hard and knocked it off balance. The wounds I had inflicted had weakened it just as I'd hoped. It didn't have the same reservoir of strength as before and fell onto its back. I aimed my hand behind me and conjured up another gust of wind that pushed me through the air and through the hole in the wall. I landed on the beast's chest and let out all the confusion and anger I'd been storing up the past week on this beast's face.

I delivered blow after blow on the demon's head. Crunch after deadly crunch echoed in the hall. The demon struggled but slowly grew weaker. Its surprised and panicked struggling became less and less energized. Its body eventually grew limp and I heard it let out one last gurgling breath. It was dead. I was sure of it this time. I felt the life leave its body beneath me.

Emotion overwhelmed me and I let out a scream. There was anger. Pain. Fear. Too many emotions to count. I felt the hardening spell wear off and the strength leave me. My body swayed drunkenly and I fell off the side of the creature. With the last ounce of strength I had in me, I pulled out my phone and hit the speed dial for Bishop. Then I dropped the phone, and just laid there, waiting for my uncle to arrive.

When he realized I wasn't talking, it didn't take long for Bishop to get here. Scout and Jacob were both with him. Jacob helped me up and shuffled through the ruined hallway with me to the living room.

"Are you okay, man?" Jacob asked me. "What the hell happened?" Concern painted his face.

"The demon from before showed up for round two." I explained. "He wasn't expecting me to be able to hit back this time. I'm just not sure why he was here. Or how the hell he was even alive. I thought you sent him packing last time?" I looked at him questioningly.

Jacob pursed his lips as he tried to think. "Demons are especially resilient. They put together these physical bodies using magic to interact with the physical world. But for the most part, they're beings of spirit."

"Which I'm guessing means even after this, he's still not dead." I groaned.

Jacob was looking over me, assessing me for injuries. He rubbed his thumb over a very large bump on my forehead. I winced as a small hum of pain washed over my forehead. "Should probably have that looked at." He put his hand down. "All you did was send it back to whatever realm of spirit it came from. And you're right, you definitely caught it off guard."

Bishop came into the room with Scout padding behind him. "That's not the only error it made." Bishop came in and held up a scale from the demon's legs. "I was able to isolate this from its body before its construct dispersed."

"What's so special about a scale from the demon?" I asked him.

"We can use it to track it back to whomever called it forth." He explained. Bishop tucked the scale into a napkin and put it into his pocket. "The authorities are on their way. I've already explained there was a break in by an extremely enthusiastic burly man violently forced his way into the house."

"And did all of that?" I motioned towards the front room. "Won't they ask questions?"

Bishop shrugged. "They might, but they won't come anywhere near the actual story."

"What about Mr. Williams?" I asked.

"Paramedics have been notified as well. And I've already used a memory hex to muddle his memories of the events. He won't remember who or what exactly broke in."

"If I didn't know better, I would say you've done this once or thrice." I said, smiling a little.

Bishop returned the smile, but shrugged. I looked over at Jacob, who mimicked Bishop's expression. Scout sat next to me, looking at me with a doggy grin. Was he in on the joke too? I wouldn't be surprised, the dog was smarter than your average bear, after all.

The police and paramedics showed up not too long after. Mr. Williams was loaded up into an ambulance and taken to the hospital. I called Claire and filled her in. The police let her and her mom go to the hospital while they kept me for questioning. I explained what had happened, while leaving out the key details. I didn't have time or the patience to get locked up in a padded room in a strait jacket. The two detectives talking to me looked at the hallway in disbelief. I was sure neither of them believed some dude in a ski mask did all this, but what better explanation was there. Hell, maybe they even thought I was a suspect, but the testimony of the entire Williams family would clear any suspicion. It was one of those cases that just wouldn't go anywhere, but not for the usual reasons. It couldn't be too often that Kong's little cousins caused trouble in suburbia, could it?

A paramedic did a quick check up on me and confirmed I didn't need a visit to the hospital, just to rest. A few bumps and bruises were definitely not hospital worthy. I'm sure they'd be confused as hell as to how Mr. Williams was carted away with three broken ribs and I came away with a bump on the head.

After way too long, they finally all left. Good, I was getting annoyed and was close to letting out several snarky quips. Plus, there was work to do. Bishop had a lead now, and there was no way in hell I was going to miss out on this. I'd beaten the demon this time. On my own. No one had to save me this time. No Jacob. No Scout. Just me. There was a swell of satisfaction that bubbled from the pit of my stomach and radiated outward. It almost made me giddy. I had trouble keeping a satisfied smile off of my face.

I walked over to Bishop and Jacob, who were talking in hushed tone by Bishop's car. "So what's the word?" I asked.

"Nothing yet." Bishop said. "I won't be able to lay down a powerful enough tracking spell until we return to the Mystic Order. Roland and the Elders will want to hear about all this."

Something bugged me about that notion. Taking this to the supernatural Justice League made me nervous. Roland Braun seemed nice enough, but I had no knowledge on the others. But Bishop and Jacob were more experienced with this kind of thing, and if they had trust in the Elders, I suppose I could too.

Nothing bad could ever happen by trusting a governing body, right?

The four of us returned to the Gum Wall where the Mystic Order secret entrance was hidden. It was getting late, so most of the tourists had cleared out. There were barely any street lights that reached this area, so it was a bit hard to see. But I knew we'd reached the wall when I saw the hints of color of the gum that plastered the wall. It was still disgusting.

"How are we supposed to open the door from each side?" I asked.

"Jacob, if you will." Bishop held out his hand, gesturing to the wall.

Jacob stepped forward to the wall. Then he started pressing the gum, as if they were buttons. I gagged. Being a wizard was disgusting, I've decided. The gum must've been some sort of opening mechanism. He pressed on several pieces of gum that didn't seem at all different from the rest. I couldn't fathom how they could possibly remember which pieces of gum were part of the sequence. Then I let my magical senses roam and reach out. Now I realized how it worked. Magic, of course. I mentally thumped my own forehead with my palm. The gum he was pressing was magically coded. I could sense something else as well. The door itself was forming slowly with each press of the gum.

"I think I get it now." I nodded. "Clever, it's a secret code only wizards would be able to see."

"And golems." Jacob added, somewhat snidely. He looked at me from the side of his eye.

"Pretty much anyone magically inclined can see the code." Bishop said. "Only those who are associated with the Mystic Order would be able to activate it."

Sure enough, the door formed into existence. A line of light carved itself into the wall and swung open with a gust of air. It was still surreal to me. The door led seamlessly into the Portal Nexus. I still didn't understand where exactly the Mystic Order's headquarters was located. Bishop explained it as a place that existed between worlds, but that wasn't something you wrap your head around in a week or two.

We stepped through the doorway. Scout's claws tick-tacked along the white tile. He wagged his tail happily, excited by all the people coming in and out of the many doorways. He may be a hellhound, but dogs will be dogs, I suppose. As long as he didn't go to the bathroom right then and there, I didn't care.

Bishop led us down a series of zigzagging hallways. There were signs that pointed to different sections of the headquarters. I saw signs that said "Gymnasium", "Library", "Infirmary", and "Hot Springs". But he didn't seem to be following any specific directions.

Eventually we found ourselves in what looked like a corporate office. Like something you'd see at any desk monkey job. Nothing magical or mysterious about it. What must've been about a hundred cubicles occupied the wide office space. I could hear the clicking of keys and scratching of pencils coming from the many cubicles. As we walked past, I saw people young and old working away at computers, typewriters, and what looked like papyrus. Most were humans, wizards, I assumed. But I also saw elves like Sylf and short muscular human-like creatures. Dwarves, maybe?

The windows lining the floor showed a beautiful sprawling landscape covered in perfectly green grass. I'd never seen grass so green, even in the most untouched parts of the country. I could see a forest in the far distance.

"Is this?" I asked, remembering the infirmary and Sylf.

"Alfheim? Sort of." Jacob began. "The scenery in the windows change daily, to keep the atmosphere fresh. Today, it's Alfheim."

We made our way past the long expanse of cubicles and found ourselves at a corner office lined on all four sides by windows. Inside, Roland Braun was writing in a notebook. His office was pretty typical of a higher-up in a corporation. He had tall potted plants in the corners behind his large wooden desk. It looked like real wood, not imitation wood. I imagined it was pretty expensive. Unless Braun had carved it himself.

Bishop knocked gently on the glass. Braun perked up at the sound, then motioned us to come in. Bishop opened the door and Jacob held it open so we could all make our way in.

"Welcome to my humble abode." Braun held up his hands and gestured broadly around him.

It really was humble. His office was very plain, almost boring. There were conveniently three chairs on the other side of his desk, already set up for us. Maybe he knew we were coming, maybe he just had three chairs. Wizards work in mysterious ways.

"High Elder, I think I may have a lead on whoever's been sending monsters after Tobias." Bishop began.

"Oh? Well then, pray tell. What is it that you found?" Braun asked, again gesturing with his hands inviting Bishop to produce the evidence.

Bishop reached into his pockets and produced the napkin. He set it on the table before letting it unfold, revealing the obsidian scale that he had picked off of the demon.

"Oh ho ho, how interesting." Braun eagerly picked up the scale and started twisting and turning it around to get a good look at it. At the same time, I could feel his own magical feelers spreading out to poke and prod the scale.

"Well I must say, I'm impressed, Tobias." Braun said with a genuine smile. "Judging by the energies I'm picking up off this scale, you managed to take down a pretty sizable demon."

"Yeah, he was a pretty big dude." I confirmed.

"Not what I mean." Braun shook his head. "The physical forms of demons aren't always relative in size to their power. Though it appears to be the case, in this instance. The demon you managed to fight off was no mere brute that any amateur warlock can call up."

"Then what was it then?" Jacob asked.

"Just from what I can tell from this one scale, this demon is of a higher caliber." Braun began. "It's definitely not a brand new demon. Might be a few thousand years old, but it means that whoever is behind this has deep reservoirs of magical energy at their disposal."

"Wouldn't we be aware of anyone with that level of metaphysical muscle?" Bishop asked.

"Usually, but not always." Braun shook his head, his face crinkling with concern.

"Our system of finding the magically-inclined is good, but it's not perfect." Jacob said. "Plenty of young magelings slip through the cracks. Many of them stumble upon some dark magic. And then bingo, bongo, you got a fresh warlock on your hands."

Braun gestured in the affirmative. "There are many warlocks out in the wild. Most don't get above petty spells and pyramid schemes. Some grow up to be politicians. But a select few grow into very dangerous and powerful warlocks. The kind that are a threat to the Mystic Order."

I tapped my fingers against my thigh thoughtfully. "So who has that level of power?"

Braun shook his head. "No one who's walking free. We act quickly on these threats and neutralize them."

Bishop narrowed his eyes. "Then that means..."

"The person pursuing Tobias comes from within the Mystic Order itself." Braun said gravely, crossing his hands in a steeple.

"Someone's operating right under your nose?" I asked, the concern painting itself across my face.

"My thoughts, exactly." Bishop agreed. "Any theories, Braun?"

"Someone scheming from within the Order would have to be exceptionally powerful. Not many outside of the Elders fit the bill." Braun said. I could tell this line of thought troubled him deeply.

I decided to take a leap of faith. "A little while ago, we overheard a group of wizards discussing something had been stolen. Seeing as how you're head honcho around here, I thought you might know something about that."

I'll give Braun credit, he barely blinked. "So, word has gotten out. The Grail has gone missing."

Bishop and Jacob both went stone-faced, which I suppose was pretty literal for the latter. "You don't mean the capital G Grail, do you?" Jacob asked.

"Yes, the Holy Grail. Born from the body of Lucifer and bathed in the blood of Christ." Braun said, his voice had changed from that lighthearted silky smooth voice to something gravelly and deep.

"Wait wait wait, so you're telling me the Christian religion is actually real? Like it's true? Every other religion is just full of it?" I scoffed, completely baffled about how casual they all were about this.

"Oh don't be silly, Tobias," Bishop said. "Pretty much every religion and pantheon you can think of is real, at least in part. People just pick and choose which to believe."

"Okay," I dragged out the word. I made a mental note to assign myself some mythology homework later. "So the Holy Grail is missing, so what? It's just a cup right?" I asked.

Braun shook his head. "Far from it, son. The Holy Grail is one of the single most powerful magical artifacts to exist on this plane of existence."

"With it and the proper ritual, one could use it to achieve incredible power." Bishop added. "Being bathed in the blood of a god, the Holy Grail possesses powers that could potentially make the wrong person into an immortal."

I whistled. Well I tried to, I actually never learned how to.

"Any theories on who within the Order would be trying to achieve immortality?" Jacob asked.

Then I remembered something. My first meeting with the Elders. One of them had given me a weird vibe. "High Elder, when I first met you, there was a man sitting on the bench that rubbed me the wrong way." I began. "Tall, skinny, short red hair, sound familiar?"

Braun grunted. "Well, that sounds like Fachnan. He's been a member of the Mystic Order for three hundred years or so now. He was recently ascended to the rank of Elder a couple of years ago."

"Ever have any reason to suspect him of foul play?" I asked. I didn't know how to explain it, but the guy had just made me feel weird. And the way he looked at me, like a lion watching his dinner.

"Not at all." Braun shook his head. "I chose him as an Elder because of his extensive experience in investigating instances of dark magic."

"I'm not trying to question your judgment, but I've gotten pretty good at picking up bad vibes from kids at school and people on the street, and his vibes are as bad as they come." I said. "When I felt him staring at me, it gave me a similar feeling to what I felt just before the demon attacked me. Almost the exact same."

Braun had a tense look on his face, like he was deep in thought. Maybe he was thinking about how he wanted to zap me for questioning his judgement on one of his fellow Elders. To my surprise, Bishop spoke up first.

"I've had my suspicions of Fachnan for awhile. Little things, but noticeable. An increase in his dealings with lesser demons, minor artifacts of power going missing, but nothing of this scale." My uncle shrugged. "I think it may be worth investigating, Braun."

Braun let out a breath through his nose, causing his nostrils to flare. "Very well. I'll launch an internal investigation into any possible connection that Fachnan might have to the Grail's disappearance."

"I'll help any way I can, sir." I said. "If this guy's dangerous, I want to help."

"Your enthusiasm speaks for you, Tobias." Braun said. "But I believe you've taken this as far as you are capable. Your uncle and Jacob will assist me, but I'd like for you to focus on perfecting your magic and staying out of the way. If you're right, the stakes have officially surpassed your abilities."

I tried to hide the flash of anger, but I don't think I fooled anyone. I wasn't some punk kid. I'd handled myself against evil twice now. I was strong and capable. I didn't need Braun or Bishop or Jacob holding my hand. To hell with them if they were going to bench me.

Jacob reached out to put a hand on my shoulder. "Tobias..."

I smacked his hand away and turned on my heel as I stormed out of the office. I didn't look back. I was pissed off. I was tired of being treated like a child. I made it towards the hallway that led back into the greater Mystic Order headquarters when someone stopped me.

It was Kat. Her hair had changed from red to grey, still shaved with patterns on the sides. She was wearing a black mesh netting that covered pretty much everything except her face. Over it she was wearing black short shorts that had splotches of white and grey on them, like they were purposely stained. And she wore what used to be a light hoodie that she had cut to end just above her stomach.

She took a long draw from a cigarette. "Hey, wanna go for a walk?"

Chapter 10

Kat had led me through a door in the Portal Nexus that spat us out somewhere in the forests of northern California. We walked right out of a tree trunk. I found myself furiously wiping off half a colony of ants that had been crawling along the bark. I definitely did not scream like a little girl either. Not me. You must be thinking of someone else.

An amused smile spread across Kat's face as she watched my archaic dance. "Not a fan of bugs?" She asked me, her voice tinted with a hint of amusement.

"Not all over me, that's for sure." I said, clearing my throat in an attempt to sound manly. "Why are we out here anyways? I didn't think you even cared much for me."

Kat's smile went from amused to sheepish. "You mean last time? It wasn't anything to do with you, honestly. I just can't stand Order politics or being anyone's errand girl."

"So you work for the Order?" I asked her.

Kat began walking down a half-formed trail that nature desperately tried to reclaim. I followed. "I don't know if work for is the right word. Work for implies that I get paid." She said spitefully. "Braun adopted me when I was very young. I've lived at Light Haven for as long as I can remember."

"Light Haven?"

"That's what most of the wizards there call it. Sounds a lot better than 'The Mystic Order's Headquarters' if you ask me." Kat said.

Bishop had always referred to it as such. Maybe he was just old fashioned. He never cared much for superfluous things.

"Living there so long, I've basically got chores, which includes picking up snot-nosed wizards for meetings and crap."

"I resent that remark." I sniffed.

Kat let out a giggly laugh. It was a nice sound, I have to admit. "So what's got you all hot and bothered? You seemed pretty peeved walking out of Braun's office."

I let out a sigh. "There's something going on and it has to do with me. And I want to help, but they just want to throw me to the sidelines while the big kids handle it all."

Kat found a mossy log off to the side and sat down, patting a spot next to her, inviting me to follow suit. "Wanna talk about it?"

I sat down with her, letting out another heavy breath. I told her everything. From my weird dream to the demon attacks to that weird shadow I'd seen outside Pike Place. It felt good to just let it all out. To be able to just vent about every little thing that was driving me crazy. Kat was very easy to talk to, despite the way she carried herself.

"On top of all that, Bishop and Braun say that the freaking Holy Grail has been stolen." I added.

"Huh, even with everything I know to be real, I thought that one was just a myth." Kat said.

She went to light another cigarette. I let out a whisper of power and with a flick of my wrist, a small gust of wind blew out her lighter.

"Seriously?" I asked, dramatically gesturing to the beautiful forest around us. "Plus, those things will kill you."

She rolled her eyes. "Magic conspiracy of epic proportions and you're worried about my lungs?"

I held up my hands. "It's the little victories, I like to think."

She tilted her head in agreement. "So what are you going to do?"

"Not sure what I can do." I huffed out a breath. "Bishop and Braun benched me while they investigate Fachnan." I waggled my fingers mockingly. "I'm just supposed to practice my little spells and stay out of the way."

"Figures those old fogies want to put the new up-and-comer out of the way so they can hog all the glory." Kat rolled her eyes. "I say we investigate Fachnan ourselves."

My eyes widened. "Woah, woah. I don't know about all of that."

"Oh come on sparkle-fingers, you're a big kid." Kat held her hands out, gesturing generally to me. "You're capable, aren't you? You took down that demon like it was yesterday's trash."

She was right. Bishop and Braun had said that demon was no lightweight. It was nothing to scoff at that I'd managed to beat it one on one. I twiddled my thumbs for a second in thought.

"Alright, what did you have in mind?" I asked her.

A devious little smile appeared on her face. "Fachnan will be busy with meetings and other Order logistical crap. He has a portal that leads to his estate in Ireland. If there's anything he's hiding, I'm betting we'll find it there."

"Are you sure its a good idea?" I asked her. "You're SURE he won't be home?"

"Positive, part of my job as the Mystic Order's errand monkey is making sure there are no errors in the big wigs' schedules." Kat reassured. "Fachnan will be too busy to return home for a few more hours. So, you in?"

I put up my hands in surrender. "Alright, let's run this." I nodded confidently.

Before I knew it, Kat was leading me down a mess of hallways throughout Light Haven. I don't know how I'd ever be able to navigate this place. Everyone had to be crazy. Though considering these people probably dealt with nightmares and monsters on the daily, maybe that was the case.

"I feel like Pinky trying to find my way around this fustercluck of a place." I scoffed.

"Well if that makes me The Brain, then we're in trouble." Kat laughed. Her smile was quick to become more neutral as we stopped in front of a black-stained oak door. The door was decorated with intricate carvings that made me think I'd suddenly walked into the 1800s. The door gave me the heebie-jeebies. I felt an icy feeling slither up my spine.

"You're kidding me, right?" I gazed in disbelief at the Super Evil Black Door of Absolute Evil. As I turned to look at Kat, the cold sinister feeling seemed to fade. "It couldn't be more obvious if he was twirling his moustache."

Kat slipped passed me and looked the door over. "It's easy to be obvious when all these old farts are naturally dense." Her fingers seemed to glow with purple light. "All the wizards who have offices and personal quarters set up their own security measures."

"So how are we supposed to get in without letting everyone know what we're up to?" I asked her. I had an image in my head of her setting everything off and having a thousand cranky wizards on our ass before we even got a chance to do our investigating.

"Relax. I've lived here long enough to get myself into trouble." Kat's hands continued tracing the carvings' grooves on the door with her glow stick fingers. "I spent a lot of that time picking apart chains and locks to places I'm not supposed to be."

"If you say so." I said. My eyes darted up and down the long hallway. I could feel my hands getting clammy. If even one person happened to walk down the hall, we were screwed.

"Duh doo, duh doo, dun doo doo dun doo doooooo doo duh doo." I sang to myself nervously.

Kat looked at me, almost disgusted. "Is that the Pink Panther theme song?"

"Don't look at me like that. I sing cartoon theme songs when I get nervous." I snapped defensively.

"Well shut it, I'm trying to focus." Kat hissed at me. "I've almost got it."

After a few more minutes of waggling her fingers and muttering curses, I felt a release of tension around the door as it slowly swung open.

"Damn I'm good." Kat stood up straight, looking very pleased with herself. "Come on, nerdy boy." She opened the door further and slipped in.

I followed. "Really? That's the best you got."

"Tell me it's inaccurate." She shrugged. "I'm not always witty but damn do I hit the nail on the head."

I shut the door behind me. Fachnan's quarters were straight out of Dracula's castle if the vampire lord had a Wi-Fi connection. Worn stone brick walls with large candles on each side illuminating the small room with dim orange light. He had a desk in one corner that I swore I'd seen in an IKEA catalogue. Two monitors displayed a generic Windows 7 screensaver. I wasn't sure where the computer's tower was, maybe hidden in the walls or something. His bed was a simple metal frame with pristine white sheets. Brave man, if it was me, those sheets would be stained to hell with food and juice spills. I am not a very clean person, and I haven't been allowed anything white as long as I can remember. He had a small dresser at the foot of his bed that couldn't have held more than a few days worth of clothes.

"Are the stone walls and candelabra really necessary?" I asked, baffled. Fachnan seemed to be the youngest member of the Elders and he was still half-stuck in the stone age.

"Yeah the older wizards always seem to be back asswards when it comes to embracing modern technology." Kat noted as she looked around the room. "They recognize the utility of the internet, but fluorescent light bulbs, now that's crazy talk."

I couldn't help but laugh at the absurdity. "Okay, so what are we looking for?"

"Fachnan has some sort of passageway that leads back to his estate in this room somewhere. There's not a whole lot to look through so it shouldn't take us too long. But it's best if we find it fast." Kat began scanning the room, turning in a circle as she looked for some sort of giveaway.

I let my magical senses reach out to the room around me. I imagined invisible hands stretching out from my body in every direction, feeling between the nooks and crannies of the room. I could feel Kat watching me as our magical feelers brushed past each other. Within a couple moment's, I felt a humming power along the far wall. I was no expert, but I had a feeling that's what I was looking for.

"Right there." I pointed towards the section of the wall that seemed to almost vibrate with energy.

She nodded and extended a hand towards the spot I had pointed. I felt a surge of energy and a glowing outline formed on the wall and the stone bricks seemed to evaporate. A corridor of luminous fog had appeared in the wall. It didn't seem to be as instant of a portal as the one leading back to Seattle had been.

"Good eye, you might have a knack for the more sensitive side of magic." Kat said.

"I'm not sure about that." I chuckled nervously.

She punched me in the arm.

Ow. She was stronger than she looked.

"Just take the compliment, ya doof." She rolled her eyes. "Let's go."

I rubbed my arm and followed her into the portal.

The portal dumped us out in yet another long corridor. I took a moment to examine my surroundings and couldn't help but let out an impressed whistle. Fachnan's castle was pretty rad. It was made of the same stone material as his personal quarters had been. Like, the exact same. He must've cut it all from the same stone. Tapestries hung along either side of the portal, which closed itself behind an ornate door painted red with silver trim. The tapestries matched, with designs of a two-headed dragon rearing up and roaring. The windows were made of stained glass depicting what appeared to be Fachnan battling various monsters. One seemed to be of a giant humanoid about to crush Fachnan with a boulder. Another had him calling down lightning against a serpent. So on and so on.

"Let's go this way." Kat motioned for me to follow as she headed down the hall. I hurried to catch up.

As we made our way down the corridor, I noticed multiple portraits of Fachnan throughout his life. Man, the guy sure liked to stare at himself. It seemed like every wall was adorned with at least one depiction of the guy, one way or another.

"So what do you know about Fachnan?" I asked.

"He's an expert in combatting and neutralizing dark magic." Kat said. "Whenever a curse or hex proves to difficult to deal with, Fachnan is usually called in to handle it."

"How's he with demons?" I asked.

"He's not much in a fight." Kat said thoughtfully. "But he knows how to hobble and bind them. Enough to make them go away, at least."

"Could he have sent them after me?"

"I think so. I've never seen him work in person. All I know is what's in his file."

It wasn't much, but it was enough to give me a reason to want to investigate him further. We kept walking.

After a couple of minutes, what felt like a static shock twinged against my arm. I looked to see a rounded wooden door set in the wall. It didn't give me a weird sickly feeling like the demon or the nagini. It didn't even feel particularly wrong in any way. I didn't get a bad feeling from it. It was completely unremarkable. But something told me it was important anyways.

"Wait," I hissed at Kat. I wasn't sure why I was whispering. We were alone after all. I pointed towards the door. "I want to check through here."

"Why? Fachnan's study is this way," She pointed down the hall.

"Trust me, something in my gut says we should check it out." I assured her. I took a step closer towards the door, reaching out for the rusted handle.

Nothing dramatic happened. I grabbed the handle, and pulled the door open. I looked down a dark staircase. The steps were wooden, nailed into the walls, but there seemed to be a space below them.

"The basement." I sucked my teeth. "Nothing bad ever happens in the basement."

"You're the one who wanted to check it out." Kat waved a hand towards the stairs. "After you."

I pulled out my smartphone, which seemed completely out of place here and flicked on the flashlight. It was a strong light, but it only lit up a few steps down.

Kat rolled her eyes. "Here, let's try mine." She aimed her fingertips down the staircase and muttered. "Lumina."

A small cloud of light seemed to seep out of her fingers and form into an almost solid cloud of pure light. It drifted down the staircase, bathing it in light. It was bright enough that it might as well have been pure daylight. The light revealed a fairly large concrete room.

"Nice trick." I tilted my head, impressed. Then I headed down into the depths.

The wooden planks of the stairs creaked dramatically as I took each step. Even with the basement illuminated I was starting to get nervous. Basements in general just have a bad energy around them. Maybe it's because every tv show and movie in existence perpetuated basements as the place where the bad things dwell. But that idea had to come from somewhere, right? After what seemed like an eternity, we'd reached the last step.

My heart skipped several beats.

In the center of the room was the image of a red five pointed star breaching the edges of a circle. Like a pentagram, except a pentagram was supposed to contain the star in the circle. On each point of the star sat an unlit candle. The smell of iron was almost overwhelming. The messed up pentagram had been painted in blood.

"I...I know this place." I felt jittery. My eyes darting around the room, looking for danger. This place had scared the hell out of me then. Now, it was real. And that made it all the scarier.

"This is the place you'd described from your dream, right?" Kat asked. She was watching me carefully. Her hands poised at the ready for spell slinging.

I could feel myself instinctually reaching out for my own magic. My fingers felt like they were charged with electricity. My body felt jumpy as hell. I could probably run a marathon faster than Speedy Gonzales.

"We need to leave. Now." I immediately turned to go. Kat stopped me, placing a hand firmly on my chest.

"No. This is exactly the kind of thing we came to find." She said, trying to cut through my anxiety with reason. "Catch your breath, and help me look around."

With that, she walked passed me and started scanning the edges of the room. I took a deep breath, slowly counting to ten in my head. It was just a room. Only Kat and I were here. There was no harm in taking a look around.

So I did. I took a knee near the edge of the breached pentagram, inspecting it closely. I didn't get any sense off of it. Not even the smell of sulfur. It seemed to be nothing more than a painting on the ground. But I knew better. My dream had taught me the true nature of this sigil. Or at least, given me a hint.

"Do you recognize this symbol at all?" I asked Kat.

"I've seen it in books." Kat began, not taking her attention away from investigating the room's edges. "A typical pentagram has the star contained within the circle, it represents magic controlled by a human will."

"But this one has the star's points breaking through the circle," I pointed out. "What does that mean?"

"It's a symbol of darkness. It symbolizes the dark magic breaking free and taking control of the mortal world." Kat explained. "It's often used in demon worship and rituals."

"So what's it doing in Fachnan's basement, and why'd I dream of it?"

"Good question. To be honest-"

Something ricocheted off the wall just an inch away from Kat's head. She whipped around, eyes widening. "Tobias, move!"

I had only a split second to react. I rolled forward, passing over the pentagram and next to Kat. Where I'd been kneeling, something came down hard on the ground, followed by a CLANG!

I turned around and saw our new friend. It was fairly small, compared to the beasts and ghouls I'd come across so far, only about four feet tall. It reminded me of a Mogwai that had been fed after midnight, but with smaller ears and a huge nose that took up much of its face. Its eyes were equally large and beady. Long lanky limbs and a small torso made up the rest of its body. It was wearing belts across its chest that housed many small daggers. It had struck at the spot where I'd been with an old axe that hadn't been sharpened in a very long time, yet had still managed to cut a couple of inches into the concrete floor. None of those details were more noticeable than the red, ragged cap that it wore on its head.

"What the hell is that thing?" I held up my hands defensively.

"A redcap, probably bound to guard Fachnan's estate." Kat cursed.

"And what the hell is a redcap?"

"A faery, one of the Unseelie Court." Kat explained. "In other words, bad news."

Kat must have been insane. This thing, a fairy? I had a feeling we did not watch the same cartoons.

"So you're the ugly stepbrother of Tinker Bell?" I scoffed. "Man, no wonder Disney didn't put you in Peter Pan."

"Me's will kills you and hang you on the master's wall." The redcap yanked its axe out of the ground. "Me's will adds your bloods to me's cap."

"Yeah, I don't think so." I turned to Kat. "Run! *Kaze!*"

Hurricane winds filled the room, ripping towards the redcap. The gust picked up the redcap, flinging it through the air. The creature seemed to ride the wind though and delicately landed on the staircase. It pulled a throwing knife from its belt and threw it with alarming precision directly at my chest.

Kat uttered a word of power and stepped between the knife and myself. The knife seemed to spark and deflect off of an invisible wall clattering to the ground in the center of the pentagram. I swallowed. That would've hurt, if I'd been alone, I'd be doing my shish kebab impression.

"Thanks." I breathed out.

"Get up, you're just asking to die sitting on the floor like that." She lectured.

"Yeah yeah," I stood up, brushing dust off my shoulder. "What do I need to know about this thing?"

"Redcaps are incredibly ruthless and crafty little bastards." Kat explained. "They're experts in the art of killing and are strong enough to go toe to toe with the likes of the demon you've fought before."

"Well, that's encouraging." I noted, humbled by the fact.

The redcap screeched and lunged towards us. I took a step forward and thrust out my open palm. "*Kaze!*"

Another rush of wind barreled towards the redcap, but it had expected the attack. The damn thing seemed to shift midair. One second, it was on a direct course to get sucker punched by my wind spell. The next, it was conveniently a few inches to the left, and coming down with its axe right towards my head. My instincts took control, and I raised up my arm defensively and yelled, "*Duro!*"

I focused the spell on my arm, and I felt my skin and muscles tighten as they hardened into something like steel. The axe clanged against my skin, causing the redcap to bounce back from the impact. It did a backflip and landed gracefully in the center of the room.

Holy crap.

Even focusing the hardening spell on my arm, I'd felt the spell almost give. If it had been only a little bit stronger, I'd have to get in line for a robot arm right after Luke Skywalker. Kat wasn't kidding. This thing made the demon and the nagini feel like lightweights.

"What's the likeliness we beat this thing?" I asked.

The redcap threw two more daggers and charged at us. I called up another gust of wind to keep the attack at bay. I was getting winded, no pun intended. I'd tap myself sooner or later and then the redcap would carve me up like a turkey.

"We don't have the power to kill it!" Kat growled. "*Raiko!*" An arc of lightning erupted from her hands and struck the redcap.

It screeched as the lightning cooked its flesh. As it convulsed, it managed to grab another dagger and throw it wildly in our direction. The dagger embedded itself into Kat's shoulder and she screamed in agony. She fell back against the wall and slid to the floor. She was bleeding heavily out of the wound, and even now I saw the color draining from her face.

"No!" I quickly put myself in between myself and Kat. With all my rage and frustration, I called out, "*Kaze maximus!*"

Primal winds filled the room and sent the redcap flying in a spiral. Stones were ripped out of the wall as the winds continued to increase in intensity. Several stones battered the redcap as it flew helplessly through the air. But it seemed only a little more than annoyed. I uttered the hardening spell while I had the redcap at bay, and instantly my body tightened and hardened. As the wind began to die down, the redcap rebounded off of the nearest wall and jumped straight towards me. I leapt to meet the creature and threw a hard right hook right for its crooked little jaw. As I felt its jaw crumble under my fist, I felt red hot pain ignite across my chest. I looked down to see a long, deep cut that stretched from my left pec to my right hip. An alarming amount of blood was oozing from the wound.

Immediately I felt the remainder of my strength sap away. My hardening spell faltered, and I fell less than gracefully to the ground. I landed on my shoulder and an eruption of pain told me it'd been broken. The redcap landed a few feet away from me, massaging its jaw. It held up its axe, examining the blood that had stained the blade. My blood.

"Tobias!" Kat cried out. Though her voice was weak. She'd lost a lot of blood. And I was losing even more. I could hear her struggling to stand. She tried to call up another blast of lightning, but it did little more than charge the air.

My vision started to swim and blur. The redcap put its axe in a holster over its shoulder and pulled out a dagger from its belt. It giggled maniacally as it approached. It kicked me hard in the chest and I rolled over onto my back. The devilish faery straddled me, speaking in a language I didn't recognize and held the blade to my throat. I tried to raise my good arm to defend myself, but the redcap screamed at me and pinned my arm to the concrete with its free hand. Its skin felt dry and leathery. I wanted to recommend it a good skincare routine but now hardly seemed like the time. If I didn't do something fast, it was going to cut my throat and watch me bleed out.

I tried to gather even the tiniest bit of magic to buck this thing off and buy myself a few more seconds, but it kept slipping away. It was too hard to focus. My mind was a haze. I couldn't put any helpful thought together.

Damn it. This had been a stupid idea. I'd known it too. But I was too pissed off with Braun and Bishop. They'd treated me like a kid. An amateur. Well, duh, Tobias. You were an amateur. They'd been doing this for decades, if not longer. I'd been doing it for what, a couple weeks, if that?

I closed my eyes. My breathing slowed and became more relaxed. I wasn't going to die a panicked animal. I was going to go out with at least a shred of dignity. I owed myself that much. I felt the redcap begin to apply more pressure as it prepared to finish the job. Any second now.

Three.

Two.

One.

Nothing happened. Was that what death felt like? Instant release? No pain, no suffering as you left the world of the living. I didn't even feel the redcap's blade against my throat anymore. I decided to take a gamble and opened my eyes.

The redcap was flailing around helplessly in midair. It still gripped the dagger, uselessly slashing the air. It was looking towards the stairs with smoldering hate in its eyes. I followed its gaze.

Standing about halfway down the steps was Fachnan. He wore white button-up shirt and black slacks with dress shoes. He had his palm aimed at the redcap and seemed to be saying something, though I couldn't make it out. The air seemed to shimmer between him and the redcap. He descended the steps, his gaze locked on the faery.

Only once he was standing right over me, did he turn his gaze to me. With his other hand, he seemed to do a vaguely magical wiggle of his fingers and I felt a wave of drowsiness overtake me.

My vision blurred to black. I remember trying to say something, but I can't remember what. All I knew was that I wasn't dead.

Not yet anyways.

Chapter 11

Dreams were always interesting to me. My friends always told me about how they dreamed of being late for work or being caught with their pants down in front of the class. My dreams almost always were some weird remix of my normal life with some characters from a tv show thrown in for some god forsaken reason. One time I had a dream that Dr. House and He-Man came to Thanksgiving dinner last year. That's beside the point.

Nowadays, I rarely dream. In fact, I hadn't dreamed since my nightmare just before my life changed forever. Apparently, my subconscious decided to break that streak.

I found myself in a storm-ridden canyon. The world was covered in a tinge of blue as dim light shown through the storm clouds. Rain plastered my hair to my head and lightning struck uncomfortably close.

"Bishop? Jake? Anyone?" I called out into the storm, but my voice was drowned in the noise of the torrent of water coming down. I'm not going to lie; I was scared out of my mind.

I walked down the valley, shielding my face as the wind picked up and the rain damn near went horizontal. It was freaking cold too, and that was saying a lot coming from someone who's lived in Seattle their whole life. I had to lean into each step or else the wind would knock me on my ass. In the distance I could hear a low, almost inaudible rumbling. At first, I thought it was thunder, considering the weather. But there was a rhythm to the rumbling. It wasn't in sync with the lightning either. I could almost make out...

Words.

It was a voice. A big, bad, scary voice.

It was saying something. "..et...m...n...!"

What I saw next, I couldn't believe, even in a dream. Something reached over the horizon. A colossal human hand reached over the edge of the world. The skin was blackened and cracked like charcoal, as if this giant had been burned alive a long, long time ago.

I was too in awe to even think about calling up my magic to defend myself. Whatever this thing was, it was huge and ancient. I saw the hand flex as it began to pull itself up. As it moved, it made a large groaning noise that I could feel reverberating in my chest. The sky and earth alike shook as its primordial voice spoke again.

"Let...me...IN!" The last word was laced with magic. From that one incantation alone, I could feel its power wash over me like a wave. From that little taste that it let loose, I felt an ocean of energy and power. My own magic was like a candle flame compared to its forest fire. It was incomparable. Something I would never even come close to comparing to in my entire life, no matter how hard I worked and trained.

That sheer, limitless power wrapped around me like a wet blanket, dampening my own abilities and perception. My mind seemed to drown in it. It was trying to consume me, trying to find a way into my mind, my soul.

The scene suddenly changed. I was in a dark room with nothing but a stone table and a light shining down. The canyon and the torrential storm were both gone. Like it had never even been there. My clothes and my body were dry.

There were two chairs at the table, one on each side. As ominous as it appeared, the table seemed safe enough. Nothing to set off my instincts or give me any reason to think it was dangerous. I looked around for any other landmarks in the space, but there was nothing. I took a deep breath and took a seat at the table.

"I was wondering when we would get a chance to meet." A voice echoed from the void. I looked around, looking for the source of the voice. But it seemed to come from everywhere and nowhere.

"Who's there?" I called out into the darkness. I began to rise from my seat, looking around wildly.

"Please, don't get up on my account." The voice seemed to focus, coming from the other side of the table. I focused my eyes as much as I could, and I saw the beginnings of a silhouette.

The figure stepped into the light slowly and dramatically, of course. My jaw hit the table hard. Have you ever watched a cartoon where the hero character meets themselves from another evil dimension? Well, here came evil dimension Tobias. He was my height, had my hair cut, was wearing very similar clothes, and even stood the same way I would. The man in front of me was damn near a photo negative of me right down to my slightly crooked chin.

He was just a little bit different. His chin leaned in the opposite direction to mine. His hair was blonde and a bit less unruly compared to mine. I was wearing a T-shirt with the PlayStation logo; he wore one with an Xbox logo. Whoever this guy was, he truly was evil.

"And who the hell are you supposed to be?" I asked.

"That's...a complicated question, to say the least." He spoke. Even the infliction of his voice was like mine, but slightly different. It felt more formal, with a sense of superiority hiding underneath.

"Uncomplicate it." I growled, trying to sound threatening. It probably would've been more intimidating if my voice didn't shake slightly. Whoever this guy was, he made me very uneasy. I felt my fingers tap against the table, a nervous habit of mine.

"There's really no need to be nervous, Tobias." The man said. "I'm not here to hurt you. I promise, I just want to talk."

"And so, I'll ask again." I slammed my hand down on the table, letting out an effort of will. A strong gust of wind burst forth and outward around us. It ruffled up his hair and clothes slightly. That'll show him. "Who ARE you?"

The man gave me a concerned look as he smoothed out his clothes and fixed his hair. "Seems like your magical talents are developing nicely." He said, before taking a seat at the table. "I have gone by many titles over the eons. They've called me the Morning Star, the Prince of Hell, the Light Bringer, the Blinding One, the Venom of God, so on and so on and so on..." He twisted his hand as if telling himself to get to the point. "Your religions have given me various names as time rolls on. Satan, Lucifer, Samael, you get the point."

He cleared his throat, and his eyes flashed. "For the purposes of this conversation, you may call me Azazel."

I went through a rapid change of emotions, from confusion to understanding, to anger and then to fear. If what he was saying was true, then that means...

"You're the devil." I said plainly, trying not to let my unease show through.

Azazel scoffed and feigned a dramatic hurt expression. "Honestly, that title was always so unflattering." He rolled his eyes. "Yes, according to your limited understanding, I'm the devil, the boogeyman, the tempter, the betrayer. Need I go on?'

My hands felt clammy, and my shirt felt a little bit too tight. The man sitting across from me claimed to be the devil, and he looked just like me. What was I supposed to make of that? He didn't seem evil or demonic or anything. That made me more worried. If Azazel was who he said he was, then he'd had thousands upon thousands of years to master the art of deception. Best case scenario, he was major bad news and I'd need to keep my guard up. Worst case scenario, it was already too late.

"What the hell do you want?" I asked. My voice shook and I found it difficult to maintain eye contact.

"Relax, Tobias." Azazel held his hands up in surrender. "I'm not here to hurt you or anything like that."

"Forgive me for not taking your word on that." I said apologetically. "Considering you are, you know," I held up my forefingers on either side of my head, mimicking horns.

"You think me a liar, a deceiver, the ultimate villain?" Azazel asked, waving his hand back and forth as he spoke.

"I think that you make Lex Luthor and the rest of the Legion of Doom look like good samaritans by comparison." I retorted.

Azazel laughed. It was eerie. His laugh was just like my own, and it seemed genuine. There was nothing mocking about it. He was genuinely amused by what I had said. "I'm sure you've heard that history books are often written by the victors, yes?" He asked me.

"I have, can't say I don't agree there." I nodded.

"Good, good. It means you're smart. You question everything put in front of you with educated skepticism. I admire that." Azazel wagged his finger with a smile spreading.

"Thanks. That means nothing to me." I spat. "Why am I here?"

"Like I said, I want to talk. That's all." Azazel held his hands up in surrender.

"Then quit with the bull and talk." I growled. "Politicians sprinkle in less fluff than you're spouting."

"Yes, well, here's the deal," Azazel began, leaning closer, arms resting on the table. "I have not set foot on this Earth since your lord and savior banished me."

"Gee, I wonder why he would do that?" I asked sarcastically.

"Oh, so you know why I was banished?" He asked in return.

"Because you wouldn't serve humanity. God told you to bow to humanity and you said no." I said.

"Do you think I should have?" Azazel proposed. "My ol' Pa considered humanity His passion project, the peak of His ability." Azazel laughed, slapping the table. "Now don't get me wrong, man has made many great accomplishments, William Shakespeare's many works, the Mona Lisa, anime, Chinese food, the pyramids of Egypt. No wait, that last one was someone else." He sucked on his teeth in thought.

"But you are also one of the most savage species to rise up across the realms." Azazel's tone shifted; it was more bitter now. Disgusted, even. "You lie, you cheat, you steal, you sleep with your neighbor's wife. You kill for the sake of killing. Wars are fought over petty politics. World War II? What an atrocity. Look at your history and tell mc I was wrong to defy God's demands."

"So instead, you proceed to be the devil on our shoulder?" I asked. "You're the dark voice in our heads that encourages us to lie, to cheat, to steal. To kill." I said the last bit with a sense of finality.

Azazel barked out a laugh. "Even now, you prove my point, Tobias. Humans are so vain they can't even own up to their own shortcomings. I haven't whispered one bad thought into a single man's head since the Garden of Eden. I may have planted the seed, but you lot sure as hell didn't neglect to water it."

I arched an eyebrow in consideration. He had a point, I supposed. I was agnostic by nature and had never considered everything bad that happened was the devil's fault, not until he was sitting here before me.

"All I want, is a chance to lead humanity." Azazel took a deep breath. "My Father hasn't given a damn about you since the Stone Age. He's left the building and left you all to do as you please with no one to check you. But I've stumbled upon an opportunity to right that mistake."

I was getting tired of repeating myself. "So again, I ask, why am I here? What does this have to do with me?"

"Ah, right, I got lost on my little rant." Azazel waved a hand. "What do you remember of your parents, Tobias?"

"Not much, they died in a fire when I was young." I said. "My uncle said they were murdered."

"This is true, but there's more to it of course." Azazel said. "Your parents individually were two of the most potent wizards on the planet, in their heyday. They were the descendants of two of the most powerful wizards in human history. Your father descended from the most famous wizard to ever live, the great Merlin. Your mother's side of the family has ties to Nicolas Flamel, famed alchemist and creator of the Philosopher's Stone."

"Hey, we call it the Sorcerer's Stone around here." I mocked. But my thoughts were running a little wild. If what he was saying was true, that means I was the product of two wizard bloodlines coming together. What a coincidence that was. It couldn't be true, could it?

"Now I know that sounds hard to believe, and it probably seems like your parents happening to meet and bearing a child are the result of astronomically low chances, and you'd be right to think so." Azazel reassured me. "Left to their own devices, they probably would have never met. But that's the fun part about being an archangel, every once in awhile, you can tip the scales ever so slightly. It was simple really, I just arranged for your mother's car to break down one day. Your father, the chivalrous bastard that he is, couldn't help but stop and help her. And voila, young love."

"Y-You arranged for my parents to meet? For me to be born?" My voice shook. That scared me. He'd been there every step of the way. "But why?"

"If I want to return to the world, I need a few things. One, an immensely powerful artifact to act as a bridge between Hell and the mortal world."

A flicker of realization crossed my mind. "The Holy Grail." I said.

"The Holy Grail." Azazel squeaked in a mocking voice. "God, who came up with that name?" He flicked his hand dismissively. "Two, wizards who can perform the necessary rite."

"Fachnan." I said. Puzzle pieces seemed to be falling into place.

A brief amusement painted Azazel's expression, but it was gone as quickly as it had appeared. "Yes, him. And last but not least, I need an exceptionally powerful host to hold my metaphysical form."

My blood felt like ice in my veins. "You mean..."

"Yes, Tobias." Azazel nodded. "You are my host. Born from the union of two immensely powerful wizard bloodlines. Born under a solar eclipse on top of it all. Bet you never knew that part huh?"

"I was born during a solar eclipse?" I asked. That sounded cool and all, but I didn't see how it was relevant.

"Yes, solar eclipses have a funny effect on the magical side of things." Azazel explained. "I don't have time to explain the metaphysics of it all, but the short of the story is, it is one of many events that can occur that coincides with the barriers between the spirit and mortal realms becoming blurred. It allows a lot of magical energies to seep through and thus, wizards born around then prove to be exceptionally more powerful. In short, with all these things in mind, you have more potential than any other wizard on the planet."

I laughed. "You're kidding right? I can't even perform a simple fire spell. You have the wrong guy, Satan."

"Given time and training, you could nurture your power and get much, much stronger." Azazel said. "But that doesn't really matter for my purposes. Once I've entered your body, I'll have the magical skill department covered. With your help,

Tobias, I can usher in a golden age for humanity." Azazel outstretched his arms in a grand gesture.

"Imagine Tobias, a world without hunger, without war." Azazel preached. "Death and disease could be eradicated. I can be the god that my Father never was. Give you all what you deserve."

As he monologued, we happened to lock eyes, and something strange happened. A rush of wind and I felt myself flying into the abyss of his eyes. What I saw was hard to explain.

I saw Azazel, as he really was. A man with bloodstained wings and large, curved horns like a goat. His skin was burned completely black, glowing cracks separating patches of his skin. His eyes had wide pupils, much like a sheep or goat. Over his normal eyes, if you could call them that, glowing cracks formed the shape of two demonic eyes on his forehead. They had a strange depth to them that shouldn't have been physically possible. They flowed like the flames of hell. He still looked a hell of a lot like me, which still freaked the hell out of me. No pun intended.

The terrain around him seemed to completely change. One moment he stood on the Empire State Building, then the statue of Christ the Redeemer, a sphinx in Egypt, the Parthenon, etcetera. What remained constant was the ruined world he stood over. Forests burned and stained the earth black, oceans dried up, what was left of humanity was subjugated to torture and slavery. I couldn't even begin to describe the atrocities I saw done to people.

What I could only assume were demons herded up whoever tried to run away and either killed them or bound them in chains. For all his talk of wanting to be the savior of humanity, what Azazel really wanted was revenge on his Father. He wanted to make a mockery of his creations and rule the planet they had called home for millennia.

As soon as it had happened, it was over. Another rushing feeling pulled me back. It felt like going down a large drop on a rollercoaster. I was back in my seat at the stone table in the void. Azazel looked at me in surprise, no, horror. I don't know what I had done, but I'd seen past Azazel's lies and illusions, and he had felt it.

His face twisted in anger, and he lunged at me. His form changed as he did. In the blink of an eye, he had transformed into the being I'd seen in the vision. The devil knocked me out of my chair and pinned me to the floor.

"You ungrateful whelp! You are but a cockroach beneath me!" Azazel's voice was distorted as he roared two inches from my face.

I coughed, turning my face as far as I could from his. "Ack, dude. Tic Tacs, Ice Breakers, something! You guys don't have toothpaste or mouth wash downstairs?"

Azazel roared as he stood up, lifting me up in the air by my throat. "Listen here, boy, willing or not, you will give me your body. My servants will perform the ritual and I will rule this world, as is my birthright. Your world will be where I make my stand against every other realm and expand my empire across this entire Plane of Existence!"

I struggled against his grip, but it didn't matter. Azazel threw me into the blackness of the void, and it shattered like glass. It suddenly became impossibly bright. Pure white light blinded my vision. I remember screaming.

Then, it all went black.

I shot up in a panic. I was hyperventilating like I'd been holding my breath for an hour. I looked around wildly like a trapped animal. I was in the Alfheim medical ward. The bioluminescent vines were the only light. It was nighttime. I felt a weight on my legs and looked down to see Scout curled up on top of them. It couldn't have been comfortable. I'd startled him, because he was looking up at me, alert. His eyes conveyed an intelligence that no other dog on Earth could convey. The dog dropped his jaw in a doggy grin and carefully crawled up the bed to cover my face in several sloppy kisses.

"Ack, cooties, dog germs!" I tried to push him off, but I was so happy to see him, I didn't actually mind the dog drool.

Scout eventually let up, sitting on my lap and wagging his tail happily. He let out a huffing sound.

"Where is everyone, buddy?" I asked him.

Scout turned his head thoughtfully, then sneezed in my face. I wiped it off, unamused. I'd been brought back to the Light Haven, but how? Last I remember, we'd been fighting the redcap and it was about to kill me when...

Fachnan.

He'd stopped the redcap. But if he was the bad guy, why'd he bring me back here? Surely, I was ripe for the kidnapping. He could've kept me prisoner in his castle. But he didn't. That confused me. I was missing something.

My thoughts went back to my dream. The devil, the freaking devil, was planning his comeback tour and I was part of his plan. I mulled over everything he'd told me and what I had uncovered myself. My lineage. His sob story. The worlds of spirits and mortals coming together. My potential. The Holy Grail.

I recalled his rundown of what he needed for the rite. He needed me, of course. I was his big centerpiece. He needed wizards. Wait, wizards, plural? Fachnan was one, maybe. Who was the other, or others? Azazel didn't seem like a guy who misspoke like that. Which means there was another player in the game. He said he already had them.

A thought came to mind, "Lightbulb."

The wizards were the only thing he specifically mentioned already having. I was the next piece in the puzzle. Our little conversation was about him trying to acquire my allegiance. He never said he and his allies were in possession of the Holy

Grail. And I sure as hell didn't see it in Fachnan's basement. I think I would've noticed the golden, gem-encrusted goblet. Azazel didn't have the Holy Grail yet. At least, it didn't seem like it.

It was my only lead. I was pretty sure I'd seen a sign in the endless hallways of Light Haven that pointed towards a library. Maybe they had a book or two on the Grail. It was sure as hell a better plan than just waiting for the bad guys to come back for me.

I'd been pretty beat up, and I'm sure they needed me in tip top shape for the rite when they were ready. Fachnan probably had no choice but to bring me back here. But where was Kat? He didn't need her for the rite, maybe he'd kept her prisoner. Or worse.

I swallowed. I had to hope she was alive. I would make damn sure she was okay, and I'd rescue her. But I wasn't ready yet. I wasn't strong enough yet. I would need to continue practicing and honing my skills. I'd been outmatched in almost every fight I'd been in thus far. It was time to get ahead of the game. That left me with a pretty clear course of action.

One, hit the books. I needed to learn more about the Holy Grail, what it could do, and where it could be.

Two, I needed a training montage. I was tired of being rescued while on the brink of death.

Three, find Kat, stop the rite, and make it home in time for dinner.

"Alright Scout, time to get to work."

Chapter 12

Sylf had come to check on me several times throughout the night. I pretended to be asleep, even though my mind was wide awake and running at a million miles an hour. Sure, I had a game plan and all, but once I locked onto something, it was very hard for my brain to sit still until the time was right.

It was about five in the morning when Sylf left again. She had a way of disappearing into the forest that was very satisfying. Those long legs, the hips, the feline grace with which she walks. I'm not drooling, you're drooling.

Right as I managed to pick my jaw up from my lap, someone entered the medical ward. They appeared through the glowing door in the trees, and I managed to turn my head away and slump as naturally as I could manage. The door closed with a snap, and I heard footsteps approach my bed. Scout picked his head up, letting out a low, warning growl as the footsteps got closer.

"I know you're awake." A voice said in a moderate Irish accent.

I opened my eyes and turned to face Fachnan, in all of his scrawny, ginger glory. He was wearing black jogging pants and a white T-shirt. It was strangely normal for someone who I'd only seen wearing borderline medieval wear. Scout was still growling, and it wasn't until I put my hand on his head that the growl subsided to something almost inaudible.

"Care to explain what you were doing snooping around my home?" Fachnan asked. He stood with his hands behind his back, eyeing me intensely, as if he were trying to read my mind.

"And do you care to explain why you have some sort of demonic ritual set up in your basement?" I shot back.

"I'm an expert on the dark arts. The 'demonic ritual set up' as you call it, was a harmless diagram I used to study the mechanics of certain dark rituals. It's not set up correctly anyhow and is perfectly harmless." Fachnan explained.

"And the redcap?" I asked him. "It's kind of weird to have a murderous goblin monster just lurking around your home."

"Believe it or not, I prefer not to keep the company of Unseelie faeries." Fachnan shook his head. "Nasty bunch, they are. I've called members of their court up before, but never as a guard dog of any sort."

"Then how'd it get there?" I asked him.

"Not sure. It certainly shouldn't have been able to get in from the outside." Fachnan tapped his chin in thought. "My threshold is strong enough to keep out most magical creatures. The only way it could've shown up inside is if someone inside the premises with enough magical ability was able to call it up."

"That doesn't exactly clear your name, you know?" I said, suspicion painted my words.

"Bold talk for the boy who illegally entered my home." Fachnan said. "Be grateful I brought you back here and didn't charge you with trespassing."

"Oh, I'm so grateful." I rolled my eyes so hard I thought they'd roll right out of my head. "And where's Kat?"

"Katherine? The girl often seen in dark clothing who lives at Light Haven?" Fachnan tilted his head. "I'm sure she's around here somewhere. Why do you ask?"

"Because she was injured by the redcap." I spat. "Why didn't you bring her back here too?"

Fachnan's eyebrow crawled up his forehead in an inquisitive look. "You must have been confused from the blood loss. Katherine was not there when I found you and the redcap."

That was strange. I knew she'd been there. Had she snuck out when I wasn't looking? Did she have some ability that rendered her invisible?

Fachnan looked down at his watch. "And with that, I must be going." He said. "If I find you trespassing in my home again, I will have you thrown in a cell."

With that, Fachnan opened the door in the tree and walked through, closing the door behind him. My face twisted in thought. There were too many twists and turns going on here. Was Fachnan lying to me? That seemed most likely. His explanations could easily be paper thin lies. The excuses he gave were circumstantial at best. And where was Kat? He had to have been lying about her being there. Most likely he'd captured her, and she was in some dark, dank dungeon in the depths of his castle. But why would he lie about something like that? Maybe he was trying to play the innocent bystander card. I'd have to go back and investigate soon, but not before more work. If I was ambushed by the redcap again, assuming Fachnan hadn't actually disposed of it, I wouldn't stand a snowball's chance in hell in my current state.

The tree's door opened again, and Bishop came through this time. His face was hard, his brow furrowed in a scowl. I heard his knuckles pop as he clenched his fists for a moment. His whole body was tense. His movements were stiff but deliberate as he approached my bed. I can't remember the last time I'd seen him that mad. Gulp.

"This is the part where I say I can explain." I offered nervously.

Bishop crossed his arms and barked out a laugh that had no humor attached to it. "Oh, you can? Well please tell me why you broke into the home of a High Elder!" His voice gradually rose and by the last word he was yelling almost as loud as he could.

"There's something strange about him, Bishop!" I said desperately. "You remember that strange basement from my dream? It was there!"

"Oh please, Tobias. You expect me to believe that the same exact basement you saw in a dream was conveniently in Fachnan's castle?" He asked me, though he wasn't yelling anymore.

"That basement was burned into my head, Bishop." I reasoned. "I'd know it when I see it. I swear to you, it was the same exact room."

Bishop sighed. "Regardless, you shouldn't have gone off on your own like that. It's dangerous. You could've run into who knows what kind of wards or guardians."

"That's just the thing! There was a guard, a redcap! Kat says they're crazy dangerous faeries from the Unseelie Court." I explained.

Bishop's face went from angry to puzzled. He held his hand up, stopping the train of thought. "Wait, Kat? Braun's errand girl?"

"Yes, she's the one who suggested we check out Fachnan's home in the first place." I said.

"And instead of doing the smart thing and steering clear of such a stupid idea, you went along with it?" Bishop said, his voice slow with concern and doubt.

"Hey, we stumbled upon something so damn fishy I thought I was on an episode of Deadliest Catch." I had a momentary debate before adding, "And there's something else."

Bishop cocked his head to one side. "What is it?"

"Right after the trouble at Fachnan's castle and I had passed out, I had a dream." I began. "It was like my basement dream, it felt so real."

"And what happened in this dream?" Bishop inquired.

I explained the dream to him. My talk with Azazel, him being my evil twin, the vision I'd seen in his eyes. If any of this scared or alarmed Bishop, he didn't let on. He just stood there, arms crossed, nodding, and occasionally grunting in thought. After I'd given him the rundown of my confrontation with the fallen angel, Bishop closed his eyes in thought.

My uncle let out a heavy sigh, his shoulders visibly rising and falling as he did. And then he spoke, "I was hoping this would never come to pass."

"What do you mean?" I asked, my voice suddenly growing tense. "You knew this was going to happen?"

"Not necessarily to you, no." Bishop shook his head. "But the same mission I happened to acquire Scout on, I encountered an Oracle in the depths of the Underworld who spoke of the return of 'The Morning Star'. She claimed the Fallen Son of God would rise again in the body of a mortal. I'd hoped it was just nonsense and gobbledygook. But it seems not only to be coming to pass, but to be centered around you."

Woah. That was...a lot. Given what Azazel had told me of his plans and goals, I was the mortal in question. Azazel wanted, or needed, my body in order to fully enter our world.

I gulped. That was scary to think about. I didn't have words for how scary that felt. But I'd come to realize that though I may be merely human, I'd learned and gained power that allowed me to throw punches in the heavier weight classes. I was a gifted martial artist, a wizard with a lot of potential, and not bad looking, if I do say so myself.

I swallowed my fear and looked up at Bishop. "We're going to stop Azazel from rising. I know we can do it. We just have to sabotage Fachnan's ritual."

Bishop closed his eyes in thought for a moment and nodded to himself. "At this point it's clear I can't stop you from involving yourself. So, I might as well help you hone your skills and grow stronger. When you're ready, get up, get dressed, and meet me in the gym. I have a surprise for you."

Bishop patted his leg and Scout jumped off the bed and followed him out the door. A surprise, he'd said. I wonder what it could be. Sylf's elven magic hadn't healed me completely, but I was mostly back in fighting shape, just a little sore. I got out of bed, careful not to aggravate the soreness in my chest and put a fresh set of clothes on.

I stepped through the door and made my way to the gym, where I would begin my work in the fight against Azazel.

By now, I'd gotten used to navigating Light Haven's endless hallways. From the infirmary to the gym, it was a right and then a left, and another left, and another, and another, then one more right. I think. Honestly, I lost track.

My uncle was standing on the far side of the gymnasium. He had changed into workout fatigues. He wore sweatpants that started off grey but were black below the knees and a simple grey T-shirt. Next to him was a metal folding chair with a briefcase that was longer than it was wide, like a clarinet or flute case.

I pointed towards the box and cocked my head to the side inquisitively. "What's in the box?" I asked.

"Come and see." Bishop beckoned me over. He seemed excited, almost giddy, to show me what was in the case.

I closed the distance between us and as I took the last few steps, he unlocked the case and motioned me to open it up. I lifted the lid carefully, making sure not to knock the case off the chair. Inside were two wooden rods. They were each about two feet long with metal end caps about an inch long on each end. By the smell of the wood, they were made of pine. Upon closer inspection, the wood of the rods were carved with intricate runes from a language I couldn't place. Greek, maybe?

They were eskrima, a weapon used in various martial arts as a non-lethal weapon. They sort of reminded me of miniature staffs. As if someone had taken a bo and split it in two. Or like police batons, but without handles. I picked them up and tested their weight in my hands. They were balanced perfectly, not too heavy or light on either end. But that wasn't all. I felt something tingle against my magical senses.

"Hello," I drawled, pleased. The eskrima were responding to my magic. As I felt for that tingling feeling again, I felt my magic slip into the eskrima. They felt like an extension of myself, quite literally.

"I've crafted these eskrima specifically to act as a channel." Bishop explained.

"And a channel is, what exactly?" I asked him.

"A channel helps wizards, new and old, focus their magic in a more controlled manner." Bishop continued. "Some wizards aren't able to perform intricate spells without using a channel to focus their magic through."

"So the channel helps a wizard...focus." I said.

"Exactly. You may be able to perform spells you couldn't otherwise or put a new twist on one you're already familiar with." Bishop said. "Take your wind spell, for example. So far, you've only been able to call up gales of wind with no real control on their size and intensity. The most you can do is point them in a general direction, right?"

"Yeah, it pretty much just acts like natural wind would." I nodded, twisting one of the eskrima around.

"With your eskrima however, you should be able to do all sorts of things with wind." Bishop rolled his wrist.

One second, his hand was empty. The next, a wooden staff as long as he was tall appeared, mid-spin. It wasn't perfectly straight or uniformly thick all the way through. It was carved with similar runes to my eskrima, but they were worn with age. He gripped it with both hands and struck the ground with one end. A thrum of power buzzed, passing over me.

"For example." Bishop pointed the staff at one of the nearby dummies. "*Ventus!*"

I felt a rush as he pulled the power in and focused it at the tip of the staff. It condensed into a softball sized ball, and then hurtled itself towards one of the dummies. The ball of wind drilled through the air and struck the dummy. On contact, the ball of wind exploded into a full-on gale, twisting the dummy into the air and hurtling it across the gym.

I whistled, impressed.

"Or it can be used more defensively." Bishop turned the staff towards me. With a muttered word, a ball of flame erupted at the tip of the staff. It grew until it was the size of a pumpkin.

"Wait!" My eyes went wide, and I held up the eskrima in a defensive X in front of me.

Another muttered word sent the fire ball roaring towards me. Without even meaning to, I pulled for my magic and channeled it into the eskrima. I shouted, *"Kaze!"* I thrust my arms out to the side just as the fire ball would've struck. Winds ripped the fire ball apart and dispersed it around me as I threw out my arms.

Bishop smiled as he rested his staff on the floor again, leaning on it slightly. I looked from him to the eskrima in my outstretched arms. They were still humming, almost inaudibly, from the energy I'd just channeled through them. I could tell from his amused expression that I was grinning like an idiot.

We continued practicing. Bishop taught me several ways I could affect my control of wind through use of the weapons. It surprised me that I had never thought to even try using wind magic in different way, even without the use of the eskrima. We kept up the training for a couple hours more, only taking a few short breaks to snack on something and hydrate. Magic is very draining on the human body, after all. But I noticed with the use of a focus, like my eskrima, I tired out a lot slower than I would've if I had been doing open-handed magic.

"Alright, let's wrap it up." Bishop said. His hair and clothes had been completely disheveled by the absurd amount of wind I'd thrown in his face. I, on the other hand, pretty much had all my arm hair burned off. Then, a thought occurred to me. A spell I wanted to try. Give it another shot, in fact.

"Hold on, just one more thing." I told him, before turning to face the lone dummy that had managed to survive our antics.

I took a deep breath and held it. My chest began to burn. It started off a smoldering campfire. Then it grew as my breath fought to escape my lungs. It was unbelievably hard to keep it in. Before I knew it, a forest fire raged in my chest. I used that feeling to fuel my magic, my drive. I pulled for the magic. I pulled for the fire. I felt it in every cell of my body. All I had to do was let it all rush out.

I lined up the shot, aiming one of my eskrima towards the lone dummy. With a triumphant roar, I let out my stored power. "*Hinote!*"

My stomach dropped as a small gout of flame belched from the tip of my eskrima before dissipating completely. In frustration, I threw the eskrima in my right hand across the room towards the dummy. It was startlingly accurate. The eskrima struck the dummy in the head and knocked it clean off. I dropped the other eskrima to the ground and fell back on my ass.

I was tired. Frustrated. Angry, even. I just wanted to shoot a freaking fireball. I looked over at Bishop, who leaned on his staff. He had a sad smile on his face.

"What's that look for?" I asked him.

"You beat yourself up too much." Bishop shook his head. He stood up straight and spun the staff in his hand. Before it'd even made a full rotation, the staff disappeared. He made his way over to me.

"You said fire was basic. Even with those damn sticks I can't make a decent fireball." I threw my hands up in surrender.

"It will come to you." Bishop patted me on the shoulder. "Focus on what you can do, and the rest will come along at its own pace."

I shrugged him off. It was the kind of thing people told you when they knew you sucked at something but didn't want to just come out and say it. "If you say so, Uncle."

"I do." Bishop nodded. "Now pick up your sticks and let's run some drills."

I did as I was told. I was angry and frustrated. But I trusted my uncle. He was the Mr. Miyagi to my Daniel-San. The Yoda to my Luke. The Dumbledore to my Harry. You get the point. With a flick of his wrist, my uncle summoned his staff and held defensively like a bo staff. I readied my eskrima.

I swung wide with my left stick, aiming for his head. The strike never had a chance at landing, I should've known better. Bishop was getting up there in years, but he'd been an expert martial artist back in the day. And he was pretty badass with a staff too. He parried my blow with a quick movement of his staff. At the instant our foci met, the staff glowed with purple runes and a small explosion of purple energy barked from the end of the staff and sent me spinning. I stumbled, struggling to keep my balance.

When I'd managed to stop doing my impression of a top, I looked at him. My eyes were wide with confusion and curiosity. "What was that?" I asked him.

"Kinetomancy, the practice of controlling kinetic energy and redistributing it." Bishop explained. "It's very useful when you're looking to send something bigger than you into the air and firmly on their ass."

A wicked grin was spreading across my face. "Show me how to do it."

"Kinetomancy is simple, but dangerous." Bishop explained. "Only the most advanced wizards use it without a focus. If you tried it without a focus and happened to lose control of it, you could easily rip your arm off."

I rubbed my arms in sympathetic pain at the thought.

"Relax, that's what we have these for." He held up his staff and pointed to my eskrima. Bishop turned from me and resumed his stance. He began spinning his staff slowly in his hands. His breathing was rhythmic and steady, in time with the spin of his staff.

As the staff spun, the runes on the end began glowing again with purple light. "Kinetomancy is not something we can simply call up out of nowhere. There already has to be kinetic energy present. As you focus on it, you draw it into your focus and drag it along as you move."

The light of the runes began to grow brighter. It was getting more difficult to look at them. And then with a swift, decisive movement, he swung the staff overhead in front of him and struck at the air. The light of the runes exploded forward and the wall at the end of the gym rumbled and visibly shuttered with a deafening boom.

"Once you've built up enough energy, you let it loose and it erupts and grows into a more powerful blow." Bishop said with finality. "It comes in handy when you end up fighting outside of your weight class as often as wizards do."

I nodded in comprehension. I took a step back and slowly swung with one of my eskrima, just going through the motion. Then I repeated it, only this time, I reached out to feel for that kinetic energy. Sure enough, my senses could feel it in the air. It was a fluid, almost liquid energy. Again, I repeated the motion, and this time I tried to catch the energy at the end of the stick like fish in a net. The energy tried to pull away, so hard I almost lost my balance. But I tightened my grip and braced my stances and pulled back harder. The runes on the rod began to glow with a green light as the energy gathered into it.

Bishop had a huge grin plastered on his face. "Good Tobias, now let it loose!"

I brought the eskrima in towards my body slowly, preparing my strike.

"*Fordun!*" With a grunt of effort I thrust it forward and a cone of invisible force erupted forward and struck the wall, drilling a small dent into it.

I had a grin of my own spreading across my face. It was quickly washed away as a wave of exhaustion came over me. I stumbled and fell to one knee, limply dropping the eskrima sticks to the ground as I went.

Bishop caught me just before I collapsed entirely. He was the only reason I wasn't completely horizontal at this point. "It's alright, nephew, I got you."

"Sorry, I think I-ugh..." I groaned as nausea threatened to give me another taste of lunch.

"It's okay. Even with the focus, you taxed yourself pretty hard today. And you're still recovering." Bishop patted my back. I let out a nasty burp as he did. "Come on, let's get you a pick-me-up."

Chapter 13

Bishop took me home. It had been a couple days since I'd been back. It felt like ages though. Bishop had given me a cup of orange juice and a chocolate chip cookie. It was surprisingly revitalizing where magic was concerned. Blood donation and magic slinging, like two peas in a pod.

After a quick snack I hobbled up to bed. I needed a break before I hit the books tomorrow. With no sense of grace, I fell face first into my pillow. I was asleep before I hit the pillow.

I slept like the dead. It was a deep, dreamless sleep that felt like an eternity. Ever since I'd been thrust into the world of magic and monsters, I'd been putting a lot of strain on my mind and body and it was finally starting to catch up.

When I woke up, it was still pretty dark out. A glance out the window showed me that the first streaks of sunlight were only barely beginning to paint the sky with brush strokes of gold. I was surprised I'd woken up so early, considering how tired I'd felt the night before. Even now, I couldn't recall what day it was.

There was a knock at my bedroom door. My uncle was the king of early risers, so it didn't surprise me. Had he heard me stir and come to check on me?

"Come in," I said. My words felt thick as they left my lips, like I'd had one too many to drink—not that I'd ever had a drink before. That would be illegal, duh. Definitely don't look under my bed.

The knob clicked and turned. The door creaked as it slowly swung open. My stomach dropped through the floor.

The disturbingly handsome devil - no pun intended - Azazel, walked into my bedroom. He was still rocking his Evil Alternate Universe Tobias look. Azazel's teeth glittered as he smiled.

"Hey buddy, find my Grail yet?" Azazel spoke with a strange, sadistic joy in his voice, my voice. The world spun as the words were spoken. I remember screaming. The spinning turned into a blur.

I shot up straight in my bed, screaming so loud my throat was raw. Bishop burst into my room, his eyes flaring with purple light and staff in hand. He looked over at me, I probably looked like crap. He flicked the staff into a corner of the room and came over to me, the arcane light fading from his eyes.

"Hey, it's okay." Bishop grabbed my shoulders and looked over me. "What's wrong? What happened?"

It took me several seconds to get my breathing under control. I wiped my forehead with my arm. I was drenched in sweat. I looked down at my bed. The sheets were soaked too, and from the smell of it, sweat wasn't the only thing. That was embarrassing.

"It-It was Azazel..." I said breathlessly. I walked him through the brief but scarring dream.

Bishop stared into the middle distance, nodding thoughtfully. "If this being truly is Azazel, then he's got to have a good reason for taunting you."

I tilted my head in agreement. "Azazel doesn't have the Grail yet."

"I'm surprised. But it would make sense as to why he hasn't made a real move on you yet." Bishop said. "And considering he probably has a small cult of followers, that surprises me. I wonder why they haven't found it yet."

I shook my head. "No clue. But I need to learn more about the Grail if we're going to find it first. Light Haven has a library right? I was thinking I could do some research there."

Bishop twitched his head. "Unfortunately, you're still an apprentice. You don't have library privileges."

I let out a baffled huff of breath. "Come on, Uncle. If Azazel is as bad as you say he is, then I'm not so sure the normal rules apply."

Bishop threw his hands up in surrender. "It's not my call, kid. The Mystic Order has rules, and I only have so much pull."

I muttered a curse. My uncle gave me a parental look. "Sorry." I said. "Fine, if I can't research there. Then I'll have to hit the books here."

"Well you're in luck." Bishop smiled deviously. "Since you're up, might as well go to school."

I let out a dramatic cry of distress as I fell back into my bed. School. I hadn't been in days. It felt silly. Unthinkable, even. "Really, Bishop? With everything going on?"

"You're still a kid, Tobias." Bishop said sternly. "School will do you some good."

I scoffed at the notion, but I knew this wasn't an argument I was going to win. If Bishop said I was going to school, then I was. There wasn't much I could do to fight it. Who knew, maybe school could be helpful.

With a satisfied nod, Bishop lightly smacked the bed with his hand and stood up and made his way out of my room. He stopped for a moment and turned to the corner of the room where his staff rested. He flicked his wrist and I felt a current of his will slither across the room. His staff flew in a controlled motion into his hand. He regarded me once more, and then dismissed himself.

I went through my morning ritual. Showering did a remarkable amount of good. Maybe it was magic, or just a natural remedy, but showering felt amazing. I felt the impurities of the last few days wash off me as the water ran down my body. Whatever it was, it was therapeutic as hell. I eventually got out, no matter how badly I wanted to stay in and let the water run over me. I patted myself dry, brushed my teeth, and did my hair, attempting to make myself the least bit presentable. Then I returned to my room to get dressed.

I picked out a pair of nearly black jeans and a worn T-shirt with Cosmo and Wanda from The Fairly Odd Parents on the front. How fitting. I tugged the pants on and shrugged into the shirt before shoving my feet into my old sneakers. I was very fashionable, I know.

I made my way downstairs, slinging my bag over my shoulder as I closed the door to my room. I wandered into the kitchen and snagged a Pop-Tart out of the cabinet and pivoted towards the door.

I waved to Bishop.

He waved back. "I'll head to the Mystic Order soon, maybe I can dig up something while I'm there. Try to focus on school."

"I'll try." I assured him. Though there was a snowball's chance in hell that was happening.

King's View High School felt more and more alien with each passing day. Kids chattered and bantered with their friends. Others were trying to swallow each other indecently. Beautiful girls and handsome guys passed me by as I walked. I imagined being with someone "normal" as I was now. Having a girlfriend or boyfriend, maybe even getting married one day. If my life was going to be as dangerous as it was, was the idea even possible?

Scout was by my side in his service dog gear. He tugged at the harness ever so slightly as his ears perked up. He let out a brief, gentle bark, as if he was trying to get my attention, but not urgently.

"Toby!" A familiar voice snapped me out of the trance. My eyes focused again and fell on the diminutive form of Claire Williams. She was wearing stylishly ripped jeans and a black sweater with the logo for Arizona State University on the front.

She wrapped me in a deceptively strong bear hug, hanging off of me with her full weight. I only stumbled a little bit as I hugged her back. After a long moment, she let me go. My friend smiled up at me. She wasn't wearing her glasses today. Contacts, maybe?

Claire looked surprisingly cheery for a girl who had gone through as much as she had since all this craziness had started. I cocked my head at her, quizzically.

"How're your parents?" I asked her.

Her smile faded to something a little more sad. "Mom's doing okay. My dad's in pretty bad shape but the doctors say he'll be just fine. My dad doesn't seem to remember much of the details."

I nodded. "Bishop said it'd be something like that. Something about mortals choosing to ignore the scary details that the supernatural world presents and choosing to believe something more 'reasonable'. I can't say I blame people, though I don't understand how they could ignore the obvious. Good to hear, though."

Claire pursed her lips. "Hey, I've been in the middle of it twice now, and even I still have a hard time believing all that's happened."

I tried to laugh, but it came out a bit forced. "Hey, I'm the one fighting the monsters and slinging the spells, and even I have trouble wrapping my head around it."

She shook her head. "I don't know how you do it."

For a moment, I weighed the consequences of omitting the details about Azazel and his plans. That didn't sit right with me, even if it might keep her safer. Claire had been in the thick of it already.

"Listen, I have some uh, homework to do." I said, putting emphasis on 'homework' to make it clear that I wasn't being literal. "Care to be my study buddy during lunch?"

Her face flickered with understanding and she nodded. Smart girl. "Sure, where at?"

"Library. Need to hit the books." I said.

"It's a date." She said. Then her face flushed with color. "Umm, I mean, not like a date."

I answered the blush with my own. The branches on the tree overhead suddenly looked very interesting.

Claire shook her head, a little nervously. "I'll see you there." She scurried off just as the first bell rang.

The first half of the school day went by without much consequence. Man, I thought school was already boring. But given all the excitement and wonder I'd experienced recently, it made practicing the Pythagorean theorem for the umpteenth time seem tedious, almost pointless. Scout's ears were pointed forward as my math teacher droned on. Was he actually paying attention? I wouldn't be surprised. He was a hellhound after all. For all I knew, he could be even smarter than I'd already thought.

Eventually, lunchtime came around. My stomach grumbled in protest as I consciously walked away from the lunch line and headed for the courtyard to meet up with Claire. Even Scout gave me a disapproving look. He'd had a leftover cheeseburger in my backpack one time and thought they were better than Thanksgiving dinner.

In the center of the courtyard was a large fountain. In the center of the fountain with several water spouts surrounding it, was a statue depicting a knight brandishing a large broadsword and shield. The sword itself was pointed towards the sky with the shield held in front of its chest. It was the school's crowning jewel.

The story was that the legendary knight had stood his ground against the forces of evil in this very courtyard hundreds of years ago, and later his comrades founded this school. That was just a blurb someone in the drama department had written about the statue though. We were in Seattle, there were no knights in ye olde Seattle.

Of course, it wasn't too long ago that I found out there were wizards and golems and demons (oh my!) in Seattle either.

I was considering the possibility of there being Arthurian knights in the American Northwest when I heard the familiar voice of Claire grace my ears.

"Toby, Scout! Hey there!" Claire's voice called from somewhere behind me.

Scout and I turned to meet her. The hellhound let out several excited barks and yips and tugged hard at his harness. I had to lean back to prevent him from dragging me halfway across the school to meet her.

"Hey, short stuff." I smiled as I made sure to exaggerate how far down, I had to look to see her.

Claire puffed her cheeks and scowled half-heartedly at me. Instead of giving in to the teasing, she decided to ignore me completely and knelt to scratch Scout behind the ears. He gave her several sloppy doggy kisses in return, licking her chin happily.

"Blegh, dog germs!" She laughed.

"Kiss ass." I huffed, looking away from him.

"So, you ready to get our nerd on?" Claire asked me with a determined look in her eye.

"Hey, this isn't nerdy. This is serious wizard business." I said, holding up a finger.

"First of all, I want you to recognize how absurd what you just said was." Claire raised a finger of her own, and then a second. "And secondly, wizard business? What do you expect to find in a public school library?"

"Well, Bishop says I'm not cool enough to hang out at the cool wizard's library, so this is the next best thing." I sighed.

"I guess that's fair." Claire shrugged. "Okay, let's go get our wizard on."

"Hey, hey, I'm the wizard. You're just my goofy assistant." I clarified.

"If anyone is the assistant around here, it's you, dunderhead." Claire stood up on her tippy-toes and flicked my forehead. Then, as if she didn't just disrespect my masculinity, she walked right past me towards the library.

I looked down at Scout. "I get no respect."

Scout cocked his head to one side and his tongue lulled out in a doggy grin. And as if he was the one walking me around, began pulling against the lead gently but deliberately in the direction Claire had gone. Even in his dog disguise, Scout was surprisingly strong. Even though it was my idea, I was now being the one dragged to the library. It was only slightly demeaning.

After a brief walk, we arrived at the library. It was a fairly modest two story building with a lot of windows on the front. There was a mural on the side of the building that depicted several famous book characters and scenes, painted by the art students a few years before I came around.

We entered through the glass doors and made our way past the front desk. The librarian was an ancient lady who made the Queen look young. She briefly looked up from her crossword puzzles, glancing at us over the rim of her triangle-lensed glasses before returning to what she was doing.

"Okay, so what are we looking for?" Claire asked me.

"Whatever they might have about the Holy Grail and anything related." I said. "I'm hoping there might be some kind of understated clue that can give me an idea of where to look for the darned thing."

Claire raised an eyebrow at me but nodded. "So maybe we should try European history..." Her voice trailed off as she went full nerd mode and began to navigate the endless rows of bookshelves in an almost trance-like state.

Claire spent a lot of time in the library. She was the Queen of the Bookworms so I suppose it shouldn't surprise me that she had an almost encyclopedic memory of the school's library. She barely looked at the books as she picked them off the shelves and began handing them to me. The books began to add up so quickly I had to drop Scout's leash to balance the growing stack of books in my hands. I didn't need to hold onto it anyways, he was more than happy to walk himself.

We made our way up and down several rows of bookshelves before she finally seemed satisfied with the two full stacks of books between us. Without even looking where she was going, Claire managed to lead us to one of many tables nestled among the shelves where we could sit and begin flipping through.

Before we even got started, she took out her notebook and began copying down the titles and authors of every book we had grabbed. I guess she wanted to be able to find them again later or look them up online. It made sense, there was no way we'd get through all of the books in the time remaining for lunch.

I picked the first book off the stack and got to reading.

Chapter 14

I love a good book as much as the next guy. But god damn, historical texts are boring. No flare, no pizazz. Just cold, hard, uninteresting facts and theories. And on top of that, everything I'd read so far even tangentially related to the Holy Grail didn't offer me anything actually useful. It was all speculation at best, and dismissed as a complete myth at the worst.

I looked over at Claire, her brow was furrowed as she read. My guess was she hadn't found anything all that interesting either. I heard Scout let out a big huff of a breath. Even he was bored.

"This is getting us nowhere." I said as I slammed the third book closed. I cast it thoughtlessly on top of the previous two books I'd already scanned.

"Well no offense, but no one in their right mind would publish anything about the Grail as fact." Claire said. She rested her head on one hand.

I pulled over the next book in the stack and flipped to the relevant chapter. Again, most of the information presented was irrelevant retellings of the various legends surrounding the Grail. I gave up on reading it word for word at this point and just lightly scanned each page. If there was something new here, it would stick out to me among the sea of irrelevant information.

Then, there it was. Something different. Something that caught my eye. It could've been nothing. But it was the first new piece of information I'd read after almost four books.

I took a breath and then read aloud.

"The Holy Grail has always been a symbol of power. But power recognizes power. The Grail is said to recognize other symbols and pantheons of power. So the Grail has traveled. It was born from the blood of Christ. It found its way to medieval Europe where it aided King Arthur and Knights of the Roundtable for a time. It kept the British in a position of unquestionable power for centuries. It followed the British as they traveled to the New World. If legend is to be believed, then it has remained in America for the last three hundred years. But not much is known who wields it now."

I turned my eyes up to Claire. She stared into space thoughtfully as she usually does when working out a particularly difficult problem.

"Well that narrows it down quite a bit, in theory." Claire said. "But even if that's the case, that's still an entire country to search."

"It's a start, at least." I shrugged. "Maybe there's something I can do to narrow it down further."

"Like what?" Claire asked me.

"Not entirely sure, yet." I shook my head. I let out a sigh as I realized what I was going to have to do. "I'll need access to the Mystic Order's library. Maybe they have a book that can tell me how to find the Grail."

"Is there such a thing as a tracking spell?" Claire proposed.

Ding. That was an idea. "Claire, you're a genius!" I let out a laugh and reached across the table to grab her head. I leaned over and planted a kiss on her forehead.

As I sat back down I noticed she looked a bit stunned. Then she shook it off and smiled. "You're just now figuring that out?"

"Bishop's at their library right now and won't be back until tonight. That gives me only a few hours to figure out how I'm going to get in there." I crossed my arms in thought.

"Okay, what can I do to help?" Claire asked.

"While I'm working out how to get into the library, could you keep digging for information on the Grail?" I asked her.

She raised an eyebrow at me. "So while you go off on a stealthy magic mission, you want me to keep trudging through these incredibly dull books?"

My mouth twisted into a nervous, pleading smile.

Claire rolled her eyes at me. "Fine, but you owe me."

My smile became something more cocky. "Thank you! Come on, Scout!" I rose from my chair and started to make my way out of the library.

The bell rung and I quickly realized that I still had half of a day of school to trudge through. I slouched as my enthusiasm was quickly washed away by the dull reality of public high school.

"Fine, school and then cool wizard stuff." I mumbled to Scout.

Scout opened his mouth in a doggy grin and looked up at me. He took great pleasure in my pain.

School dragged on for an eternity and a half. Teachers rambled on about irrelevant information that would be of no use to me in life. Even Scout lost interest after a while. I trudged through the rest of the day with the perseverance of a man hopelessly stuck in the friend zone.

Finally, the last school bell rang. It was a heavenly sound that hit my ears and abruptly shook me out of a haze. I was among the first of the sea of kids to breach the front doors of the school and back into the free world. Even though I was in a pretty big hurry, I still had no idea how I was going to sneak into the Light Haven's library.

I wasn't quite sure what kind of security the library would be under if any at all. But I had to expect at the very least that there would be prying eyes watching for wascally new wizards trying to sneak in.

Lightbulb.

"Well, the grumpy old farts can't catch me if they can't see me." I scratched my chin as the idea put itself together. "Come on, Scout. I think it's time to take the training wheels off for a bit."

There was a junkyard not too far from the apartment complex where I lived. It made the rent a little cheaper so that was one benefit. But it dawned on me how useful it'd be for some discrete magic practice. There were piles of junk all around me. Random debris ranging from torn-up dolls to the shells of cars protruded from the mounds of indiscernible garbage. I unclipped Scout's leash and let him have free range of the junkyard. It was an independent yard that didn't have any employees besides the owner and he was the kind of guy who just sat in his office and watched soap operas on TV all day. Plus, I slipped him a twenty.

While Scout investigated various mounds of indeterminate objects, I was looking for something rather specific. It took a while but I eventually found several mirrors of various sizes and shapes among the debris. Only one of the mirrors was intact; a large oval-shaped one almost as tall as me. It had an ornate carved silver rim with a lot of frills and flower shapes. The rest were rectangles of various sizes with varying degrees of damage. More than half were damaged to the point that they were unusable if I was trying to observe my appearance.

But that wasn't what I was going for. I had something way cooler in mind. I spread the eight mirrors in equidistant points around a small clearing among the junk. When I stood in the middle, I could easily be seen in each mirror. My eyes coasted along, checking each mirror one more time. There I was.

Then I closed my eyes, taking in a deep breath as I gathered my power. I imagined myself fading from view, becoming completely invisible. I mumbled random syllables in an attempt to focus my power on the spell. I felt a rush as the spell took hold. As I opened my eyes, I noticed my form starting to blot out. My vision became slightly blurrier. Then something tugged my gut and I felt the energies buck loose. I saw my body come back into view as the energy released itself as arcs of blue lightning struck against the mountains of junk.

I flinched as the lightning whipped and cracked at my surroundings. "Yikes, that's never happened before." I took a deep breath. I didn't expect to get it on the first try, but I hadn't expected the spell to buck me off like that.

I tried it again. And again. And again. Each time the spell practically exploded and dissipated. With each failed attempt, I felt the fatigue grow a little more. Maybe trying to make myself completely invisible was a bigger feat than I gave it credit for. In my head it seemed pretty simple, but perhaps what I intended for the spell was a little far outside my skill level.

"Okay, so I can't make myself invisible," I said to myself. "So maybe I have to go for something a bit subtler."

If I couldn't make myself invisible, maybe I should go for practically invisible. I didn't need to be completely hidden from view. I just needed to go unnoticed, right?

So, again I gathered the energy around me. It sizzled and cracked as the viscous energy threatened to slip out of my grip. But I was determined and far from worn out. Have you ever watched a cartoon or an anime where it's very obvious who the main character is because all the background characters are completely unremarkable? Well that's what I was going for. I just wanted to hide in the background. The unruly energies suddenly began to settle as it formed around my intent. I continued mumbling nonsense that vaguely sounded like Latin to focus on the spell. As I chanted I focused on a word to lock the spell to. Many different words flooded my mind's eye.

There it was.

I opened my eyes and chanted, "*Decivus*."

The world around me seemed to change. Nothing particularly remarkable. The mounds of junk blurred in my vision, as if looking through fogged-up glass. The mirror directly in front of me, which was only a few feet away, was the clearest thing in view. The mirror displayed the same image as before. I was just standing there.

But it was different at the same time. Even though it was only a reflection, the effect I intended still seemed to apply. I couldn't quite make my eyes settle on my image in the mirror, and whenever I didn't look directly at it, it became an inconsequential detail of the background.

I let out a whoop of excitement and stopped abruptly. My voice sounded muffled, as if I was trying to speak to someone through a pillow while standing across the road. Interesting, I hadn't intended on the spell dampening sounds too, but I wasn't going to complain. The spell was a success. I pumped my fist in the air. That sudden movement must have been too much because the spell suddenly dissipated and I felt the magic that had hidden me melt away like Nickelodeon slime.

"Okay, so note to self, no sudden movements." I said.

I took a couple of deep breaths and gathered my magic again. I had to test this spell thoroughly and make sure it worked exactly how I needed it to. Once more, I muttered the word of power and felt the mask of irrelevance wrap around me. With a hesitance to the movement, I took a simple step forward. As I moved, the world became momentarily clearer but blurred once more as I stopped moving. My image had become more distinct in the mirror as I took the step.

"Okay, so moving around at all is going to make the spell weaker." I noted.

This time, I took a much slower step. The spell didn't waver this time. So the sneakier I tried to be, the better the spell would hold. It made sense that the spell wouldn't just let me walk in willy-nilly.

A satisfied grin plastered itself on my face. The spell worked and I didn't even need any help from Bishop or anything. The only downside seemed to be that I had to actively concentrate on the spell to keep it up. I'd have to be absolutely focused to pull this off, otherwise the spell would slip and there's a chance someone would see me. Now all that there was left to do was a trial run. I wanted to make sure the spell actually worked how I thought it did. I released the spell and the world immediately became clearer.

I clapped my hands once and called out, "Scout! Time to go!"

The dog immediately came bounding for me through a small tunnel in one of the piles of trash. Much to my disgust, in his mouth was a dead rat the size of a schnauzer. I wish I was kidding. The rat had to weigh almost ten pounds.

"Seriously?" I crossed my arms at him.

I swear the dog rolled his eyes and then simply opened his mouth to drop the rat at his feet. I chuckled, clipped his leash to his harness, and we made our way out of the junkyard.

There was a convenience store not too far from the junkyard that I decided would be my test site. I walked by the entrance and made my way to the side of the building. As I walked I took note of anyone inside the store. From the looks of it, it was just the cashier and two customers. Piece of cake.

I knelt down to Scout's eye level and spoke quietly. "Alright Scout, make yourself scarce for a bit while I give this spell a go."

Scout let out a yip that I assumed was agreement. I took off his leash and stashed it in my pocket as best as I could. Without further instruction, Scout ran down a nearby alley that was completely cloaked in shadow. I could barely see his silhouette in the darkness but after a few feet, I swear he just disappeared.

"Spooky." I said, impressed with the dog. With my furry companion out of the way, I prepared the stealth spell once more. The sun was starting to set and not many people were walking the streets, so I wasn't shy about performing the spell in almost open view.

"*Decivus.*" I whispered, almost silently.

The spell took hold after only a couple of moments. I felt the magic wrap around me like a heavy cloak. Just as it had done before, the world had become a slight blur around me. I took a step forward. Not too fast, but not too slow either, though. The spell only slightly gave way. I took a second, slightly slower step, and the spell held. Pleased with myself, I began walking at a pace a bit slower than I would normally keep if I was just taking an evening stroll.

The world around me kept that vague blurriness to it. I made my way towards the entrance to the convenience store, and as I did, I made sure to keep an eye on my surroundings. If the spell was working as I intended, people wouldn't notice me walking by and could run into me. And I imagined that wouldn't go over well with the average passerby.

I was at the front door of the convenience store now. I reached out slowly for the handle of the door. This would be interesting. How would my spell interact with anything I touched? I pulled back my arm, slow enough to maintain the spell, but fast enough so that I wouldn't attract any attention by being too slow. It was a careful, frustrating balance.

As I opened the door fully, one of the patrons walked out with a bag of snacks and a case of beer under his arm. If he noticed me holding the door open, he didn't let on. He passed me by without so much as a sideways glance in my direction. I smiled, quite pleased with myself. I walked into the convenience store and let the door close behind me. The only sign I had come into the store at all was the chime of a bell hanging above the door. But even that could've been blamed on the guy who'd walked out.

The remaining patron, a young man a little older than me, was too focused on deciding between Snickers or Milky Way to notice me. I took a few laps around the convenience store. I was keeping the proper pace to maintain the spell but I kept up the routine long enough to think someone might notice. I couldn't help but chuckle to myself as neither the customer nor the clerk seemed to even notice I was in the store with them. At one point I even waved my hand slowly in front of the young man's eyes while he was looking at the selection of candy. Instead of waving me away or asking what my problem was, the guy seemed to just take one big step to the side so that I wasn't obscuring his view.

"Oh ho ho, I'm liking it." I whispered to myself. The spell worked. So long as I didn't move too fast or make too much noise, it seemed like people treated me as just part of the background.

With the spell thoroughly workshopped and the sun starting to set, I decided that it was time to go home and wait to enact the next phase of my plan. I snuck back out of the convenience store and found Scout digging through some trash. Crazy mutt, he was going to make himself sick. I attached his leash and pulled him away from the trash. Then we walked down the sidewalk and made our way to the apartment.

When I arrived back at the apartment, I found Bishop in the kitchen making Hamburger Helper. He looked up and smiled at me as he stirred the pasta in the pan.

"It's about time you got home." My uncle said.

He stepped away from the stove for a moment and set down a bowl of wet dog food on a rubber mat in the kitchen. Scout jumped around in excitement for his delicious meal. I was barely able to get the mad dog out of his service dog harness. After he was free of his bonds, the dog rushed over to his food and hurriedly began to chow down.

"Wash your hands," Bishop said. "Dinner will be ready in a couple of minutes."

I nodded and did as I was told. I sat down at the table and Bishop walked over with two plates. He set one down in front of me and sat down with his own. I dug into my food like a starving animal. Workshopping that new spell had really done a number on my reserves, though not as much as my spells had previously.

"So, how was school?" Bishop asked me in between bites. Scout had finished his dinner and curled up near my uncle's feet.

"Dull," I groaned. "Nothing even remotely interesting happened."

"That's good." He said, muffled by a mouthful of food. "Just keep up a low profile."

"Do you have any leads on the Grail yet?" I asked him, trying to fish for any information I could get.

Bishop shook his head. "Not yet. There's a lot of books in that library. Even the most relevant books are going to take a couple days to comb through."

Yikes. If the library was as impressive as Bishop made it seem, then I was in for a long night myself. "Need any help?" I offered.

Bishop cocked an eyebrow and waved his fork at me. "Nice try, punk. I already told you, it's off limits to apprentice wizards."

"All I'm saying is that seems counter productive to the whole 'learning magic' thing." I waved my own fork at him. "Libraries are supposed to be for students to learn."

He shrugged. "Maybe. But like I said, I don't make the rules."

I sighed but turned my focus back to my dinner. The rest of dinner time was spent in silence. After we'd finished eating, I took both plates and washed them. I glanced at the clock, it was a quarter after eight.

"I think I'm gonna tuck in early." I hooked a thumb towards the stairs. "I didn't sleep too well last night, so I need to catch up."

Bishop nodded at me. "Alright, I don't think I'll be far behind you. Staring at books all day tired out my eyes."

"Okay, night." I waved and hiked up the stairs.

Now all I had to do was wait for Bishop to go to bed and knock out. Then I'd sneak out, make the trek to the Gum Wall and find Light Haven's library.

Chapter 15

I heard the steady rhythm of my uncle snoring rumble throughout the apartment just after 10 p.m. Careful not to make any noise, I got out of bed and slipped into black sweatpants and a grey T-shirt. I completed my stealthy ensemble with an old pair of tennis shoes and a black hoodie. Before I left my room, I doubled back for a moment to grab my eskrima, which were in a leather pouch on my bed. The pouch itself had straps that tied around my leg so they'd be in easy reach. Now equipped with my magic focus, I was ready to go.

I tiptoed down the stairs, careful to avoid the creaky step as I made my way downstairs. Directly between the stairs and the front door was the lying form of Scout. The dog was splayed out on the tile of the entryway and if he noticed me, he didn't let on. I made a conscious effort to step over the dog, careful not to even graze him. Without incident, I slipped out of the front door and closed it in near silence.

It was a cold night. And I was underdressed. The fangs of the frosty air bit through my sweats easily. There was no point in risking going back inside for thicker clothes, so I tried to think warm thoughts. Warm showers. Hot Pockets. Soup. Heated Blankets. The Human Torch. It didn't help much, but it gave me something to focus on.

The walk across town took almost two hours and I got plenty of strange looks as I made my way to the Gum Wall. I looked like a man on a mission and my outfit made it seem like my mission might be considered illegal. By some miracle, no one cared enough to stop me. I found my way to the Gum Wall and pressed the secret combination of gum pieces under the light of my phone screen.

The magical doorway carved itself into the Gum Wall and gave way. With one step, I was no longer in Seattle and back in Light Haven. The bright lights of the Mystic Order's Headquarters combined with the pristine white marble rooms almost blinded me.

"Agh, Jesus..." I cursed as I shielded my eyes while they adjusted.

Light Haven was evidently busy any time of day. It made sense considering that wizards from all over the world frequented the magical complex. It was going to be hard to keep a low profile with Light Haven so busy. I cursed myself but figured it'd be too late to back out now. I left the Portal Nexus and made my way down the halls until I stumbled upon a directory. Frankly, I wish I hadn't bothered. The directory posted on the wall displayed the layout of Light Haven's halls. As I'd previously suspected, Light Haven wasn't just an incomprehensible maze of rooms and halls.

Light Haven's layout was constantly changing. The directory displayed rooms shifting from one position to another. Hallways were appearing and disappearing, growing longer, shorter, and branching off into countless directions.

"Well, this is going to be more complicated than I thought." I stroked my forehead as a mild headache began to throb.

I put a finger to the directory and did my best to trace my position to the current position of the library. Once I'd reached the library, I tapped the directory in thought. Out of nowhere, a thrum of magic echoed from the directory and a spark of blue energy darted towards me. My vision was hit with a flash of blue light, and when my vision had refocused, I noticed something quite interesting.

Starting at my feet, the floor tiles began to glow with blue runes. They went down the hallway to my left and took a right down another hall. That was a surprise. I hadn't expected wizards to know a thing about GPS. But you wouldn't catch me complaining either.

I followed the glowing tiles with enthused curiosity. It was like a video game where the path to the goal was highlighted for you. As I walked along the path, the tiles behind me lost their glow, returning to normal. I passed by several other wizards as I made left and right turns down the long hallways. Hell, I even made a loop-de-loop at one point, which seemed like it should be impossible. Another young wizard, maybe only a few years older than me, passed me mid-loop, and didn't seem phased by the gravity-defying hallway. So I just had to assume this was part of the new normal.

After a surprisingly brief walk, I saw my path coming to end at a T-shaped intersection. Where the three hallways met was a set of double doors with the word "Library" shimmering above it. The words glowed with a fluid light and as I focused on them, I noticed the letters were changing. Every second or so, the word was changing languages. Spanish, Russian, Japanese, and others I couldn't recognize. But no matter how many times the letters changed, I could read it perfectly.

"Gotta admit, that's pretty neat." I said, cocking my head to the side in recognition.

I watched the doors for a few minutes, trying to gauge the foot traffic. Only a few others came in and out. An old, scholarly wizard. One of the Ljósálfar, a young handsome guy with bristly hair that reminded me of a bundle of twigs. Two female wizards who looked to be approaching middle age. I tapped my fingers on the side of my leg. I was getting antsy, and standing here watching the door was almost as suspicious as just walking right in.

I took a deep breath, pulling together my magic. Two more deep breaths and then I lightly clapped my hands together. I whispered, "*Decivus.*"

I felt my magic swirl in the air as it wrapped around me. The world grew blurry and muffled, which told me the spell was up and working, hopefully. I took an experimentative step forward. The echoing tap of my shoe on the tile felt quiet, almost distant. The blurriness didn't waver at all. It was improving with each use. I moved forward at a steady stride.

Right before I walked into the intersection, a tall, robed wizard crossed my path. I hurriedly halted my forward momentum and shuffled a step or two back. The sudden motion caused the blurriness to fade for a second. But with a conscious effort, I pulled the spell back into place. That was a close one. If I'd began walking a second sooner, I would've bumped into that person and blown my whole scheme.

I let out a sigh of relief and then carefully looked down both hallways to make sure that I wouldn't accidentally play bumper cars with anymore passerby. No one was there. I steeled my resolve and stepped forward and through the doors of the library.

I was definitely not prepared for what I saw.

Try to think of the biggest library you've ever been to. Now make it ten times bigger. Even then it wouldn't begin to compare to the sheer magnitude of Light Haven's library. There were bookshelves as far as the eye could see in every direction. The shelves themselves extended high into the sky. Yeah I said sky. High above me, there were clouds floating silently around the shelves. Stars shone in between the fluffy forms that lit the library below. The shelves continued well past the clouds, they just kept going up and up. I couldn't see where they ended.

I lifted my hand up to close my hanging jaw. I had to wonder, when would I stop being impressed by the magical world? Hopefully never. Were we somewhere like Alfheim? Or did the library act on TARDIS rules, being bigger on the inside? I'm sure I'd learn eventually but it hardly seemed important right now.

"Now how am I supposed to find what I'm looking for?" I thought to myself.

There were an inconceivable amount of books here. How was I going to track down any information on the Holy Grail or a tracking spell to find it? I looked around for any sign of something useful. There had to be a directory or an index or something that could help me locate what I was looking for. As far as I could tell, there was no front desk or map to guide me. Not even a return slot. Everyone around me just seemed to know where to go. They moved with purpose from one shelf to another, pulling books down and returning others.

Other books seemed to be carried through the air by strange lights. I focused my eyes on a nearby book floating through the air and noticed that there was a miniscule humanoid figure with wings carrying the book. The small figure appeared to be a college-age girl with bright purple hair. She didn't seem to be wearing any clothes but the glowing light she gave off helped her retain any modesty. Her wings were beating as fast as a hummingbird and the young lady didn't seem to be struggling too hard to carry the book.

"Pixies, huh?" I shrugged. "Neato, but not helpful."

I stepped towards the nearest shelf and took a book off at random. I flipped the book open and turned a few pages. I'm sure the information was quite interesting and generally useful, but I couldn't read a damn word. It was in some archaic language that didn't come off as human to me.

"It's Fae writing." A voice from behind me said. "That book in particular is written by the satyr, Puck."

My skeleton damn near crawled out of my skin at the sound of the voice. I turned to face the voice's owner, my spell crumbling as I lost my concentration.

It was Jacob. He leaned comfortably against a bookshelf a few feet away from me. He had a smug grin on his face. Or was it pride? He stood up straight and walked over to meet me.

"How'd you know I was here?" I asked him. "I was sure that spell worked like a charm."

"Saw you come in through the Seattle portal." Jacob explained. "And it did work, by the way. Pretty impressive veiling spell, did you teach yourself how to do that?"

"Yeah I threw it together after a few hours in a junkyard." I was still trying to steady my breathing. Jacob had caught me way off guard.

Jacob stretched his face into an impressed expression. Then he furrowed his brow in concerned thought, before shaking it off and turning his attention back to me. "Well your hard work paid off. If I hadn't seen you disappear in the first place, I don't think I would've noticed you."

I had to admit, that made me feel good. I was a sucker for positive affirmation. "So, are you going to kick me out?" I asked him.

He shook his head. "That depends, what are you doing in here?"

I explained to him my search for any information on the Holy Grail, as well as a spell that would help me find it before Azazel's agents did. Jacob had a troubled look on his face. There was a brief moment of silence while he gave himself some time to mull the information over.

"You really should let the higher-ups deal with this, Tobias." Jacob said, though it sounded half-hearted.

"You've known me for years now, Jake." I told him. "And if you've been paying even the slightest bit attention, you know I can't sit on the sidelines when trouble's afoot. Not if there's something I can do about it."

Jacob nodded. "I know, I just wanted to be able to say I tried."

I held up the book loosely in one hand. "So can you read this?" I asked him.

He nodded. "Yeah, but it's not much use to you. That's a book on herbs."

I pursed my lips and gave the book a look. Without looking back at the shelf, I put the book back. "So, where can I find the books I'm looking for?"

Jacob cocked his head to the side. "This way. Just keep your hood up and your head down." He motioned for me to put my hood up. I did. "Most of the scholarly types won't even notice you if you don't make any noise."

I nodded. "Got it."

Jacob returned the nod. "Good, now follow me."

Jacob left the row he'd found me in and began walking past the other rows to my right. I had to jog for a couple of seconds to catch up with him. He was moving fast. It was impressive for a guy his size. But after a few moments, I'd caught up to him.

"Why are you helping me, Jake?" I asked him. "You could just rat on me and have me locked in a room somewhere until this is all handled."

"Because, I was in your position once. A long time ago, all I wanted was to prove myself." Jacob told me. "Back then, I wished someone had stepped in and helped me. No one was there for me then, but I'll be here for you now."

My face contorted into something thoughtful. Jacob had never mentioned anything like that before. Of course, he'd kind of been hiding a lot from me, and for good reason.

"But above all else, you're my friend, Tobias." He told me. "Sure, maybe at first, you were an assignment. But then I got to know you. You treated me like a brother. When kids would bully me for my size or my messed up face, you were always the one who got in way over his head to defend me. We went to birthday parties together, field trips, sleepovers. I haven't thought of you as an assignment in a long, long time."

Jacob smiled at me. What he said was true. There were many times where kids in school would make fun of him for his big nose or his oversized stature. On more than half of those occasions had ended with some kid's nose bloodied and my ass planted firmly in the principal's office. I'd always known Jacob to be a gentle giant, and in part, that was true. But I knew now that he had to let the kids jab at him and call him names. Because if he'd ever fought back, he could've killed any one of those kids. Not only is that frowned upon morally and legally, but it would've put him in a position where he couldn't protect me anymore.

Jacob stopped walking and raised a fist, signaling me to do the same. We stopped in front of an aisle that was identical to every other one we'd walked past. Jacob turned and began walking down the aisle. I followed. There was no one else perusing these particular shelves at the moment.

"There are several books on tracking spells in this aisle." He told me. "Start looking. The pixies are constantly rearranging the books in each aisle, so I'm not sure exactly where it is."

"Of course." I sighed. "There's no one we can ask for help or anything. These pixies can't just pull the book down for us?"

Jacob shook his head. "Most pixies are free-spirited by nature. But these guy are major snobs. All they care about is their work and nothing else. They barely even notice us here."

"Well that's insulting." I grumbled. "They might as well be robots. Where's the fun and fantasy in that?"

"Well it's not called 'funtasy' for a reason." Jacob said.

I blinked. I put down the book I was looking at and turned my gaze to him. "Wh-What did you just say?" My voice was laced in equal parts confusion and amusement.

Jacob looked back at me sheepishly. "It was a lot funnier in my head." He said.

"That sounded so wrong." I said in a lecturing tone. "Never again."

Jacob shrugged and turned his attention back to the shelves. A second later, his eyes lit up. He pulled a slim book from the shelf. It wasn't really a book, more something akin to a folder with a fastener on the fold that kept papers in place inside.

"That's it?" I asked him. "I was expecting something more wizardly. Big tome with glowing letters and stuff."

"Most are like that, yes." Jacob said. "But others are a bit more modest."

He lightly tossed the folder over to me. I caught it carefully. I flipped through the pages for a moment. Thank God. It was written in English. I tucked the folder under my arm.

"Now we just need a text on the Holy Grail." I said.

"That one is going to be a bit of a nuisance." Jacob groaned. "Believe it or not, there's only one book about the Grail in this entire damn library."

I rubbed my face and tried to wipe away the exasperated look I'd donned. "Well, maybe I should start reading this," I held up the folder. "While you look for the other book."

Jacob raised an eyebrow at me. "So while I'm marching up and down the aisles of this library, you're going to sit on your ass and read?"

"You know what you're looking for, I don't. I need to absorb as much as I can about tracking spells and we're on the clock. If there was a better alternative I'd take it. But time isn't on our side."

Jacob nodded, smiling. "Only busting your balls, dude." He nodded upwards from where we'd come from. "Back down that way and to the right are some work tables. Settle down there until I come back."

I nodded in agreement. "Thank you, Jake."

"Of course. What are brothers for?" He said. I could hear the satisfaction in his voice as he called us brothers. Then he turned away and sped down the aisle. I turned the opposite way and made my way to the tables.

It didn't take long to find the tables. There were about a dozen round tables with five or six cushioned chairs each. The farthest one from me was mostly unoccupied and I made my way to it.

I took a deep breath, sat down and opened the folder.

Chapter 16

After reading the last page of the booklet, I flipped it closed. I took a breath while I processed what I'd read. The main thing I learned from Tracking Spells and You was that a tracking spell was a bit more complicated than any spell I'd done before. It wasn't as simple as saying a magic word and casting the spell. It was more akin to a ritual. There were steps to be taken and components to be gathered.

I wondered if the spell could be used to find people. Like Kat, she was still missing. Fachnan probably had her trapped in a dungeon underneath his castle. But he played dumb when I asked him about her. Convincingly so, was it really possible that he had no idea where she'd disappeared to.

I shook my head. I had to focus on the matter at hand. If I saw this ordeal through, I felt confident that Kat would turn up. And she seemed like a strong, smart girl. I turned my focus back to the details regarding the tracking spell.

While slinging wind spells and making my skin into armor was pretty neat, there was something extra cool about this spell. I took out a small notebook and pen from my pocket and began writing down the steps and components I would need to make this spell happen. I deposited the notebook back in my pocket and tucked the pen behind my ear.

Jacob arrived after a few minutes, carrying a large tome. It was exactly what I was expecting out of something from this library, unlike the folder I'd already read through. It was a very thick text wrapped in aged brown leather. Jacob set it down in front of me, and even from a short drop, the weight of the tome made the table shudder slightly. The robed figure sitting across from me didn't seem disturbed by this, and just continued reading through their book.

The cover read "The Holy Grail by Merlin Caledonensis".

"I'm going to guess this is THE Merlin?" I looked up at Jacob.

Jacob sat down next to me. "Yep, he wrote this in the last few years of his life by request of the Mystic Order." He held up another book, this one a lot less dramatic and plain compared to the large tome. "I also found this. Thought it might interest you."

I accepted the second book from him. On the front cover it simply said, "The Hierarchy of Magic and the Cosmos". It was printed in very simple looking gold lettering. Strangely enough, there was no author credited.

"Thanks." I said before putting it down, returning my focus to the large tome. "Okay, let's crack this baby open."

I flipped the book open. The leather-bound book creaked as I did. I was sort of hoping a cloud of dust would puff out for dramatic effect, but nothing like that happened. I guess it made sense. It wasn't like the book was being kept in an old abandoned castle somewhere, after all.

On the first page, I read the following:

The Holy Grail is a magical artifact of unknowable power and origin. While many believe it was created by the touch of the son of God's lifeblood, there are other theories. My colleagues theorize it may be of faery-make, though we are unclear if it was a gift to man or if man stole it from the Fae. Another theory suggests it is a fragment broken off the body of one of the Old Gods. Due to the nature of the Grail, there is no way to define its true origin. What we do know about the Grail is that it is a conduit for power. It has a seemingly infinite amount of utilities in ritual magic. In my time observing the Grail's use by King Arthur Pendragon, it can be used to make a man into a minor god. Using its power, King Arthur was capable of wielding the full might of Excalibur. The effort of which would cause any other mortal mind to crumble. King Arthur utilized the Grail in a ritual that gave him physical and mental strength on a cosmic scale that made him the most powerful mortal on the planet for hundreds of years.

While not as spectacular, the Holy Grail would later be used to give the British a foothold in the New World. Contrary to popular belief, the British were initially unable to push back the Native Americans out of their territory upon arrival to North America. This was due to the Natives' use of magic, which Britain had long since strayed away from for decades up to this point in time. Desperate to claim the land for their own, the British eventually were willing to try, what they considered to be, unorthodox methods. The Holy Grail had since been considered simply an unimportant object of power. Its power being more symbolic rather than literal. With consultation from wizards of the king's court, they used the Holy Grail in a ritual to alter the nature of the Natives' relationship with their magic.

I paused for a moment to consider what I'd read. It was consistent with what Azazel had told me about the Grail. It was a versatile tool, indeed. I rubbed my eyes as they started to sting. Reading was rough on the eyes, especially when I was already tired. I flipped a few pages in the tome, and read on:

According to various accounts I've recorded over the centuries, the Holy Grail seems to possess some sort of intelligence. A will of its own. It follows power. It values leadership. It favors those who seek to do justice for the world. It seeks out those who would fight for the light. But

*more than anything else, it is often found where it is most
needed.*

*Despite this, it is not infallible. Agents of darkness have
gained hold of the Grail's power before. And it is said it will
happen again. A hundred years from now, a prophecy tells of
the second coming of The Blinding One. A rite will be
performed, and a conduit of two powerful wizard families
will be the catalyst by which he returns. When the blood of
the conduit is spilled and the Grail is no more, the Morning
Star will be a blight upon our Earth once more.*

I shuddered. Azazel's plan was right here, in black and
white. It really had been prophesied that all this would go
down. They might as well have had a picture of my face
imprinted next to these words. Damn. I was liking this less
and less. I flipped through a few more pages. There had to be
something in here that was useful to stopping the ritual.

Nothing. It just went back to useless history. I cursed and
slammed the book shut. Jacob flinched. The robed figure
across from us didn't even stir. They seemed too absorbed in
their book.

"What did it say?" Jacob asked.

"That the second coming of Azazel has been prophesied
for at least a hundred years." I muttered. "And Merlin seemed
pretty confident it was likely to happen, considering he wrote
it down and all."

He put a hand on my shoulder and squeezed lightly. It was his way of trying to reassure me. It didn't.

"Prophecies aren't a sure thing." Jacob shook his head. "Just because someone prophesies that something is going to happen doesn't mean it is. Did the book say anything else?"

I sorted through the information mulling around in my head. "The Grail apparently can think for itself. It can find a way to be exactly where it needs to be."

I chewed on that for a second. "If this prophecy is true, and I really am the one who will become the host of Azazel, could that mean the Grail might think it needs to be in Seattle?"

Jacob furrowed his brow. I could tell the idea troubled him. "It'd truly be impossible to understand the inner workings of the Grail's consciousness. I doubt even any of the High Elders would be able to come close, and they understand magic and magical artifacts better than anyone on the planet."

"That's an extremely roundabout way of saying 'yes'." I said gravely.

"Why do you think its a yes?" Jacob asked me.

"Because if we truly don't understand how it might think, then it might have a reason for wanting to be exactly where it shouldn't be." I explained. "And at this point, we have to expect the worse. That both I and the Grail are sitting ducks in Seattle, just waiting for Fachnan and any cronies he might have to snatch us up."

"So we get you out of Seattle." Jacob held his hands up. "Remove you from the equation, problem solved."

"No, not problem solved." I shook my head. "Remove me from the equation and they'll just add me back in later after they've gotten their slimy hands on the Grail."

"So we-" Jacob began, but I was quick to cut him off.

"No, we can't just keep running forever. If Fachnan has the Grail, who knows what he can do with it. Even without me in the picture. He'll have both the magical and non-magical worlds as hostages until he gets what he wants. Me." I paused for dramatic effect. "We need to get the Grail before he does. So he has to play on our terms. If we do that, we can bait him into making a mistake and capture him. Then we lock both Fachnan and the Grail away and throw away the keys."

"We should talk to Bishop." Jacob frowned. "He's more experienced than either of us."

I let out a big sigh, my body visibly rising and falling as I did so. "Yeah, we definitely should."

One of Jacob's eyebrows slowly rose up his face. "But..."

"But I want to do this without his help." I said. "Partially because I'd have to explain how I found the damn cup in the first place. Partially because he'd scold me about how dangerous it was. And finally, I need to prove myself."

"You have nothing to prove, Tobias." Jacob said, his voice tinged with concern.

"Yes I do." I shook my head in a loose, exasperated motion. "I haven't amounted to crap since my parents died, man. My grades have been average at best. I never excelled at any sports or anything else worth a damn. Bishop doesn't say it out loud but I know he wants more from me. If I can do this, it'll show him I've come into my own. That I'm a wizard worthy of him, and my parents too."

Jacob crossed his arms and took a moment. I could tell he was processing the feelings I'd expressed. Finally, he spoke. "Alright, fine. But we play this smart. I'll help you gather what you need for the spell, and then we do it together. You, me, and Scout will track the Grail down together. And then we immediately get into the hands of the Mystic Order. Got it?"

"Got it." I nodded, then said, "Thank you, Jake."

Jacob tilted his head towards the last book he'd brought. The Hierarchy of Magic and the Cosmos. "There's something in there that I wanted to show you."

I picked up the book and began flipping through pages. It gave brief summaries of various magical creatures and deities and how they all interacted with each other. It was interesting to think about.

Jacob pressed his hand down on the fresh page I'd turned to. "There. I want you to have an idea of the kind of mess you're entering, and the true scale of the world you've dove into."

I moved his hand out of the way to observe the page he'd stopped me on. There was a lot going on in the picture. I saw various creatures and people, no, gods, depicted in a series of large rings, floating among the stars. Even though it was obviously a still image, the figures and rings seemed to move slightly if you didn't focus on anything in particular.

"What is this?" I asked him.

"This is a visual representation of how some of the biggest players relate to each other in terms of power and responsibilities." Jacob said. "It's not often the Mystic Order has to tango directly with any of these guys, but when we do, it's important to keep the stakes in perspective."

I pointed to the innermost ring. "Okay, so who are these guys?"

There were several figures orbiting the innermost ring, but four stuck out to me the most. They seemed larger and more defined than the rest.

"The Sky Fathers, some of the most powerful of the known Old Gods." Jacob said, then pointed at the four prominent figures. "The most notorious among them being Zeus, Odin, Ra, and Wākea."

In the center, enclosed by all the other rings, was a figure completely obscured by white light. "And that must be good ol' capital G, right?"

"We believe so. But it's hard to say. No one alive has ever met Him." Jacob said. "But look farther out, at the outermost ring." He dragged his finger from the Sky Fathers to the outermost ring and stopped on one figure in particular.

My heart skipped a beat. For a split second, I saw myself. But as soon as I focused on the image, it changed. The figure was a dead ringer for the monster I'd seen in my vision during my conversation with Azazel.

"That's..." I began.

Jacob nodded. "Right, Azazel."

"Why's he all the way out here with the rest of the chumps?" I asked.

"Oh, don't get the wrong idea. Azazel is no chump, he wields massive power, but he's far from the most powerful thing out there." Jacob said. "If we're going to do this, I just wanted you to know the scales we're playing on, and what's at stake. Azazel is far from all-powerful, he can be beaten, but we have to play it smart."

I nodded. "Okay then, thank you Jake." I closed the book.

"Of course." Jacob picked up the book and he put it into a stack with the tome and folder. Then with no sign of physical effort, Jacob picked up the heavy books and turned to take them back to the shelves. "Stay here while I put these back. And then we'll get to work."

So I sat there and waited. I occupied myself by reading my notes on the tracking spell over and over. The spell would need several components. Some I could find lying around the house. Others I'd need to shop for. They were fairly simple articles, so it wouldn't be too much trouble. But it'd take time.

I kept waiting. It was taking awhile for Jacob to get back. Too long. I tapped my fingers on the table nervously.

Index. Middle. Ring. Pinky. Tap, tap, tap, tap.

Index. Middle. Ring. Pinky. Tap, tap, tap, tap.

Index. Middle. Ring. Pinky. Tap, tap, tap, tap.

How long had it been since Jacob left? Twenty, thirty minutes? I looked around. And that's when something became very apparent. The library was empty. Before, it had been bustling with wizards, elves, dwarves, and pixies. Now, it was a ghost town like so many libraries were nowadays. The next realization that came to mind was the complete and utter absence of any color to my surroundings. Everything was streaked in gray. No light shown, yet there was no darkness either. It was like looking at a old black and white photo. Then one more thing became very, very apparent.

I was, in fact, not alone. Sitting across from me was the robed figure who'd been quietly reading while I'd been reading through the books. They were the only thing around me that still retained its color. I stared at the figure as my mind raced at a kajillion miles an hour yet I was drawing a complete blank. It was like my brain was pressing on the gas and hitting the brakes at the same time.

The figure broke the stand off. Their hands rose to their hood, and they slowly drew it back. It didn't take long for me to recognize the figure. After all, he had such a regrettably handsome face.

"Hello Tobias." Azazel said.

Chapter 17

Azazel sat across from me, a satisfied, no, mocking smile plastered across his face. The robe he wore dissolved away like chalk being washed away by the rain. Underneath he was wearing a nearly identical outfit to my own. But instead of all black, he wore all white. How poetic of him.

The initial shock wore off and I jumped to my feet and pulled out one of my eskrima in one fluid motion, knocking my chair over in the process. *"Kaze!"*

Normally my wind spell manifested as a giant gust of wind that started at my palm. But by using my focus, I was able to shape the spell however I imagined it. A miniature twister erupted around Azazel and threw him high into the air. Blades of wind lashed out from the tornado, flinging chairs and books around. I swung my eskrima, directing the tornado and it exploded sideways and hurtled Azazel into a bookshelf, sending even more books flying. The shelves crunched and splintered, shards of wood flying in every direction. I felt several stinging cuts up and down my body.

I wasn't done yet. I swung my eskrima overhead, gathering kinetic energy as I went. I focused on the image of a giant mallet in my mind and the energy seemed to shape itself around my focus as it did. "*Fordon!*"

I slammed the invisible mallet of force down on the bookshelf where I'd thrown Azazel and it exploded into dust and debris. I was engulfed in dust as books flew past me. I panted, taking several deep breaths in quick succession as I recovered from the effort. I did my best to slow my breathing down, it didn't do me any good to breathe improperly.

I muttered angry syllables to myself, still breathing heavily as I did. "Take...that...you...funhouse mirror freak."

"Ha...that was a good punch. You've been practicing." Azazel's voice echoed through the dust.

I wasn't surprised that I hadn't instantly killed him with my attack, but there was a small part of me that was disappointed anyways.

Okay, a big part of me.

Alright, pretty much all of me.

To spare myself the theatrics, I swiped my eskrima from one side to another, muttering a word of power as I did. One big gust of wind exploded outwards and dispelled the dust. Azazel was sitting in the debris of the bookshelf. I kid you not, he was sitting at a small table with a tiny cup of tea in hand. He held it with his pinky out. The devil himself took a small sip of the tea before setting the cup down and smiling towards me.

"What do you want?" I asked him. I held the eskrima up, pointed right at his head.

Azazel held his hands up in mimed shock. "Tobias, I'm hurt. I just wanted to check in with my favorite person and see how things were going."

I looked around and waved vaguely at our surroundings. "Dream?" I asked.

"Something like that." Azazel nodded.

That was a little reassuring, for what it was worth. It meant Azazel was in no better a position than when we'd last spoke. I felt more confident, in light of that. Even still, I didn't put my eskrima down.

Azazel stood up and the tea cup and the table disappeared in a puff of smoke. He twisted his body around and scanned his surroundings. He had a confused look on his face. I saw him tapping his fingers on his leg.

"Lucky for you, I haven't been able to discern where you are. Otherwise I'd already have my followers after you." Azazel nodded slightly to himself. "That's alright though. It seems as though your wizarding skills are blossoming quite nicely. You even have a focus." He held a hand towards my eskrima.

With a shudder and a whoosh of motion, the spare eskrima flew from the pouch and into Azazel's hand. He turned it over a couple of times and seemed to be examining it. The runes carved into the wood glowed with the colors of a sunset as he did.

"Quite interesting. Versatile, not too dominant in defense or offense. And a good whacking tool, should you need it." Azazel said thoughtfully. "Not what I would have chosen for you, but they'll do just fine to start."

I flicked the eskrima in my hand and muttered a word. A gust of wind tore the eskrima in Azazel's hands free and flung it towards me. I caught it in my free hand and held it by my side.

"If you're just here to taunt me, piss off. I have better things to do." I waved dismissively.

Azazel didn't take the hint. "I wanted to take this opportunity to extend my offer to you again. Join me, willingly, and I promise I'll make your existence a living paradise. You won't have a damn thing to worry about with me in the driving seat. Hell, I'll even extend the offer to your friends, and your little dog too."

"If you actually think I'd take that offer, then you don't know me at all, Azazel." I shook my head at him. "Makes me wonder how compatible we could really be."

"Oh I think we're plenty compatible." Azazel wagged a finger at me as he started circling me. He chuckled to himself.

"You want to make daddy proud. You're resentful that you have to prove yourself at all. Part of you just wants to say 'screw it all' and let the whole world burn."

I felt my eye twitch. He was trying to appeal to my darker nature. It was typical. Stereotypical, in fact, for a creature of his origins. Azazel was a monster of temptation. I'd read the Sunday school stories. If he really was the devil he claimed to be, he'd been tempting people, and successfully, for centuries.

So I think I must've given him quite the surprise when I said, "Why don't you just piss off already?"

"I see. Despite the inevitability of what's to come, you still choose to resist." Azazel sighed and turned away from me. "Very well, Tobias. I'll see you soon."

Azazel raised a hand and snapped his fingers.

I jumped up from my slumber in a sudden panic, knocking my knees painfully against the bottom of the table. I muttered a curse and rubbed my knees, hoping to ease the pain. I was back in the library. The real library. The color was back. The people were back. Notably, the robed figure that had been sitting across from me was gone. Had he ever been there? Or had he always been a projection that Azazel had zapped into my head?

I turned to see Jacob walking back over to me. He must've noticed I had awoken suddenly because he looked at me with a bit of concern. "You okay, Tobias?"

I decided it was better not to mention yet another Satan dream. It wouldn't exactly ease Jacob's mind about what we were doing. I filed it under "need to know" and shook off the nervousness that Azazel had left me with.

"Yeah, sorry. Just a bad dream." I waved dismissively.

"It wasn't that one of Trump in drag, was it?" Jacob asked, his tone very grave.

I forced a laugh. "No, no. Not this time."

"Good." He nodded. "Then let's get you out of here. No reason to stay any longer than necessary."

I returned the nod. I muttered my cloaking spell and felt the world blur around me. Jacob led the way and kept my path clear so I didn't accidentally bump into anyone. That would've been awkward for sure.

We snuck back out of the library with ease. It was easy. Too easy. For my peace of mind and to get a little practice in, I decided to keep up the spell. It didn't hurt to exercise my magical muscles. How else was I going to perfect my Vegas act?

I followed Jacob down the halls. Just like everyone else I followed around here, he seemed to have an uncanny understanding of the machinations of Light Haven's corridors. He took turns without hesitation and walked like someone who knew exactly where he was going. We turned another corner and I could see the doorway that led to the Portal

Nexus just straight ahead. I prepared to drop the cloaking spell. Our trek back had gone off without a hitch.

Almost.

"Jacob, hello there my friend!" A deep, familiar voice called out from somewhere behind.

I frantically grabbed the reins of the spell and held it together. We both turned around and standing down the hall we'd just come from was High Elder Roland Braun. He wore long white and red silk robes that covered his feet and obscured his hands. His long dreads hung over his shoulders and he was wearing, I kid you not, rose-tinted glasses. They were small old-timey spectacles that seemed even more fragile on such a large man.

Braun began walking towards us. Again, I was about to drop the spell. But something inside me, call it instinct I guess, screamed at me to keep it up. So I did. Jacob turned to meet him and I crouched behind him, slightly off to the side to avoid tripping him if he started walking again.

"Oh, hello High Elder." Jacob said. "You're not usually out and about."

Braun cleared something from his throat. "Yes, well, I had some business to attend to."

"Anything you can share?" Jacob asked.

Braun's eyes wandered and fell on a spot just a few inches above my head. I caught myself holding my breath. For whatever reason, my instincts were sending out a warning.

"We may have a lead on whoever has been sending things after Tobias." Braun said, though he seemed distracted. His eyes shifted back to Jacob. "The demon who has attacked Tobias on two occasions is known as Leonard, he's been noted as a servant of Azazel in more than one text."

"He didn't look like the depictions of Leonard I've studied." Jacob said, surprised.

"Unfortunately for us, demons aren't so consistent as to keep the same form for more than a few millennia." Braun said. "He may also have picked a form more suited for combat. But it is him, the scale retrieved from his body matches our records."

Jacob nodded, though something about his expression seemed concerned. "So what does that tell us?"

"Well, I was doing some investigating into our archives on demons. The only file we have on Leonard was mostly compiled by one wizard in particular." Braun's expression was gravely serious. "Can you guess who?"

"Fachnan." Jacob said.

"Exactly." Braun grimaced. "And how convenient is it, that Fachnan just so happens to be taking a leave of absence for the next couple of weeks."

That was mighty convenient, I thought. Could it be that Fachnan was taking that leave of absence in order to focus on his plans to resurrect Azazel? Probably, but something was still bothering me. I filed it under "To Discuss Later" and continued to listen.

"So what's your plan, High Elder?" Jacob asked him.

"Well, Fachnan has temporarily disabled his portal that connects Light Haven to his castle so we'll have to march up to the front door the old fashioned way to take him into custody." Braun explained.

"Well, let me know." Jacob said. "I'd love nothing more than to help take the guy in who's been causing so much trouble for Tobias."

Braun put a hand on Jacob's shoulder. "Thank you, Jacob. You've grown into quite the guardian. I'm proud of you, and trust me, I plan to have you right by my side when we capture Fachnan."

"Of course, sir." Jacob nodded respectfully.

Braun took his hand back and clapped. "Well, alright then. It's time I get some rest. There's a lot of boring paperwork to do tomorrow."

"Good night, High Elder." Jacob did a sort of half bow, awkwardly inclining his head towards Braun, and then turned to walk away.

Just before I moved to follow Jacob, I happened to glance at Braun.

My heart stopped cold.

He was staring directly at me. My eyes locked directly with his. For several agonizing seconds, we just stared at each other. There was a glow to his eyes. I could feel it cutting through my spell. Braun smiled down at me. Subtly so, in a way that he could pass off as if he were thinking of something funny.

Then he winked at me. A small, inconsequential thing that could've gone unnoticed to anyone else walking by. And then he just snapped his head back forward and walked right past me. I shook myself back to reality and turned to follow Jacob into the Portal Nexus.

As soon as we made it through the Seattle portal, I dropped the spell. The world came back into focus in a rush. I was breathing hard. I'd been holding my breath ever since Braun had made eye contact with me.

"What's wrong, Tobias?" Jacob asked.

I leaned against the wall opposite of the Gum Wall and slid to the ground. "He saw me, Jacob. He knew I was there."

"How do you know?" Jacob asked. "Maybe it's just nerves man."

I shook my head. I wiped my forehead with my sleeve. It was drenched in sweat. "No, we locked eyes man. He saw me. He winked at me"

Jacob thought about it for a moment. "Well if that wasn't concerning enough, there's something about what he said that's got me thinking."

"What is it?" I asked, looking up at him.

"Braun's never been one to suspect on circumstantial evidence." Jacob explained. "He's smart, and he's always trusted his fellow Elders. But ever since you even mentioned Fachnan to him, he's been suspicious of him."

A thought came to mind. "How goes the search for Kat?"

He looked at me, confused. "What do you mean?"

"When I went to Fachnan's castle, Kat was with me." I explained. "When we were attacked, Fachnan was the one who saved us. But since then, Kat's been missing. Seeing as she's a member of the Mystic Order, I would've thought there'd be some initiative to find her. I assumed Fachnan had captured her, but Braun didn't mention her at all when talking about him." I paused to think. "When I spoke to Fachnan in the infirmary, I asked him about Kat, but he said she'd never been there at all. I assumed he was just playing dumb. But now, I'm not so sure."

Jacob crossed his arms in thought. He had a look of concern staining his face. "I mean, I haven't seen her for awhile now. But no one's looped me in on any search party effort."

"Something just doesn't add up." I shook my head. "It's been a couple days now. I would've thought things around Light Haven would be a little more riled up. But everything seems to be business as usual."

Jacob twitched his head in agreement. Then his face twisted with displeasure, almost sick. "It may be possible," He hesitated. "It may be possible that the High Elders may be trying to keep things quiet. After all, Fachnan is tied up in this more than I think Braun is comfortable with. If even a hint of corruption amongst the High Elders got out, there could be chaos."

Jacob offered his hand, and I took it. He heaved me to my feet and I dusted myself off.

"Not to mention it probably doesn't look good to have one of your young wizards missing and another having been attacked multiple times now. Not to mention the whisperings we've heard around the Order about the Grail going missing. Sounds to me like they're trying to keep a crisis from breaking out." I said, more so thinking out loud than actually adding to the conversation.

Jacob nodded. "Why can't you apply these critical thinking skills to your homework?"

"Now you sound like my guidance counselor." I said. "Beside the idea of civil unrest amongst the members of the

Order, it wouldn't do our cause much justice if Fachnan realized we were onto him. Or at least, any more onto him than he thinks."

"So as much as it sucks, this apparent lack of concern from Braun and the rest of the High Elders might be a good thing. As good as it can be, at least." Jacob concluded.

"I guess so." I agreed. "But it means we can't rely on him or Bishop to act swiftly. They're too wrapped up in the politics."

"I suppose that's where we come in." Jacob smiled.

It was a wicked grin. The kind often seen on someone who was about to do something crazy and ill-advised. Despite that, I returned the smile in kind. And we got back to work.

Chapter 18

There's nothing a high schooler like me loves more than a good Saturday. No school. No responsibilities. Just a day open to whatever I wanted to do. Or so I had hoped. I was able to sleep in after my late night at the library. I didn't wake up until almost noon. I reached out to my nightstand and fumbled for my phone. I knocked an empty soda can and some loose papers over before I finally managed to find it.

Jacob had called me almost an hour ago. When I hadn't picked up, he'd sent me a text. It read:

"Tobias, let's meet at the YMCA. I've gathered the supplies we need for the tracking spell. Bring Scout with you. I have a feeling we could use the extra set of eyes."

I rested the phone on my chest and groaned. So much for a free day. I mean, I knew I had responsibilities today. Jacob and I would be working the tracking spell today. As long as all went according to plan, there shouldn't be too much trouble.

With an effort of will greater than any magic I'd conjured so far, I forced myself to get out of bed. I didn't want to keep Jacob waiting. I sent him a quick message:

Copy that. Just woke up. Gonna get ready and then I'll meet you there.

I hurried into the shower. I didn't waste any time enjoying the warm water, as much as I wanted to. I sudsed up, rinsed, and hopped out. Though it took everything in me not to just stand under the hot water for an hour. I pulled on a pair of blue jeans and a charcoal-colored T-shirt that read "I paused my game for this". I found a black denim jacket in my closet and threw it on too. I laced up my Converse and started for the stairs.

My eskrima in their holster caught my eye. I'd thrown them in the corner of the room. I weighed my options but decided it was a better idea to bring them along. Last thing I wanted was to get caught with my pants down. I strapped the holster onto my leg and hurried down the stairs.

As if he knew I'd be taking him with me, Scout was sitting at the bottom of the stairs with his leash and service animal harness at his feet. He was smarter than your average bear after all, so it only made sense. I got Scout all suited up and we left the apartment.

The local YMCA, I hadn't been back here since before I had been attacked by the demon the first time. It was only fitting that the next phase started here. I had a feeling things were going to be getting real hairy, real soon. I stood in front of the Y for almost fifteen minutes. No sign of Jacob. Scout was sitting patiently by my side. I could learn a thing or two from that dog. He was a master of patience. Waiting. Unlike me, he wasn't prone to restlessness. I was tapping my fingers against my leg and my eyes were constantly scanning.

Another fifteen minutes went by. I checked my phone. No missed calls or messages. Where could Jacob be? I was starting to worry. I looked down at Scout. He was calm, tongue hanging out as he panted. Now I was starting to get really antsy. I was about to make myself scarce when I heard a noise.

"Psst," Something hissed at me.

I spun around, looking for the source of the noise.

"Psst!" There it was again, more urgent this time.

I followed the sound and eventually locked onto the corner of the YMCA building. It was Jacob. He was poking his head out from the corner of the building. It was hard to see from this distance, but he looked a bit banged up.

Scout and I jogged over to him. I'd been right. There were cracks in his clay skin and scuff marks on his face and arms. His clothes had been torn up and were barely hanging on.

There was a duffel bag hanging over his shoulder. It seemed to be mostly intact.

"What the hell happened?" I asked him.

He winced as he sat down against the wall. "It's not looking good man. Azazel's allies are getting riled up. I got jumped by three demons on my way here." He motioned to the bag hanging on his shoulder. "I managed to keep this stuff from getting too messed up. Should still work for our purposes."

I frowned. No wonder Jacob had been late. He'd been jumped by monsters who were probably out looking for me. He'd been hurt because of me, and that didn't sit right with me. But then my frown turned back into something more neutral, and then a slight smile. I had a feeling that Azazel and friends knew we were getting ready to make our move. They were getting restless too, nervous even. But that told me something. Whatever they had planned, they weren't expecting us to make our move so soon. That put a smile on my face. We had the advantage.

"Are you okay, Jake?" I asked him.

Jacob nodded. "It'll heal up over the next day or so, nothing to worry about."

"Okay then." I twitched my head at the bag. "So what exactly do we have there?'

Jacob coughed once and then with a grunt of effort put the bag between us. He unzipped it and motioned for me to look inside.

I leaned over to take a peek inside the bag. It...wasn't what I was expecting, if I was being honest with myself. I had expected to see glowing crystals and mandrake roots and what not. Instead, inside were a bunch of items one might buy from a yard sale. Hell, I wouldn't have been surprised if Jacob HAD bought them in a yard sale. Inside the bag was a Christian Bible, a carton of Tang, a candle that apparently smelled liked "Morning Dew", a kaleidoscope, a plastic collectible Iron Man cup, and a clay bowl that initials and a date engraved on the side. In addition, there was also one of those toy dogs that walked on its own and a fresh box of rainbow chalk.

"What is all this crap?" I looked at Jacob, my face contorted by a mixture of confusion and concern.

"It's not crap." Jacob said. He sounded legitimately offended by the comment. "They may seem mundane, but they're legitimate articles we can use as components for the tracking spell."

"Okay, how so?" I asked, trying to recall the exact details of the spell from memory.

"Did you actually pay attention to what you took notes on?" Jacob asked me accusingly.

"Hey, that's a pretty good impression of my Math teacher." I pointed out.

Jacob facepalmed and I quickly reined in the smartassery.

"The tracking spell requires multiple items related to both the object or person you're trying to track, as well as the caster of the spell." I recited as I pulled out the small notebook where I'd written down my notes.

"And...what else?" He dragged the words out in an attempt to lead me on.

I flipped to the pages where I'd jotted down the notes, quite messily, I realized. Never take notes in the middle of the night without first chugging an energy drink. I squinted as I attempted to decipher the hieroglyphics.

Jacob tried to wait patiently but I could tell it would only go on for so long.

"Got it." I tapped the page. "Generally, there are six components for a simple tracking spell. One major focus item related to the item in question, as well as five minor foci based on the five senses."

"That's right." He gestured at the items. "So how do you think these items correspond to the spell?"

I studied the items again and thought carefully. It only took a few moments to deduce their significance. "The candle for smell, obviously. Tang for taste, the kaleidoscope for sight."

I paused to touch the clay bowl that had probably been a ceramics class project. It was rough, it hadn't been painted over yet. "The bowl for touch, and..."

I turned my attention to the Iron Man cup. It stumped me. I didn't get the impression of it being for sight or touch. So what the heck was it for? "Uh..."

Jacob smiled, amused by the roadblock I'd evidently hit. He picked up the cup, making a dramatic show of holding it high above the ground. Then he simply let go of it. The cup hit the ground and began to hop around, making a lot of noise as the plastic bounced back and forth on the ground.

"Sound." Jacob said, seemingly amused by the clever thinking.

I turned my attention to the Bible. "Which means this is the major focus item, right?"

Jacob nodded. "Good to see something sticks in that smooth brain of yours."

I rapped my knuckles against my forehead. "Me brain work good." I said with a heavy lisp. Then I frowned and pointed towards the toy dog and the chalk. "What are these for then?"

"The chalk is to draw a circle, where we link the foci and gather the magic." Jacob explained. "The dog...well, you'll see."

I pulled out the box of chalk and opened it. I held my hand under the opening and let a blue piece of chalk fall into my hand. After I made sure to tuck the other pieces back in properly, I put the box down. I picked out the most in tact section of sidewalk, making sure it was free of cracks and debris. Then I drew a wide circle that took up the entirety of the slab.

"Okay, so what's next?" I asked, holding up the chalk.

Jacob held out his hand for the piece of chalk. I handed it to him. Within the circle, he drew a five pointed star, much like you learn to do in school. I had a brief flash of uneasiness. It reminded me of the pentagram I'd seen in the basement of Fachnan's castle. Except the star was contained within the circle, rather than poking out the sides. Jacob put the chalk down and then pointed to where each point of the star met the circle.

"Now, place each of the minor foci at a point of the star." Jacob said.

I did so. I placed the Tang at the farthest point from me, and then placed the candle, kaleidoscope, Iron Man cup, and clay bowl at each point in a clockwise fashion. With that done, Jacob thumped the Bible and placed it directly in the center. On top of the Bible, he placed the toy dog. I was still confused as to what it was for. He pulled out a small Bic lighter, flicked it to life, and lit the candle. In a few moments, it began to smell like what a big candle company thought "Morning Dew" smelled like. Personally, I didn't think it smelled like much of anything, but that probably wasn't too important. I saw Scout's nose twitch as he investigated the smell.

"Okay, now the rest is all you." Jacob explained. "You'll need to focus on gathering energy into the circle while you picture the Grail in your mind."

I stopped him. "How's that gonna work if we don't know what the Grail actually looks like?"

"Remember, magic is all about intent. You don't need to get the image exactly right in your head. So long as you convey what exactly you're looking for, the spell should focus in on the actual Grail."

"Okay, fine." I shook my head and closed my eyes. I focused on my breathing for a few moments, paying meticulous detail to my breaths coming in and then going back out. This wasn't the quick, ka-boom type of magic I'd been used to so far. This was something more delicate and more complicated. It would take more focus than usual to get the spell off the ground.

I held my hands slightly raised over the circle and began muttering to myself. The syllables were mostly nonsense, meant to sound magical and mysterious, but they did the trick. I felt a stir in the air as the energy began to gather within the circle's boundaries. I imagined it as a large nebulous thing bound within a glass cylinder.

Jacob must've felt the spell forming because he spoke with an approving tone, "Good Tobias, now close the circle."

Without opening my eyes, I touched one hand to the chalk border of the circle. It's hard to describe, but I felt the circle become...secure in a way. I no longer had to expel effort to keep the magic within its boundaries. Now I just had to focus on the Grail itself. I pictured it how it had been depicted so many times in movies and books; as an oversized, jewel encrusted goblet with carved gold and glass sides that looked like it'd be impossible to drink from. It was very dramatic and no doubt nothing like the actual Grail, probably.

With my mystic senses, I felt the magic I'd gathered lash out like a fishing line into the void. My eyes followed the unseen cord of energy as it slithered through a sea of energies. I could feel my spell closing in on something. Something I could only describe as a wellspring of immense power. It was magic, but unlike anything I'd felt before. It felt older, somehow. There was a purity to it as well. It was hard to put into words. My magic fishing line swirled around the wellspring, though it took additional effort as the energies threatened to casually dismantle my spell. I renewed my focus and my tracking spell struck true. It lassoed around the wellspring and I felt the magic tug as it pulled taut.

"Got it." I grunted without opening my eyes.

"Good, now bring your focus to the toy dog in the circle." Jacob spoke gently, so as not to disrupt my focus.

I was still unclear of the toy dog's purpose, but I did as I was told. I imagined the other end of my arcane fishing line as a leash of sorts as I brought the toy dog into my mind's eye.

With another effort of thought and will, I tied the cord to the toy dog in imagination. There was an audible snap within my mind as the toy dog became bound to the Grail.

Jacob must've sensed it, because he let out a bark of laughter. "It worked!"

My face was still twisted in concentration. "Can I let up now?"

"Yeah, you can let go now." Jacob confirmed. "The spell will sustain itself for awhile."

I let out a gasp, releasing the tension that had built up within me, both physically and magically. Even without looking for it, I could feel the spell still attached to the toy dog.

"Okay, now can you tell me what this is for?" I flicked a hand at the dog.

"Well, for a tracking spell to work, you need a couple things once you've gotten it up and running. First, the target. In this case, the Grail. Secondly, you need a tracker. Something to lead you to the target. It can be something like a pendulum, or a compass, or even..." Jacob waved at the toy dog.

"A novelty toy." I said.

Jacob shrugged at me. "Hey, if it works. It works."

I wasn't one to argue with results. I picked up the toy dog and found the power switch. As I did, the dog's legs began to wiggle back and forth and it began making a very loud and repetitive yapping sound.

I glared at the yapping toy with disapproval.

Jacob caught the look and chuckled. He beckoned me to set the toy dog down and I did so. Normally, these types of toys wander around aimlessly. But to my surprise, the toy turned and began to waddle back the way I'd come. Scout was watching it with wary interest. The toy's incessant yapping was sure to get on his nerves too.

With hurried motions, Jacob snuffed out the candle and packed it along with the other items we'd used for the spell. He slung the bag over his shoulder and pointed towards the toy dog, which was moving way quicker than it should be able to.

"Follow that dog!" Jacob said with a satisfied glee to his voice.

Without needing to be prompted, Scout was the first one up and moving. Jacob and I had to jog for a moment to catch up to my dog, who followed the toy dog with great interest. I wasn't surprised to get a few strange looks from the passerby as we followed the toy dog. We probably looked like idiots. Oh well, there were worse things.

It didn't take long for us to realize the toy dog, or rather, the spell, didn't have an understanding of how roads and buildings worked. The spell guided the toy on the most direct route to the Grail, obstacles be damned. There were multiple occasions where we had to pick it up and move it around the obstacle in question.

Despite the toy dog's increased speed, the trek took quite awhile. My mouth was dry and my feet were starting to hurt. While I was starting to tire, I noticed Jacob was moving faster. There was less pain behind each step. The cracks and scuff in his clay skin were starting to heal. Being a golem definitely had its perks.

As we walked, I noticed that our surroundings were beginning to look quite familiar. But for the life of me I couldn't figure out why. The toy dog seemed to get its second wind; its little legs wiggled faster and it was covering more ground. Finally, we rounded a corner.

My heart skipped a beat.

"You've got to be kidding me." I said, my voice full of disbelief. My feet were stuck in place on the sidewalk as I looked up at the large building that the toy dog was making a beeline for. I couldn't believe it had slipped my mind.

I looked up at the Burke Museum of Natural History as the distant sounds of a yapping dog grew quieter in the distance.

Chapter 19

There was less than an hour before the museum closed. Jacob and I flashed our student IDs at the ticket counter and they let us in for free. Which was a good thing because we were both dirt broke. The woman at the ticket counter gave Scout a suspicious look until she saw his vest. All the while I was kicking myself for not remembering the museum sooner. They had a freaking exhibit on European history and mythology, including a whole display dedicated to the Holy Grail.

"Stupid, stupid, stupid…" I muttered angrily to myself. I was walking so fast I was nearing a jog.

Jacob had put away the toy dog when we'd reached the museum. I doubted we needed the guide at this point. He struggled to keep up with me. It didn't take us too long to reach the back of the museum, where the exhibit was. We passed by suits of armor and tapestries and other artifacts from ye olde England. At the very end of the exhibit was the boulder that displayed the legendary sword wielded by King Arthur: Excalibur. But we weren't here for some model of a legendary sword. We were here for what lie past that.

Past the sword in the stone were several pedestals. Each one displaying a different rendition of the Holy Grail. There was a wooden chalice much too wide to seem practical for regular use. A wine glass that was tall and thin; so much so that a light breeze would probably knock it over. There was the clay bowl that I remember thinking didn't even look like a cup. And at the center of them all was the one I'd imagined when focusing the spell; the one with a golden base, glass sides, and jewels fused to the gold.

"This is really it?" Jacob asked.

I gestured vaguely towards the bag. "Ask the dog just to be sure." I said, glancing from one Grail to the next.

He did so, pulling the toy dog from his bag, flipping the switch, and setting it down. The toy dog began its yapping and waddled over to the pedestals. Without pointing out any of the cups in particular, the dog spun in a circle, yapped a couple more times, and then shut off.

"I guess that settles it." Jacob shrugged.

"Now we only have to figure out which Grail is ours." I said.

Jacob grunted. "Perhaps we should wait until after the museum closes."

I shook my head. "We can't afford to wait. Azazel's forces are on the move and we could be sitting ducks if we wait around here."

"Won't do much good if we get caught stealing the Holy Grail either." Jacob said. "An hour won't kill us. And if the museum is empty, we'll have better luck sneaking our way outta here."

"Fine." I growled.

Jacob twitched his head towards a secluded corner behind a table that was displaying several pieces of jewelry. "We'll hide back there. Bring up your veiling spell if we need to." Jacob looked up towards the ceiling and I realized he was noting the positions of the two cameras in the area. "Those cameras don't look like they cover that spot, so we should be good."

It was settled. We made our way behind the table as discretely as possible. Luckily the museum was already starting to empty out, so it wasn't like there were many prying eyes. We hunkered down behind the table and got comfortable. I missed when monsters and demons were trying to kill me every few days. What happened to that? This wizarding stuff was starting to feel a bit overrated.

We had to wait behind that stupid table for way too long. I mean, WAY too long. There wasn't a whole lot of space behind that table and the wall it sat parallel to. Jacob, Scout, and I were folded up more than a paper swan in an attempt to fit into the small space. Jacob was worse off than I was. His shoulders were hunched uncomfortably past his head so that he didn't peek out over the table.

Finally, we'd waited long enough that I was confident that the only people around were us and a security guard who'd just passed by on his rounds. I stood up awkwardly from behind the table. I didn't have any room to use my arms to help myself stand up, so I had to rely entirely on my legs. I helped Jacob up and he had to stumble awkwardly to avoid stepping on Scout's tail. The dog gave Jacob an annoyed look, regardless.

"Eh, sorry." Jacob held his hands up apologetically.

The sun had just set, leaving only the moon to cast its silvery light through the windows. Rectangular shafts of light fell upon the exhibits. It was a surreal sight, all those artifacts from ye olden times lit by the moonlight. We made our way out from behind the table and approached the Holy Grail display.

"Now to pick out our very own Holy Grail." I reached for the jewel-encrusted Grail that acted as the display's centerpiece.

"Wait a second." Jacob whispered.

I looked at him, confused. "What is it, Jake?"

"I don't think that's the one."

"And why not?" I asked him.

"My magical senses aren't as strong as that of a wizard's, but when I tried feeling for that Grail's magical energies, I got nothing." Jacob clarified. "Open up your senses and feel for the power."

"Oooookay." I said, skeptically. Though he probably was right. I just wanted to get out of here before we were caught.

I closed my eyes and let my own magical aura mingle with the world around me. Even now I wasn't sure how to describe it. It didn't parallel any senses in a way that made an easy comparison. I couldn't see the energies, so it wasn't sight. The energies offered no sound, so it wasn't hearing, either. It sure as hell didn't taste or smell like anything either. The closest I supposed was touch, but that didn't feel like an apt comparison either.

Imagine bodies of water coming together and how the warm and cold, the pollution or lack thereof, might mix. I suppose it was something like that. My magic was polluted by my own humanity. My hopes, my fears, my dreams, and my aspirations all were reflected in my magic.

Then I felt the Holy Grail's magic.

It literally knocked me on my ass. I fell back onto the marble floor hard. I'd be sore later, but it was hardly my concern at the moment.

The magic that the Holy Grail produced was blinding. It blew straight through my magical senses and hit me in every other sense I had. My sight was obscured by burning white light. My ears were ringing with a sound that I couldn't even begin to describe. My entire body was tingling with a feeling like ants crawling on my skin. I smelled flowers on the first day of Spring, fresh water springs babbling about, and strangely enough, chocolate. The taste was similar, but with a metallic tinge on the edge of it all.

But despite all of that, it HURT. That raw power. That wellspring of magic was so overwhelming all my body knew to do was fire off every pain receptor in my body. Yet at the same time I felt completely numb. It was a maddening sensation. The pain was there, yet I felt nothing. It made no sense, but it didn't seem to matter.

I didn't hear him move, probably because I couldn't, but I felt Jacob's broad hand cover my mouth and stifle the shocked scream that I hadn't realized escaped me. I squirmed mindlessly against his grip. I couldn't explain what was going through my mind. Everything was just too loud, too bright, too intense. I couldn't focus.

I was shocked to feel something hit me hard across the face. A new sensation of pain stung on my cheek, while the Grail's burning power seemed to subside. My vision came back into focus, and the way Jacob was holding up his other hand, I realized he'd slapped me. Freaking hard too, I might add. I flexed my jaw and was relieved to find nothing felt broken.

"Uh, thanks." I said. My words came out slurred and the sound of them felt distant.

Jacob offered me a hand. I took it, and he pulled me up. "Are you okay?"

I shivered, feeling the phantom sensation that perceiving the Holy Grail's magic that was left behind. My mind felt...scattered, and I struggled to focus. I shook my head, trying to jostle everything back into place.

"Are you okay?" Jacob repeated, slower this time.

"Uhhh, yeah. Yeah. I'm okay." I felt everything start to fall back into place. I was still a little shaky, but it'd have to do.

"What happened?" He asked me. He was still speaking slower than normal, which helped me keep up.

"The...The Grail..." I trailed off and I shook my head again. "We're definitely at the right spot, I'll tell you that much."

"You sensed it?"

"And then some." My eyes widening as I nodded in the affirmative.

"Well you need to pick it out so we can dip." Jacob looked over his shoulder, nervously. "No doubt that guard heard you."

"Ugh, fine. Fine." I growled.

I delved into my memory. Even remembering that light, that power, felt far from good. It burned brighter and hotter than the sun. It was like nothing I'd felt before, and I don't know if there'd ever be anything that surpassed it. But that wasn't important. That didn't help me. I needed to see through the light, to discern which Grail was real. I gathered my own magic in my mind and shaped it into something like a barrier from the memory.

I pushed against the light, the power that toppled enemy kings, that was the scourge of innocents and monsters alike. That power was uncaring, unyielding. It did not discern between good and evil. Only the hand that guided it could. I pushed deeper and deeper, until I saw a shape take form in the light. I reached out for that shape. That shape that had caused us so much trouble. I felt it in my hand and I clamped down hard.

My eyes flashed open and in my hand, was the modest clay bowl. I looked at it in disbelief. It wasn't what I was expecting, to say the least. It had been the least grand of all the others. But as I touched it, I could feel the thrum of its power.

"This is it." I turned to show Jacob the bowl.

Scout sniffed at it curiously, then took a step back.

Jacob looked from Scout to the Holy Grail in my hand. He held out a hand and I tossed it to him. The reaction was immediate. His whole body seized, his back arcing in what would've been a painful angle for a normal human. It only lasted for a second though. His body loosened up and he fell to a knee.

Scout and I both rushed over to him, my dog sniffing in his ear and offering several delicate doggy kisses. I helped him stand and supported him. He was still holding onto the Grail with a death grip.

It was my turn to ask. "Are you okay?"

He nodded to me. "The Grail is a huge reservoir of magic. I guess it takes a second for magical constructs like myself to adjust to contact with it."

"Let's put it in the bag." I said. "No reason to risk either of us getting whammied by that stupid cup again."

"I won't complain." Jacob nodded. He unzipped the duffel bag, and with notable effort, he dropped the Grail inside. He zipped the bag back up and looked back to me.

"So what now?" I asked him.

"We take the Grail back to Light Haven before someone can jump us for it." Jacob said.

"I'm not going to argue with that plan." I agreed.

Then, something came over Jacob. His facial expression changed from something serious and calculating to what seemed like a horrible realization.

"What is it?" I asked.

"A tracking spell. It's so simple." Jacob said.

"Yeah? That's why we did it, right?" I said, uncertainty painting my words.

"Exactly. It's simple. It's the first thing that Braun would've done to find this thing." Jacob continued.

"Uh, right." I said. "I'm not following."

"So if that's the case, then why hadn't they found the dang thing sooner?" Jacob asked. "What are the odds that we were the first ones to try it? And succeed, no less?"

Oh, now I got it.

Jacob held up two fingers. "There's only two possibilities. Neither of them are good." He put one finger down. "One, they were actively avoiding trying to find the Grail." Then he put the second finger down. "Two, someone was preventing the tracking spell from zeroing in, until they knew you'd be the one to try it."

A cold, sinking feeling began to fester in my stomach. Had we been played?

That's when my phone rang. It felt so out of place, all things considered. But I pulled the phone out of my pocket. The screen displayed a picture of Claire. Don't ask me to explain why, but I had a seriously bad feeling. I almost didn't answer.

I swiped on the screen and held the phone up to my ear. "Claire?"

"Toby, where are you?" Claire whispered. Her voice was shaky, like she was crying, or she was scared.

I looked around at the museum. "Uhhh, long story, why?"

Claire let out a distressed sound. "I was at the school library late, doing research on the Holy Grail like you asked when the lights went out. And I started hearing strange noises outside."

My stomach dropped.

"Claire, just stay calm. Find somewhere to hide and just stay put. Jake and I will be there soon." I said in a hushed tone, trying to keep my voice calm.

"Okay Toby, just plea-" The line cut with a violent burst of static.

I looked down at the phone, and then over to Jacob. "It's Claire. Something's after her."

He cursed. "The school is across town. We'll never make it."

I looked from him, then to Scout, then back to him. Then back to Scout. The dog got the idea before I had. Scout braced himself and then I felt a surge of power burst outward from where he stood. The dog began to grow and change. Scout growled and roared as he changed. It looked painful. I could hear bones cracking and shifting. Scout's body grew thick with muscle as a trail of fire trace his spine. His front paws shifted into something more like hands with large black claws.

Scout roared as he finished his transformation. I smiled at the big dog. I turned to Jacob and twitched my head at the hellhound. "Get on."

Chapter 20

Here's something I bet you didn't know: hellhounds can MOVE. Jacob and I had climbed onto Scout's back, and to my surprise, the flames didn't burn us. But that was hardly the most apparent detail at the moment. Scout moved so quickly down the streets of greater Seattle that I could barely make out any details as he ran. We passed by cars that must've been going fifty miles per hour. Scout turned corners with extreme precision, his claws digging into the asphalt in order to turn on a dime.

"Now THIS is pod racing!" I laughed maniacally as Scout charged down the streets.

"Are you serious right now?" Jacob screamed over the sound of the whipping winds.

"Oh come on, man! This is great!" I yelled over my shoulder. "So what's the game plan?"

"If Azazel's goons are really making their move, then they're are going to be a lot at the school." Jacob explained.

"How many do you think?"

"It'd be foolish to expect less than at least a dozen of them." Jacob said, a little more grimly.

Damn. The idea of a dozen mooks on par with Leonard occupying the school was not a pleasant image. Even if they were more comparable to the Nagini, which hadn't been nearly as tough, I didn't like our odds. This was going to get way out of hand.

Even with the thrill of the hellhound ride to distract me from the looming threats, something was still eating away at me. Given the urgency of everything going on, the hunt for the Grail had progressed poorly, despite the apparent skill and power the Mystic Order had at its disposal. Either the Mystic Order's politics were so muddled it took them far too long to get anything done, or someone was purposely pulling strings to hang up the whole investigation.

Fachnan, being our prime suspect, was in the perfect position to do just that. I didn't have all the details but I had to believe it was possible that Fachnan was doing something to keep the Elders from acting swiftly.

Alternatively, there was only one other person that I knew for sure had seen me sneaking in and out of the library obtaining the information about the tracking spell, but that person didn't exactly strike me as the evil puppet master type.

But at this very moment, none of that mattered right now. I had the Grail in tow, and Claire was in trouble. Get her out of danger, and deal with the fallout later.

Before I knew it, Scout had skidded to a stop in front of the school, tearing up the concrete as his claws dug in. Jacob and I hopped off and I scratched under his chin affectionately. The dog sat back on his haunches and kicked one of his back legs in a satisfied manner. The ground rumbled ever so slightly with each kick.

"Good boy, Scout. Good job." I said in my best puppy dog voice. Then I noticed Jacob looking at me. "What?"

"Are you really giving a hellhound, guardian and warrior of the underworld, chin scratches and baby talk?" Jacob said slowly, as if I was dumb.

"Well yeah," I gestured at him, obviously. "He's a good boy."

Jacob shook his head dismissively. "So what's the plan?"

"I was hoping you'd have one." I tilted my head up at the school. "Seems quiet."

"Don't let them fool you. They're in there." Jacob twitched his head to Scout. "He can sense them too. I say we form a tight circle, the three of us, and wedge our way in. There will be at least a couple guarding the front door. Maybe a few more guarding other entrances, the rest will be looking for their target."

I shook my head. "No, just the two of us."

"What do you mean?" Jacob asked me.

"I'm sending Scout back home. If there was ever a time to loop Bishop in on my mess, now would be the time." I explained.

Jacob's face contorted into an ugly expression as the thought ran by him. I could tell he'd feel a lot more comfortable having Scout to watch our back. But he also knew a dozen or more demons and whatever other mooks were way too much for just the three of us. With an experienced wizard on the way, we might just make it out of this alive.

"Okay." Jacob nodded gravely. "Then maybe we should wait until Scout gets back with Bishop."

"No!" I damn near screamed at him. I twitched my head and exhaled, bringing my anger back under control. "No, if we wait, they could find her and hurt her, or worse."

Again, Jacob looked very uncomfortable. There was no way in hell it was a good idea for us to take on the hoard of bad guys alone, just the two of us. But Jacob and I both knew that I was going in there, whether he was there to help me or not.

"Fine." Jacob muttered.

I nodded at him. Then I looked to Scout. The hellhound was listening intently. "Scout, we need you to find Bishop.

Bring him here. Claire is in danger and we're not going to be able to do this without either of you. Do you understand?"

It was an alien motion for a dog, even a hellhound, but Scout nodded at me. The big dog then planted a giant doggy kiss on my face. I sputtered and shook my head, covered in hellhound drool. Then the dog stood up and took off at blinding speeds. It was less than a minute before the hound disappeared into the darkness.

With Scout gone, I looked over to Jacob. "Well, you ready?"

Jacob tilted his head to one side, almost indifferently. "I'm not doing anything else tonight, I suppose."

I reached down and pulled out my eskrima, holding them ready at my side. This was going to get real noisy, real quick, so I wanted to be ready. I could feel a stir of power, and I noticed that Jacob's arms were taking on an appearance akin to sandstone. There was a faint green glow to them as well. He was getting ready to throw down. I recalled when he had fought against Leonard when all this crazy nonsense first started. There was a childish glee at the thought of kicking ass next to Jacob. We'd been friends, brothers even, for years and years. We'd always had each other's backs, so this was more of the same. Just sub out the bullies for demons.

"So how are we doing this?" I asked him. "Are we going in loud, or we going in sneaky?"

"I don't think going in sneaky is going to do us any favors at this point." Jacob said. "We want their attention, and they'll notice us sooner or later. Might as well be on our terms."

We walked up to the front door. There was no sign for alarm. I gave Jacob one last look, a wicked grin spreading on my face. I took a step back into a sturdy stance, winding back one of my eskrima as I did so. I took a deep breath, and swung my eskrima underhanded towards the door. As I did so, I focused on gathering kinetic energy, forming it into something akin to a battering ram.

"*Fordun!*" I followed through on the swing and the kinetic energy I'd gathered up exploded against the double doors.

The doors exploded inward, making a sickly, loud crunching noise as they ripped off their hinges and flew into the hall. They banged and bounced against the floors, the ceiling, and the lockers on either side.

I stopped to admire my handwork for a moment. I didn't think I'd hit it that hard, but I sure as hell wasn't complaining. To my surprise, nothing else happened. There was no hissing and screeching or rushing forth of eldritch horrors. Jacob and I took a careful step forth into the school.

Nothing happened. And then nothing kept happening. And then nothing happened some more. My eyes swept across the intersection of halls. I scanned the left hall, then the center hall, and then down the right. There was nothing.

I held up my arms in disbelief. "Oh come on!"

Then, as if on cue, I saw a shape lunge from above. It hit Jacob on the back and sent him stumbling forward. Jacob cursed and raised his arms to grab at the thing on his back. It was hard to see what the shape was, but I could see arms flailing as it raked at Jacob's back. I raised one of my eskrima level with the creature attacking my friend. I began to speak a spell but a sudden impact against my back sent me tumbling to the ground.

Red hot pain erupted on my back as something slashed at the space between my shoulder blades. I cried out in pain and swung blindly behind me with my eskrima. I got lucky and managed to strike my attacker. It wasn't enough to knock it off of me but I was able to knock it off balance. While the creature was stunned, I got my arms under me and rolled over, the creature tumbled away as I did. I managed to get to my feet and locked onto the creature. I didn't even take a moment to take its details in.

With a swing of my arm, I collected kinetic energy at the end of my eskrima, shaping it into a mallet and I swung it down on the creature. "*Fordun!*"

It splattered into a mound of chitin and green blood that burned the ground around it. I realized now it was some sort of bug creature, presumably a demon. I couldn't make out its appearance anymore, due to the aforementioned squashing, but I could still see twitching wings and the remnants of insectoid limbs. The green blood bubbled and sizzled idly, and damn, it smelled like crap.

A roar of anger snapped me back to attention. Jacob had gotten a grip on his bug demon and flung it into a section of lockers. It made a terrible screeching sound as it did, and began to pick itself up before Jacob struck it with his large fist in a blur of motion. The creature splattered similarly to the one I'd squashed. Acidic green blood dripped to the floor and sizzled some more.

"Yikes, shoulda brought some Raid." I noted.

"As far as guard dogs go, they weren't much to write home about." Jacob shrugged. He pointed toward my back. "You okay?"

I juggled my eskrima in one hand, and with the free one felt my back, inspecting the damage. The creature hadn't cut deep, thanks to the denim jacket I'd been wearing, but both it and my shirt were ruined. The shallow wound was bleeding plenty, but it wasn't so bad as to draw immediate concern.

"I'll be alright." I muttered, wincing as the wound stung from my touch. "Ruined a perfectly good denim jacket though, never mind the shirt."

"Good. Coulda been worse." Jacob said. "I'm not sure how much noise that made, but we shouldn't sit still for long."

I nodded at him. "Claire was in the library when she called, so we should check there first."

Together, we went down the center hallway. No other demons attacked us, though I had a sneaking suspicion we were being watched. We could hear skittering and chittering sounds in the dark expanses of the school's hallways. There's something about schools at night that always felt weird. They just weren't meant to be inhabited once the sun went down. So many empty rooms and echoing hallways reminded me of a mummy's tomb, in a weird way. The image of my history teacher half-wrapped in toilet paper shambling out of a classroom muttering something about brains or curses flashed through my mind.

Hey, I was nervous, cut me some slack.

We emerged from the entrance building into the courtyard. In the center of the courtyard stood the fountain, its spouts turned off, and the legendary knight lit by the moonlight. If you looked at it at the right angle, it almost looked like the knight was stabbing at the moon itself. The image gave me a sense of renewed vigor towards our goals here. It was somehow reassuring that we were under the knight's watchful gaze.

The library was off to the right of the courtyard. I was tempted to just cut straight through the courtyard, but Jacob raised his arm to stop me.

"Last thing we need to do is expose ourselves where the enemy can attack from all sides." Jacob whispered. "We'll hug the walls of the buildings as far as we can up to the library."

"Good idea." I had a thought of something swooping down from one of the nearby trees to disembowel me. I gulped.

We did as Jacob suggested, and walked against the walls of the buildings that surrounded the courtyards. Luckily there were pretty much no significant gaps between buildings between us and the library. So if something really did try to swoop down and rip my guts out, I could duck and it would pancake against the wall like a cartoon. That was a funny image, and it eased my nerves a bit.

Nothing attacked us as we approached the library. Which struck me as odd. Jacob said there'd be something like a dozen bad guys roaming the school. So where were they? We weren't far from the front of the library now. In a few moments, we'd be inside and we could nab Claire and get out of here. God knows I wish it had been that easy. Right when we were about to approach the door, something screamed. It wasn't a scream of terror. Not even close. It was a scream full of anger and challenge. I turned to the source of the scream, but before I could even lock my gaze on it, another scream rang out in the night. And another. And another. And another.

Things came into view. I counted four gargoyle-like demons with scrunched up pig faces perched in the nearby trees, their molten red eyes glowed in the darkness. Two insectoid demons, about the same size as the ones Jacob and I had squashed before buzzed and landed on the ground in front of the trees. They reminded me mostly of roaches, but they had horns that resembled that of a Hercules beetle. Three large ape-like monstrosities with the faces of lions landed on the ground in front of the insect demons. They were a bit bigger than Jacob, but not by much.

Finally, a demon I was all too familiar with, emerged from the shadows. I mean, literally emerged from the shadows. The demon I'd come to know as Leonard took form from the shadows of the courtyard, oozing into his familiar form. He must've been going for a nudist look up until now, because unlike our previous encounters, he was wearing armor the color of obsidian and he brandished a large axe to match.

"Tobias Caesar Leight, I don't think I need to tell you it is in the best interest of both you and your friends to surrender now." Leonard said.

It wasn't meant to be threatening. He said it as a matter of fact. If we didn't surrender, he and his posse would attack and my friends would most likely die. And me, well, no doubt Leonard here was under strict orders to make sure I survived. Though that didn't mean he needed me in mint condition.

So they'd been watching us after all. They had just been waiting for us to get into position before they revealed themselves. And judging by the fact they'd made a theatric entrance rather than just jumping us all at once, they must've been pretty confident. There was no doubt in my mind that in a straight fight, Jacob and I would be pounded to a pulp faster than you could say "orange juice." Get it, because pulp? Don't judge me. It took everything in me not to cry like a little girl right now.

I held one eskrima pointed straight at Leonard, while my spare was held back by my head, ready to whip out a lance of kinetic energy if it came to that. Though I wasn't sure if I'd be able to do much against this many enemies.

"You and I both know that isn't happening, Leonard." I said his name in my best mocking tone. "Seriously though, what kind of name is Leonard for a demon anyways?"

Leonard uttered an ugly sound from deep in his belly. And I realized he was laughing. It was a grotesque corruption of what a laugh should be: full of joy and happiness. This was full of sick and sadistic amusement.

"Jest however you wish, Leight." Leonard chuckled. "Though it will not save you from your fate. And it definitely won't save that little girlfriend of yours."

Then I realized something. Including Leonard, I counted nine demonic nasties staring us down. Jacob had said that for this sort of operation, he would expect the demons to come in a group of at least twelve. We'd performed pest control on two of them, and if there were nine here...

I swung my head back at the library doors, though I couldn't see anything inside. Could there already be a demon lurking in the library, hunting for Claire?

I looked back to Jacob and whispered, "I think there's one already inside the library. Claire could be in trouble."

"Well we can't exactly just ask these ones to sit patiently while we rescue her." Jacob grunted through his teeth.

"I know, but we can't stay here and banter with them either." I said. "We're going to have to divide and conquer. Do you think you can hold this clown squad off while I go find her?"

Jacob grimaced. He did not like the idea. But we didn't have much choice if we wanted any hope of getting out of here alive. "Maybe for a few minutes. Give me a distraction and then run for it. Find Claire and let's make like leaves and get the hell out of here."

I didn't think that was how the saying went, but I decided now wasn't the best time to debate that. Alright, if the demons wanted me, we sure as hell weren't gonna make it easy on them.

I called up my power. It was going to take a lot to knock these guys off balance. I took several deep breaths, with each inhale, I brought more magic into me. After about ten seconds, I had enough power stored up to give myself a migraine. Then with a defiant shout, I thrust my lifted eskrima forward with a step.

"Kaze maximus!"

Chapter 21

As soon as I'd shouted the spell, the winds kicked up instantly. With the aid of my focus, I was able to shape the spell exactly to my liking. A small tornado of gale force winds erupted right in the middle of Leonard and his squad. The gargoyles wings were caught in the gale and were flung from their positions in the trees. The insects followed suit and were whipped around wildly. One was flung into the sword of the nearby knight statue and cut cleanly in half.

Nice.

Leonard and the lion-apes didn't seem too disturbed by the winds, though they did stumble around a bit and generally seemed off balance. Jacob rushed forward, getting his golem on. His entire body took on a sandstone texture and he leaped into the air dramatically, carried by my winds. He grabbed the remaining insect demon out of the air with impressive dexterity. He fell straight onto one of the lion-apes and stabbed the horns of the bug into its skull. The impact crushed the bug's body and knocked the lion-ape to the ground. The dead ape demon's body twitched and gushed blood like a damn garden hose.

I whistled, but I didn't have time to watch further. I rushed to the library doors and ripped them open. I sprinted in until I was past the front desk and looked around. It was dark and quiet. Well, save for all the noise and commotion going on outside.

I considered calling out to Claire, but I didn't want to risk her exposing her location to the demon. It was better to find the demon first, smash it, and find Claire afterwards. I picked an aisle of shelves and started walking, my eskrima raised and ready to fling spells. I had to move fast; Jacob wouldn't last long. A loud crash to my right caught my attention, and I whipped around to the source.

Through the bookshelf, I could see the subsequent shelves crashing against each other, and getting closer to me. I ran down the remainder of the aisle and dove forward to avoid becoming a book-and-Tobias sandwich. I hit the ground in a roll, managing to come out on my feet. I aimed an eskrima in the direction the shelves had fallen from.

A spider-like beast with the face of a wolf and the size of a bear crawled over the fallen bookshelves. It raised a scorpion tail into the air. The tail was long enough to carve a scar into the ceiling, small chips of debris falling onto its back as it did.

"Oh come on...why did it have to be a spider monster?" I groaned.

The thing snarled a challenge at me and struck at me with its tail. I had only a moment to react.

"Back off Charlotte, you don't want to make me angry. You wouldn't like me when I'm angry." I said, taking up a defensive stance with my eskrima held near my chest and head.

Charlotte the demon didn't seem amused by either reference and let out a chittering roar in reply.

"*Duro!*" I snapped.

My skin hardened until it shone like steel. The demon's tail struck me but slid off my hardened body. Eww, phrasing. I parried the tail to the side, knocking the thing off balance and lunged forward. I whipped my eskrima at the creature's face but it caught my weapon in its teeth. We played a brief game of tug of war until I remembered my second eskrima. Duh. I swung with my free arm and by collecting kinetic energy into it, strengthened the blow to deadly proportions. Well, maybe for humans. The spider demon fell flat to the ground and released my first eskrima from its grip. I backpedaled a few feet before it could recover.

My skin returned to its normal durability as I steadied myself and aimed my eskrima at the creature and shouted, "*Kaze!*"

Wind erupted from the tip of the weapon and roared towards the monster. It might've been big, but it wasn't terribly dense. The winds, while nothing compared to the gale I had whipped up outside, was more than enough to send the creature, and a boat load of books, flying towards the far wall. The demon regained its composure and opened its maw. Webbing shot out of its maw and latched onto one of the fallen shelves. It used the tether to regain its footing and resist the winds.

Damn, I was really hoping to do my own interpretation of Picasso with its guts on the wall. Oh well. I ditched the wind spell and rushed forward. I had to put it down quick. I jumped into the air, lined up the shot, aiming my eskrima at the ceiling at just the right angle, with my free eskrima aimed right at its head.

"*Kaze!*" I snarled.

A brief gust of wind roared from my eskrima aimed at the ceiling and sent me flying straight down at the thing's head. In that split second, I refocused on gathering kinetic energy and focused it at the tip of my downward-facing eskrima. I did my best to shape it into something like a cone, but I could feel my control slackening. It wasn't going to be perfect.

But it proved effective.

The combined force of the kinetic spell and the wind spell made for quite the spear. My eskrima sunk into the demon's head, all the way up to where my hand gripped it. But I didn't come out unscathed, as I'd struck the demon, its scorpion tail had managed to slice a large cut into the side of my arm. It burned. Holy hell it burned. I cursed as it fell limply to the ground. I pulled my eskrima free of its skull and wiped the blood off on my pants.

There was an almost transparent amber liquid coating my wound. Oh man, was that thing poisonous? That wasn't good. The room swayed and it took all my willpower to keep myself standing upright.

"Claire!" I yelled, though it came out hoarse and hollow. My breathing grew heavier. "Claire!"

"Toby?" Claire's voice rang out, surprisingly close. I turned around to find her emerging from a supply closet.

She was sweating nervously, but she seemed unharmed. She wore grey sweatpants and a lumberjack jacket that I had loaned her at some point and never gotten back. Her long blonde hair was curled up into a messy bun held together by a couple of number 2 pencils. I stumbled over to her and wrapped my arms around her. I slouched and leaned into her as the tension left my body. Or maybe the poison was starting to settle in.

"Thank God you're okay." I rasped. My eyelids felt heavy.

Claire pulled away from the hug and looked me up and down. Concern painted her face and I could feel her holding me steady.

"Toby, what's wrong with you?"

I gestured vaguely towards the demon. "Poisonous. Nicked me right as I killed it."

"We gotta get out of here. They're all over the place." Claire said in a hushed voice, as if there were more demons in the library. Though I faintly knew that wasn't true.

"J-Jake's keeping the rest of them busy." I stumbled on the words. "Need to get out there and help him clear a path for us to escape."

"You're in no condition, Toby." Claire looked me up and down.

"We don't really have many options." I said. "If I don't get out there to help him, none of us are making it home in time for supper."

Claire muttered a curse. It was strange, she wasn't really one to curse. I shook my body out a bit, trying to loosen up and refocus. I didn't have time to be dying from demon poison right now. There was a loud crash from outside, and that pretty much snapped me back to reality.

"Okay, just stay behind me." I told her sternly. "Jake and I are gonna lay the smack down on these guys just enough to carve us a way out of here. I promise you, I will get you out of here alive. When I move, you move, capisce?"

She nodded, though it looked like she'd rather run away and cry. Me too, sister. But there was no time to cry. I'd cry later. Cause holy hell was all of this absolutely terrifying. I put one of my eskrima back in its holster and grabbed Claire's hand.

We ran for the front door and emerged upon a war zone.

I knew Jacob was badass, but holy crap, I had no idea just how badass. Besides the demons we'd dispatched before I'd gone into the library, he'd ripped apart two of the gargoyles and beaten one of the lion-apes to a pulp. He held one of the remaining gargoyles by its leg and was currently using its body as a club to beat the remaining lion-ape to a pulp.

Leonard was watching the fight go down while the remaining gargoyle circled Jacob high in the air. Anytime the gargoyle tried to come in close, Jacob swung at it with the body of its fallen brethren. But as he fought, I noticed he was badly hurt. His clay skin was cracked and chipped in several places. Instead of blood, a green gaseous light leaked from openings in his body. He couldn't take much more of this.

I looked back at Claire again. "Stay back, I have to help him."

Claire nodded at me frantically.

I turned back to the fight and raised my eskrima. I gathered my power and shouted, "*Kaze!*"

Instead of a rush of wind, the world did a somersault. Nausea overwhelmed me and I fell to the ground hard, my eskrima clattering to the ground noisily. I heard Claire shout, but the sound was instant and muffled. Between all the magic

I'd been throwing around and the demon's poison, it seemed I was pretty much spent.

I could still see Jacob fighting the demon where I'd fallen. He'd heard my shout, and damn it, I'd just screwed him. He turned to face me and his face twisted with despair.

"Tobias!" He shouted.

But the second he'd looked away from the lion-ape, it seized its chance. The demon swung one of its oversized arms at Jacob. It hit him square in the chest and sent him flying. He cried out as he flew and crashed into the wall of the library.

I turned my head to face Claire. "R-Run…" I choked.

Before my vision faded to black, I saw Leonard's ugly ass foot step down in front of my head, facing Claire.

Oh God.

Chapter 22

I was getting real tired of passing out. If it happened even one more time I'd have to get my head checked. I wonder if they had punch cards for that kind of thing. The humor left my body as I awoke. I couldn't see. Something tickled against my eyelashes, and I realized I must've been blindfolded.

I tried to remain calm and take in any details I could without my sight. I was laying down, my limbs stretched out and tied to some sort of metal X-shape. It was really cold. I shivered, and realized that I was damn near naked, save for my boxer briefs. Yikes, that was embarrassing. The poison's effects seemed to have faded. Or a more uncomfortable thought, had my captor's cured me of it?

Okay, time to get down to business. I twitched my head around, trying to take anything in I could. That wasn't much, until a familiar voice rang out.

"Toby?" Claire called in a rather loud whisper.

"Claire, are you okay?" I asked, trying to keep my voice level. I didn't bother trying to whisper.

"Yeah, I'm okay." Claire's voice came out choked. She dropped the whisper too, and I could tell she was trying not to cry.

"Can you see? Where are we? And where's Jake?" I didn't mean to ask the questions in such quick succession, but I was trying to learn as much about what was going on as quickly as I could.

"Yes, I can see. I'm tied up in the corner. Jake's tied up to your right, he looks hurt, but he's breathing." Her voice was shaking, yet she kept up on relaying the information to me. "We're in some sort of basement, you're in the middle of some magic symbols. It-it smells like blood."

So we were back in the basement in Fachnan's castle. I cursed. Despite all of our efforts, we'd still ended up here. And damn it, I'd dragged Claire and Jacob along too. Claire hadn't said anyone else was in here. So obviously Fachnan was off doing something else while I shivered my half-naked ass off.

"Okay, okay." I let out a few shaky breaths as I tried to get my wits about me. I wondered how Leonard and his cronies had gotten us here anyways. The only way I knew how was through Light Haven's portal system. But I had a feeling that wasn't it.

I went for my magic. It had become instinct by now. Maybe I could fling myself free of the bonds with a wind spell? Or toughen up my skin and rip out of the ropes? But I didn't get the chance to try. As soon as I'd reached for the power, the metal cross under me began to burn with intense heat.

I screamed as the metal burned against my back, my arms, and my legs. It was the most incredible pain I'd ever felt. The pain forced me to drop the power from my grasp. A moment after I did, the burning ceased, and I went limp again.

"Are you okay?" Claire asked, the shakiness of her voice subsided as she expressed her concern.

I grimaced, gritting my teeth as the echoes of the pain tingled against my skin. "Uh, yeah. Yeah. Note to self, no magic while stuck to the stupid cross thing."

"I could've told you that." A voice said.

Alarm bells went off. One, because we were no longer alone. Two, that wasn't Fachnan's voice. It was the voice of a girl. A girl I'd come to know quite a bit as I'd learned more and more about the world of magic. I cursed myself as I remembered her resentment, her anger, even the innocent mischievousness. All that, and I hadn't even considered that Kat had been pulling the strings behind the scenes the entire time.

"Hello, Katherine." I tilted my head to the sound of her footsteps descending the wooden staircase on the far side of the room.

"Tobias, a pleasure." Kat said, her tone quite amused. Or was it pleased? "I have to admit, I enjoy this look. What a shame it's under such unfortunate circumstances."

I shifted uncomfortably, wishing I could cover up.

"Even after all I've seen, Kat, I just don't understand why." I said. "Why are you doing this? Do you realize what you're doing?"

"Oh, I do, Tobias. The Mystic Order, for years, has prattled on about protecting the worlds of magic and mortals alike. Keeping order, peace, and so on. Yet still, people die. Mortals are still treated like cattle by vampires and succubi. And in turn, the mortals do their damndest to ruin the world and its nature so carefully curated by the Fae. It's high time for a shift in power. And who better to do that, then the rightful ruler of both worlds? The Fallen Son of the Almighty, who wanted nothing more than to guide humanity in the proper direction since the day we rose from the mud."

I wouldn't have been surprised if Kat had been a drama student at some point, because she had a flair for the dramatic speeches.

"And what about Fachnan?" I asked her. "Is he just some red herring in all of this?"

Kat whispered a word and I felt a surge of energy right before my blindfold was flung off in one swift, clean motion. Thank God, I was tired of not being able to see crap. The basement was just as I'd remembered it. I looked to my left, where Claire sat in silence, watching what was happening. She was battered and bruised, but otherwise she was okay. Her hands were tied behind her back. There was a cloth around her neck, probably meant to keep her quiet but she'd wiggled out of it at some point. To my right, Jacob lay slumped against the wall bound in chains. His skin was almost entirely in sandstone form, large cracks zig-zagging around his body. There were several points where his skin had completely chipped off and green light leaked out, albeit slowly and weakly.

Then I turned back to where Kat stood, just at the bottom of the stairs. She wore her typical goth garb, ripped up leggings and a band T-shirt, though I didn't recognize the name. Next to her, stood Fachnan, though he didn't seem to be all there. His eyes were glazed over and he swayed back and forth.

Kat smiled, still eyeing me up and down. "Fachnan's been so lovely and helpful towards my scheme. Though it took quite a bit of convincing, I think I was finally able to work my magic on him."

So that's what it was. Fachnan was under her spell. He'd been doing her bidding for who knew how long. Acting all suspicious and villainous to keep any attention falling on her.

She'd even taken advantage of his castle and his knowledge of dark magic to make all of this possible. But there was another alarming detail. From what Braun had told me, Fachnan, being a High Elder of the Mystic Order, was an incredibly powerful wizard. Like, really powerful. So if Kat was able to mind whammy him, that meant she was way more powerful than she let on. Hell, she was probably on par with Braun himself, if not stronger.

Ruh-roh. That didn't spell good news on my chances on figuring a way out of here. Even if I were to figure a way out of my bonds, I'd have to find a way to fend off both Kat and Fachnan. I just wasn't on that level yet.

But...

I glanced over at Claire. I had to get her out of here. Get her somewhere safe. And the only way to do that was by going through Kat, Fachnan, and whoever else she had on standby. But without a battle-worthy Jacob, or my eskrima, that wasn't going to be so straightforward. My best hope for survival at the moment was to stall. Maybe Jacob would stir while I did, or I'd come up with a better plan than to just run my mouth.

"Do you really think that Braun and the rest of the Mystic Order are just going to let your plans play out?" I asked her. "I bet they're on their way right now."

Kat smirked, the expression corrupting the otherwise beautiful features of her face. "The Mystic Order is otherwise occupied. With Fachnan's help, I was able to disrupt the spells that keep Light Haven aligned with its portals. They're currently drifting aimlessly in The World Yonder. It will be hours before they can properly tether the complex again."

Gulp. I wasn't exactly sure what all of that meant, but I got the idea that the Mystic Order wouldn't be sending a cavalry anytime soon. Well, so much for that idea. I struggled to think of anything crafty or interesting to say, and just sort of, mumbled incomprehensibly. I took a second to compose my thoughts, then spoke up again.

"So you're Azazel's little honey bunny on the mortal coil, right?" I asked. "Sending Leonard after me twice, the nagini who attacked me at the school. Hell, I bet you even had the redcap set up to jump us when we came here the first time to remove yourself from any suspicion that might've started on rise."

"You're right on track as far as Leonard and the redcap are concerned. If Fachnan hadn't had a brief moment of clarity, the redcap would've succeeded in its mission and then some." Kat confirmed my suspicions. "But, the nagini, now that wasn't me."

I squinted at that. "Well, then who was it?"

Kat shrugged. "Good question. Sadly, a mystery that will never be solved."

I filed that away for later thought. Seems like Kat and friends weren't the only ones who were gunning for me.

"So what's your stake in all this?" I asked. "You help Azazel into our world and then what? Who's to say that the devil himself won't dispose of you as soon as you're no longer useful?"

A brief moment of doubt flickered over her confident expression. "I've served the master for years now, carefully planning each and every detail of recent events so that we'd be ready for any contingency. He's shown me the way, taught me magic long forbidden by the Mystic Order, and helped me attain power. He promised me a seat at his side in his new world order. An ally such as myself isn't so easily thrown away."

Damn she was confident in her position among Azazel's cronies. It didn't seem like any seeds of doubt could be planted in this soil. Kat was too far gone, my words were simply falling on deaf ears.

I opened my mouth to speak again, but Kat was quick to cut me off.

"Enough." Kat slashed her hand across her chest in a dismissive motion. "The time for talk has passed. Now, it's time for the return of Azazel."

"Now, wait a second!" I stammered, my voice cracking.

Kat ignored me, and moved over to a corner of the room. In the corner was Jacob's bag. She knelt down and unzipped the bag. From it, she retrieved the Holy Grail. That modest, unassuming bowl of clay. You'd never be able to pick it out amongst a hundred like it unless you were magically inclined. How funny that it was the cause of so much conflict.

Then, to my alarm, she made her way over to Claire. As she walked, she reached behind her with her free hand, and pulled out a long, sinister-looking knife.

"Hey! HEY!" I yelled. "What the hell are you doing?!"

"The ritual calls for the blood of an innocent." Kat explained. "It's the only reason your little girlfriend here is still alive."

"If you kill her, I swear to God, Kat, I will kill you!" My voice came out rough and loud. My face contorted with pure, unadulterated anger and desperation.

"Relax, lover boy." Kat mused. "I have no reason to kill her, and a captive audience of one will be just perfect for my lord's return."

Claire squirmed, backing into the corner of the room as much as she could, desperately trying to get as far away from Kat and that malevolent blade. "T-Toby!"

"Katherine!" I roared in protest. "Don't touch her!"

Kat ignored me.

"Toby, help!" Claire's cried. Tears were streaming down her face now.

"Claire, it's going to be okay!" I tried to reassure her.

I had no choice. No matter how much it hurt, no matter what happened to me, I had to stop this here and now. I had to use magic. I called up my power. That painful burning sensation erupted all across the backside of my body. I wanted to scream. I wanted to cry. I'd never felt pain like it before. Imagine a million tiny needles stabbing into you. While you were on fire. While being electrocuted. While blades ripped into your skin. All of that together didn't even begin to describe the pain that tore through me. All the while I was trying to gather any ounce of magical energy. But it was like trying to hold onto water or air. Every time I think I was about to gather a usable amount of magical energies, it slipped away, stirred by the pain. It was useless, but I kept trying anyways.

Damn it. Damn it. Damn it.

Kat knelt down in front of Claire and grabbed her arm. Claire whimpered as Kat manhandled her. Kat rolled her eyes. "Oh, quiet down, Tobias. I already said I wasn't going to kill her."

Claire continued to squirm, and Kat cursed. She couldn't line up her blade perfectly with the soft skin of Claire's bicep. "Fachnan, hold her still!"

Fachnan, who might as well have been sleepwalking, held out his hand in Claire's direction. I felt a tension in the air, and then Claire's body went rigid. She gasped as she struggled to move, but she simply couldn't. Fachnan was using his telekinesis spell to keep her still.

"Thank you, dear." Kat giggled. And then turned back to Claire. "This will only hurt for a second, sweetie."

Then she ripped into Claire's arm with the knife, a quick and clean slice across her skin. A whip of scarlet liquid lashed out and splashed against the wall. I could hear stifled moans of pain from Claire, and another tear streaked down her face. If she wasn't paralyzed, I'm sure she would've been screaming. Kat pressed the Grail to her arm and blood dripped into the bowl. After a few moments, Kat seemed satisfied and rose again. Fachnan dropped his hand, and Claire went limp again. She sobbed quietly.

"Damn you, Kat." I growled.

"I can assure you I'm not the damned one here." Kat chuckled. "And now, the ritual can begin."

Crap. Crap. Crap. I'd failed. And now everything I'd feared was coming to fruition. Kat moved outside of the circle and back to the far side of the room, next to Fachnan. She set down the Holy Grail at the point of the corrupted pentagram closest to her. With a nod to Fachnan, they both raised their hands over the Grail and began to chant.

"*Diaboli reditus mancupim mundus...*" They both chanted. Their voices were weirdly modulated, echoing strangely as they chanted.

Okay. Okay, time for my grand escape. It was now or never. I could feel massive amounts of energy beginning to stir, forming around the Holy Grail. I had to act. Even a small spell, just a gust of wind to knock the Grail over.

"Diaboli reditus mancupim mundus..."

I reached for my magic again. But instead of pain erupting across my body, I felt the magic simply get swept away and into the spell that Kat and Fachnan were working. Oh, crap. I tried again, and still my magic was lost in the metaphorical storm of magic.

"Diaboli reditus mancupim mundus..."

Come on. Something. Anything. Maybe Jacob would wake up.

"Diaboli reditus mancupim mundus..."

I struggled against my bonds, panicking now. They were fastened tight. I simply didn't have the leverage to break free.

"Toby..." I heard Claire's voice.

No. No. No. No. No. This couldn't be happening. I had to do something. Anything. Was this really it? Was I going to become the devil himself? Please, God, no.

The world began to spin, and my vision began to blur. I wanted to scream, but if I did, I couldn't hear it.

"Diaboli reditus mancupim mundus..."

Chapter 23

When the world came back into focus, I realized I was now standing up right. No, that wasn't right. I slowly cast my gaze across my surroundings. I was floating, just a few inches off the ground. Everyone looked at me in awe. Katherine and that fool, Fachnan, scrambled to kneel before me. That girl in the corner behind me, Claire, was crying. She was scared. Why was she scared? I felt GOOD.

It felt like electricity was coursing through every muscle in my body. I felt invigorated. A glance down at myself and I realized that there was electricity coursing through me. Every few seconds, an arc of electricity would zig-zag across my body. I tightened my muscles, flexing. I unleashed a combo of several jabs and crosses in front of me, really trying to get a feel for my body.

"My lord," Katherine's voice spoke up.

I looked down at her, and smiled. "Oh, my dearest Katherine. You have done well."

I drifted towards her, kneeling in midair. I lightly grabbed her chin and brought her eyes to mine. I brought my lips to hers, and kissed her. She made a startled sound that quickly turned into something more satisfied. She leaned into the kiss. It amused me, satisfied me, to hear that sound come from her; the one who had been so loyal to me. After a few moments, I broke away from her and rose back to my full height. As I pulled away, I noticed her follow me, yearning for more. I felt a sense of satisfaction at that. She was a pretty little number after all, and she'd done much to assist me in my endeavors. Loyalty like that should be rewarded after all.

"Uh, um, t-thank you m-my lord." Katherine stammered. "Is it time to begin the reshaping of this world?"

I examined the lean muscle of my arms when I looked at her. "Why rush? I can raze this world and remake it at my leisure. It's been millennia since I've walked this soil. I might as well enjoy myself for some time."

She nodded frantically. "Of course, my lord."

The girl was absolutely precious, especially when she was nervous. But enough toying with her. It was time to take my body for a test drive. I extended my hand forward, my fingers extended and concentrated on gathering a whisper of my power. In an instant, a six foot long lance of white light formed in my outstretched hand. I gripped it and slashed it through the air, experimentally. I could feel it ripping through the magical energies in the air, manifesting as a huge gust of wind that knocked Katherine and Fachnan backwards slightly.

Then I swung the sword of light over my head towards the ceiling, putting some effort behind the swing this time. My blade didn't make contact with the stone ceiling, but as soon as I had finished the swing, the ceiling suddenly exploded upwards, the whole ceiling. And then the floor after that, and then the one after that, and then the one after that, and so on and so forth. The sound was tremendous. Bricks exploded upwards and ripped against each other. Furniture was crushed and destroyed by the exploding bricks. After only a second of time had passed, I'd successfully gutted the entire castle.

Debris began to rain down, but I raised my other hand upwards. Again, I muttered a whisper of power, and a wave of force, perfectly shaped to the borders of the castle, exploded upwards. Any falling debris that was directly overhead, instead flew back into the air and over the walls of the castle.

"Hmm, not bad." I looked myself over. "Given time, my powers should fully settle in to this new form."

"So what would you like to do now, my lord?" Katherine asked me. She seemed to be regaining her composure.

"Well, first I thi-"

I was interrupted by one of the remaining walls of the castle exploding inward. I looked towards the incoming debris lazily. I called up a shield of pure heat around me. When the debris got an inch away from me, instead of smashing against me, it simply vaporized into superheated particles and flickered harmlessly past me.

A hellhound flung itself through the dust and debris and went straight for Katherine. She let out a curse and flung an arc of lightning at the beast. The blast struck through but wasn't nearly enough to stop the oncoming beast. It only roared in pained anger and landed on top of her. In a flash of white teeth, the hellhound grabbed Katherine by the arm in its massive jaws. It flung her back and forth, like a dog playing with a chew toy, and then threw her into the wall behind me. I heard her body crumple limply to the ground. She made no sound. Then the beast locked its eyes on me. I smiled as it roared a challenge. But it didn't move.

Another figure had leaped through the dust at the same time as the hellhound. It was a man I recognized all too well. He was a tall man with aged muscle. His salt and pepper hair was cut neatly and undisturbed by the explosion he'd caused.

Bishop Leight's eyes were ablaze with purple light. He aimed his staff at Fachnan and before the enthralled wizard could do anything to defend himself, Bishop shouted a word and unleashed force and purple flames upon Fachnan. The Irish wizard went down and was out for the count. What a pity, but he truly was useless.

Bishop turned to me, his eyes still blazing like miniature purple suns. They were full of rage. I could tell he knew the ritual had been a success. I certainly didn't look the same as I had before, in a magical sense, at least.

"Bishop! You came!" Claire cheered through her tears.

"Hello." I said simply.

"Azazel!" Bishop roared. "Leave my nephew's body now! Or I swear, I will destroy you!"

I cocked my head sideways. "Am I supposed to be intimidated by you, wizard? Simply because you dispatched my servants in an ambush?"

"No, you should fear me because I'm Bishop Rodrick Sebastian Leight, bane to the Gorgons Three, tamer of the hellhound Auscultarian! I'm a senior wizard of the Mystic Order! I've infiltrated the Underworld and returned to tell the tale! I am Bishop the troll slayer, recognized by the Seelie Fae as a wielder of the Spring Flame!" Bishop shouted. "And you're still vulnerable from the ritual that brought you here, which means you can be dispatched as easily as the pest you are."

I chuckled. The chuckle turned into a laugh. I laughed, louder and louder. The laugh became something hysterical. "You think a mere wizard could best me alone?"

"Damn it Tobias, why couldn't you just listen to me?" Bishop muttered to himself. Then louder he bellowed, "*Igni!*"

He thrust his staff toward me. Purple flames erupted forth and roared towards me. I raised my blade of light and casually flicked it to the side. The flames split around me as I did so and rushed right past me. But it had been a distraction. The hellhound, Scout they called him, had closed the distance while I had been distracted by the fire and rushed at me, fangs bared and claws extended. The beast slashed at me with its claws and I raised my arm defensively. Its claws slashed through my flesh, which quickly began to heal, but then it clamped down with its jaws. It dragged me to the ground and attempted to pin me with one of its paws on my chest while it ripped into my arm.

"Agh, damn mutt!" I cursed.

I placed my free hand just under his jaws and roared out a word of power. Pure force unleashed itself from my palm and wrenched the dog away from me, sending it hurtling into the air. The beast flailed wildly, desperately clawing for anything to grab onto. I rolled away and just before the beast would've hit the ground, I held up my arm and unleashed another blast of pure kinetic energy. It hit the mutt head on and flung it towards the wizard.

I felt a surge of energy form around Bishop. He'd called up a shield of translucent blue energy that deflected Scout into the now useless staircase. The remains of the staircase exploded from the collision and splinters flew in every direction. Bishop raised his staff again and shouted his fire spell once more. Another surge of purple flame rushed from the tip of his staff. The flames consumed me instantly.

I'd crafted an aura of magical energies around my body. The flames stopped just a half-inch from my skin, repelled by an invisible mesh of energy. The magical fire passed over me harmlessly and was soon snuffed out.

"I grow real tired of your games, wizard." I said, my voice was cold.

I raised my hand towards him, gathering power in my palm. First, I'd rid myself of the wizard. And then, I'd rid myself of the girl and the golem. I could sense Bishop preparing a defensive spell. I was about to unleash the ball of light I'd created in my hand when I heard small footsteps running up behind me. I turned just in time to see Claire swing one of my old eskrima directly at my head. Where had she found the eskrima anyways? I'd been too surprised to react in time and her strike landed true. It hit me hard across the jaw and the power I'd gathered dissipated.

I stumbled and touched my face where she'd struck me. It hurt. It hurt like hell. I rubbed my jaw, grabbed it, and shoved it to one side. There was a sharp cracking sound as I put my jaw back in place. The girl was strong, I'll give her that.

"That was a big mistake." I rose to my full height and glared down at her. Electricity sparked across my skin as I gathered my power and my anger.

Claire dropped the eskrima and immediately began to cower, backing away. "Wait a second…" She whimpered.

Bishop let out a defiant roar. I flicked my hand absently in his direction and an unseen force pinned him to the wall. I heard the clatter of his staff falling to the ground as I approached Claire.

Her pretty face was contorted into something ugly by her fear and despair. Her face was wet with tears and mucus. It was quite the pathetic sight. If I hadn't felt so angry, I might've felt some sympathy for the girl. I extended my hand towards her and called up a white hot ball of fire the size of a baseball.

"Be honored." I said. "You will be the first to die for my new world."

I roared as I unleashed the ball of flame. Claire screamed bloody murder. She screamed and begged for her life as the ball approached her. I couldn't understand a word she was saying behind all that sniveling and sobbing.

"Please, Tobias!" Claire screamed. Her words rang out, and something very, very strange happened.

The world stopped. The flames dispersed. I couldn't move. My body felt rigid. No, it felt like I was carved out of stone, never meant to move a muscle. My breath didn't catch in my throat because I couldn't even remember how. What the hell was happening? Claire didn't move either. She was paralyzed, mid-scream. I could see a tear that was flung into the air, just hanging there, defying gravity. What had happened?

My surroundings shattered like glass and the shards disappeared into a white void. Sudden and unimaginable pain erupted in every cell of my body and I screamed. I felt my fingers raking at my face, my chest, and my arms as I desperately tried to rip myself apart. The pain was too great. I felt it driving me to the brink of insanity. It felt like every cell in my body was set on fire and not allowed to burn into nothing. I couldn't take it anymore. I let out one final scream as I dug my fingers into either side of my face, and pulled.

The force behind it sent me rolling away, as if this white void had a solid floor. I sensed someone else had been flung in the opposite direction. My head hurt, but not as bad as it did before. It felt like someone was tapping my head with a hammer every couple of seconds. Not hard enough to actually hurt me, just enough to send a pulse of pain through my head. I imagined a small little goblin snickering and then whacking my head with the small hammer, taking much joy in the endeavor.

I groaned as I picked myself up and rose to my feet. My entire body felt sore and tingled strangely. What the hell had happened? I'd been fighting with Bishop and Scout. It sounded strange, but it was true. Then Claire had hit me with my eskrima for some reason, and then I...

No, that had been Azazel. Kat's ritual, it had worked. Azazel had managed to possess me after all. It was so strange. It still felt like I had been in control. Like I was still me. Just that my priorities had seriously changed, but I couldn't tell the difference. But as soon as Azazel had turned on Claire, I must've woken up. I couldn't imagine wanting to ever hurt her. Plus, she was a girl, and you don't hurt girls. That had been the defining moment. Azazel was still weak, and when he did something my subconscious didn't agree with, it shattered the hold he had on me, if only temporarily.

Maybe ten feet away, Azazel was still getting his bearings. He groaned and growled and grumbled as he rose, rubbing his forehead. He was still donning his "evil Tobias" look. We were both only wearing plain black boxer briefs. It'd be awkward if it wasn't, y'know, the king of Hell I was dealing with.

"Azazel, you bastard....!" It started as a growl, but quickly rose to a shout.

Azazel shook off the daze and locked eyes with me as he stood up. He still had that satisfied look on his face. It truly drove me crazy how the devil bastard was always so smug and confident.

"Tobias, I have to give you credit." Azazel clapped slowly. "I've never met a mortal mind who could outright break free of a fallen angel's mental domination. Though, this is only a minor obstacle. Surely you know that I'll have to beat you back down."

"Well, you made the mistake of hurting my friends, my family." I said. "Only so much of that I can take before I have to check your ass. Now it's just you and me."

Azazel laughed. It was disturbingly genuine. "And you think that you can beat me into submission, alone?"

"Oh I know I can." I pumped my fist into my open palm, and then cracked my knuckles. I switched hands and did the same with the rest of my knuckles.

"A duel, then?" Azazel asked, clearly amused. "You want to test your magical talents against me in open combat?"

I let out a laugh. "Oh, no. No. This is my head, which means I'm in charge of the rules around here. And I say, no magic." I smirked.

Azazel barked out another laugh. "You think you can just stop me from using magic?" Azazel extended his hand forward and I sensed him trying to gather power. But nothing came to him. His eyes widened as he stared down at his outstretched hand.

My smirk turned into a full-on grin. While the devil was still stunned at his inability to use magic, I rushed him. I closed the distance in a matter of seconds, taking full advantage of Azazel's disbelief. Then, I decked him. Hard. I put all my weight into a downward swing of my fist, striking him across the face, and knocking him to the ground.

I breathed hard. It seemed unfair that I could still get tuckered out in my own mindscape. Azazel roared in rage as he twisted around on the ground, a motion that reminded me of breakdancing, and swept my legs out from under me.

I hit the ground hard and Azazel attempted to jump on top of me. I rolled away a second before he landed and managed to get to my knees. We both leaped at each other and collided in midair. We hit the ground again in a tumble and scrambled to get an edge on one another. But the gamble I'd made proved to pay off. Azazel may have been hell on wheels when it came to magic, no pun intended, but I don't think he had ever really had to fight someone hand to hand, and I'd been training for years in mixed martial arts.

I managed to get on top of Azazel and I threw down several blows to his face and chest. He roared in anger but wasn't in a position to do much counterattacking. His arms were moving frantically in an attempt to disrupt my assault, and I used that to my advantage. I let up on my flurry of blows and grabbed one of his arms with both hands, holding on as tight as I could. I threw my right leg over his body as I twisted and landed on my back, perpendicular to Azazel's chest. I held onto Azazel's arm and pulled, raising my waist into the air as I did.

In practice, once your opponent tapped out, you would release the arm bar. But this wasn't practice. This was the real deal. I used every ounce of strength I had, pulling Azazel's arm as far as I could while pushing against his elbow with my waist. Azazel roared in pain and struggled against me, but it was no use. I had all the leverage. It only took a few moments before a sickening pop and crunch echoed through the void.

Azazel let out a scream of pain. I released my grip and did a reverse somersault away from him. I'd already gotten back to my feet by the time Azazel managed to stand, holding his broken arm. Before the devil even had a moment to react, I swung my leg at Azazel's head, hitting him with a roundhouse kick that was aided by all the weight and momentum I could put behind it.

To my surprise, Azazel caught the strike with his good arm and grabbed my leg. He let out a roar of pain and rage and swung around, flinging me into the air. I hit the ground hard and rolled on my side.

I coughed and I was surprised no blood came out. I'd hit the ground pretty damn hard. Azazel let out an inhuman bellow of anger and rushed toward me, his broken arm flailing uselessly as he did. Before I had the chance to react, he was already on top of me. He struck me several times with his good arm. Between each strike, I tried to do something to get him off of me, but he just struck again. Each blow scattered my thoughts more and more. I'd underestimated him. Even without magic to rely on, he was still a formidable opponent.

My face had swollen and I tasted blood. I could barely see through my swollen eyes. Damn it all. Even after all this, my big comeback, I was still going to lose. I'd still lose myself within Azazel and his massive power. Azazel laughed at me. It was no longer something smug and cool. Azazel had descended into madness.

"You maggot! You worthless scum! You dare resist me, bind me in your mind? You raised your fist against me? What a fool!" Azazel bellowed as he struck me again. "When I'm done with you, I'm going to kill your uncle. Then I'll kill your friend, the golem. After that, the hellhound. Oh, but Claire. Claire I'll hold onto. She will be my little tool to use as I please. I will break her and soon she will beg for more. She will crave my touch. And only then, will I kill her in the most painful way I know how."

My eyes widened in rage and I let out a guttural sound that was on the brink of being inhuman. Then with a tone so calm, it scared even me, I said, "*Hinote!*"

One moment, there was nothing except us and the void. The next, a pillar of flame erupted from me and flung Azazel a few feet away. A second later, I was standing. Even though I don't remember making the effort to do so. I let out another defiant scream and flames erupted around me in every direction.

Azazel's eyes widened in shock and...fear. Again, he attempted to call up a magical counterattack, but no power came to him. Again, I screamed and the flames surged forward and trapped Azazel in a circle of fire. I stepped forward, seemingly impervious to the fire that I'd summoned. Out of the corner of my eye, I could see fire flowing over my body, licking between my palms and making my hair flow as if the wind was blowing.

"You're in MY mind." I said, again with disturbing calm. "I'm the one in charge here. And I say, you're not welcome here. I banish you, Azazel! Leave this place and go back whence you came!"

I aimed my open palm towards Azazel and shouted, "*Hinote! Kaze hinote!*"

Fire and wind erupted from my hand and struck Azazel like a battering ram. He screamed like a tortured animal. The mindscape began to blur around us as I intensified my magical strike. Explosions, wind, and screams roared in my ears. It felt as if I'd be lost in the chaos swirling around me. The noise became so loud that it was nothing more than a ringing sensation that hit me in every sense of my mind.

The white void faded to black nothingness, and then, it was simply over.

Chapter 24

I opened my eyes, blinking a few times to disperse the post-sleep blur that masked my vision. Claire's face was the first thing I saw. Her eyes were red and puffy. She'd been crying, a lot. Bishop was there too, he looked battered but otherwise okay. His face was crinkled with worry that soon changed to relief. Then there was Scout, back in the form of a German Shepherd, who upon seeing my eyes open, began slobbering all over my face.

"Ugh, doggy slobber…" I said weakly. My throat felt dry. I choked and coughed.

Claire helped me sit up and I took a second to look around. Azazel had completely destroyed Fachnan's castle, from what I could see in this small basement. The demonic symbols that had been drawn on the floor in blood had been smeared and destroyed. I'm not sure when that happened.

"Wh-What happened?" I shook my head, trying to shake off the fog clouding my thoughts.

"Umm, that girl, Kat, I think. She and that guy with the red hair did some ritual thing with the Grail," Claire grimaced, looking away from her wounded arm. "Then you changed. Well, it wasn't you, exactly. It was..."

"Azazel." Bishop spoke up, finishing her sentence. "Azazel had successfully taken over your body by the time I'd arrived. I tried to fight him, but my magic wasn't strong enough to touch him."

I nodded, the pieces seeming to fall into place.

"Then in the midst of the chaos, I managed to slip my bonds and hit Azazel with this." Claire held up one of my eskrima. An echo of pain throbbed in my jaw. "He turned on me, and was about to burn me. Then, before I knew it, you were passed out on the ground."

I turned to my left, where I remembered Kat had been thrown by Scout. My eyes widened. Kat was gone. I looked frantically around the room, and sure enough, she was nowhere to be found.

Bishop nodded, a disappointed look on his face. "I believe she slipped away during the chaos. No doubt she figured Azazel would make quick work of us and she would return for him later."

Damn, so she was still out there. I noticed Fachnan still lay unconscious on the ground. Perhaps he'd have some answers for us, later.

My eyes widened in realization. "The Grail!" I looked around frantically. A sharp sensation of pain stabbed me in the back and I was forced to stop.

"Relax, Tobias." Bishop held up a hand, motioning for me to stop moving. "You're still in a fragile state, better not to move too much."

"But-!"

With his other hand, he showed me the Holy Grail. It was streaked with dried blood. I let out a sigh of relief. At the very least, we had managed to keep control over the Grail at the end of all this. I shuddered as I imagined what Kat could accomplish if she had managed to sneak off with the Grail.

"Can you stand?" Bishop asked me.

I used my arms for support and managed to get my legs under me. I slowly rose, shaky and stumbling a bit, but Claire stood close to me so I could lean on her for support. I felt dizzy as hell. Everything felt distant, like a dream. I hated feeling like this. I hated that Azazel had been in my head. What had happened to him in the end? Maybe I could ask Braun about it.

"How the hell did you get here, anyways?" I asked. "Kat told me that Light Haven had been like, I don't know, de-synced from its portal system."

"Light Haven isn't the only way to travel from place to place. It's just very convenient." Bishop explained. "When Scout found me, we immediately returned to the school. But by the time we arrived, Leonard and his cronies were long gone. But Scout had your scent, so to speak. So I opened a portal into The World Yonder and tracked you here, then I opened another portal back into our world, and here I am."

I was about to ask him what the hell The World Yonder was. Kat had mentioned it too, but another dizzy spell made my head swim. I slouched, and I felt Claire struggle under my weight. But she didn't drop me. I distantly heard Bishop's voice speaking, but I couldn't focus my vision on anything, so I was pretty blind to what was happening. After a few moments, I felt someone pick me up like a baby.

I didn't pass out, I swear. But I was so incoherent I might as well have been. I remember a shaft of light appearing, then we might've been in a forest or something, and then...

Okay, then I passed out.

The next time I opened my eyes, they were immediately burned by something bright. I shielded them weakly with my arm. That's when I noticed the IV in my arm. My first assumption was that I'd been brought to the infirmary run by Sylf, the elf who'd already patched me up a couple times now. But the infirmary hadn't been so damn bright. It took a few moments for my brains to put everything back into order. My vision focused fully, and I realized the bright ass light was coming from a fluorescent ceiling light.

I looked around, there was an IV bag hanging from a hook to my left. I noted white tile floors, white walls, white tiles made up a dropdown ceiling. There was a curtain to my right obscuring most of the room from me. To my left was a wide window that took up most of the wall. It was night time, but I could see the silhouette of Seattle's skyline in the distance. Sitting in a chair between the window and my bed was the sleeping form of Claire.

I smiled. Even though she didn't have to, Claire had stayed close by my side to watch over me. Despite the fact she'd been through a lot, or that hospitals smell weird, or that that chair she was slumped in was probably very uncomfortable, she had still stayed. Claire was good people.

I recalled my fight with Azazel within the depths of my mind. How I'd confronted the devil himself in a fight for the survival of me and the ones I'd loved. I'd almost lost, until...

Until I'd used fire magic for the first time. I could recall the invigorating rush of fire spewing forth from my body in every direction. The way I'd used it against Azazel as a reflection of my rage, my love, and my pure stubborn will. I'd never managed to call up fire before, even if it had only been in the confines of my own mind. If it hadn't been for Claire's courage in the face of pure evil, I may never have been able to cast fire. It was true what they say, there is no greater source of strength in life than friends and family.

Claire began to stir from her sleep, snorting once, before shaking her head. Her sleepy eyes focused on me. They widened upon realizing I was awake and she jumped on top of me in a tackling hug.

"Toby, you're awake!" Claire cheered. She was crying again, I could hear it in her voice. But I was pretty sure it was a good cry.

I heard the bark of a dog, and Scout in his service dog uniform emerged from somewhere underneath my cot. He jumped on me too, but politely let Claire hug me, uninhibited.

"Ow! Ouch!" I howled in pain. My body was sore as hell.

Claire pulled away and then realized she had her full weight on me, "Oh!" Embarrassed, she scooted off of me and sat on the bed at my side.

Scout got off of me too, but was laying close to my side, opposite of Claire. He was inching forward carefully, trying to get as close to my face as possible. He was making excited, quiet yipping sounds.

I groaned but tried to take it like a man. Though I suspected that illusion had long since faded.

"So what am I in for?" I wondered. I seriously doubted I was in for "recovering from demonic possession."

"Umm..." Claire put a finger to a chin as she tried to recall the information. "Severe dehydration, I believe. Which you were very dehydrated, and it's not like we could tell them that the devil had taken your body for a joy ride."

"True enough." I agreed. "Any idea on when I can get the hell out of here?"

"Day after tomorrow. Your body was pretty banged up, so they just want to keep you for observation. But it doesn't appear that Azazel left behind any serious injuries."

I made an annoyed sound. I had no interest in spending an extra day laid up. I wanted to know what was going on in the aftermath of things. Then I realized I'd forgotten to ask something.

"Where's Bishop, Jake, and Fachnan?" I asked her.

"Well, Jake and Fachnan were both in rough shape. But Bishop said there was nothing a normal hospital could do for them, given their unique conditions. So Bishop coordinated with the other wizards to get your guys super secret base back to normal. Then I think he took them there." Claire explained.

What she said tracked. Jacob was a golem after all, a normal hospital wouldn't be able to do a thing to help him. It'd be like trying to hammer in a nail with a screwdriver. Or trying to get a psychiatrist to perform open heart surgery. Or teaching a monkey to fly a spaceship. Then there was the matter of Fachnan, whose injuries were more mental than anything else. I had to imagine that getting mind whammied wasn't exactly easy on one's psyche.

I thought about everything that had gone on. The demons, Azazel, Kat, and the nagini, and everything in between. I recalled Kat mentioning that she had nothing to do with the nagini. But if she hadn't, then who did? If she had known who sent them, she hadn't let on. I twisted my face into a frustrated expression.

Claire must've read my mind or something because she put a hand on my shoulder and squeezed. "Toby, you need to rest. Don't worry so much about what you can't control. I'm sure the time will come for us to get answers. But for now, you should sleep."

I sighed. "You're probably right. It's just...a lot. Only a few days ago I was worried about rushing an English project in time to turn it in. Now, hell, I socked the devil in his metaphysical face. Who knows what's going to come next? I imagine this isn't a door I can close again."

"Well, whatever comes through that door next. Just know that you won't be alone in facing it." Claire smiled that infectious grin of hers. "I don't know what I can do to help, but just know that I'll be there."

I could feel my emotions welling up in my throat. I made a choking sound, doing my best to pass it off as a laugh. I wish I could express to her how much it meant to me to know she'd always be by my side. Claire was special, always has been. She was not only beautiful, with those unassuming girl next door looks, but she was smarter than most and far braver than anyone would've expected from her.

I could feel my eyelids getting heavy once more. I tried to keep my head up, but it was a fruitless effort. I leaned back against the pillows as my eyes began to droop. I distantly felt the brush of her hand against my hair as the sweet embrace of sleep held me close once more.

Chapter 25

I woke up on the last day to an envelope sitting on the table next to my hospital bed. There was perfect gold lettering on the back. It simply read "Tobias." I opened it up, with no regard for neatness, practically tearing the whole envelope apart. Inside was a handwritten letter. I recognized my uncle's handwriting.

"Tobias,

I'm relieved that you're okay. Claire has been keeping me in the loop regarding your recovery. I'd have brought you back to Light Haven, but there's a whole lot of chaos going on here and I didn't want you barraged with questions from the bureaucrats until you had recovered enough.

If I've timed this right, you are due for release today. I've made arrangements for the hospital to release you without my being there. Come to Light Haven as soon as you are ready. The High Elders have requested your presence.

B."

Tucked in with the letter was some cash that I could use for a cab. Which was good, because my allowance had pretty much run dry.

I did my time sitting on my ass in the hospital. I took part in all the pleasantries, including embarrassing examinations and deceptively good pudding consumption. That being said, I rejoiced when they finally released me. Bishop was waiting for me at Light Haven, and I had to face the music that the High Elders were playing. I squirmed at the thought of facing them all. But what had happened wasn't exactly my fault, right?

Claire saw me out, but she planned to stay behind to visit her father, who was still recovering from his demon-related injuries. I couldn't blame her, and it wasn't like she could come with me to Light Haven, anyways. It didn't seem like a place where vanilla folk were allowed to visit. I took a cab to Seattle proper, the sights and sounds of the bustling city life passing by. The Space Needle stood tall in the distance. It was a spectacle to be sure. I rolled down the window for Scout, just enough for him to poke his head out and enjoy the wind blowing in his face.

It wasn't long before we'd arrived at Pike Place. I paid the cabbie what I owed him and closed the car door behind me. I made the short hike to the Gum Wall. There were a few tourists who were admiring the germ-ridden landmark, but they didn't seem to notice as I punched in the combination that opened the portal to the Mystic Order's HQ. The glowing doorway carved itself into the wall and opened up to me. As discreetly as I could, I walked through.

Usually Light Haven was bustling with activity. Wizards, elves, dwarves, and pixies were usually rushing around left and right, the multitude of voices devolving into a senseless noise, and for a moment, it was just that. But as soon as everyone saw me walk through, it got very, very quiet. Everyone stared at me. No one moved, literally. Humans, and I imagine other races of the magical variety, even when still, would sway ever so slightly. They'd blink, their chests would rise and fall as they breathed. But for a few agonizing seconds, there wasn't even a single breath. I could feel dozens of pairs of eyes bore into me. There was an uneasy tension in the air, and it was all centered around me.

Scout leaned against my leg, reassuring me with his presence. He let out a low whine and I patted him on the head so he knew I appreciated the gesture. I had a good feeling that the story of what happened to me had gotten out and spread around the patrons of Light Haven. That probably wasn't good. No one was trying to kill me, which was refreshing, but no one was shaking my hand either. I let out a huff. Someone had to make the first move, so it might as well have been me. I started walking out of the Portal Nexus, the sound of my footsteps accompanied by the clicking of Scout's nails against the tile floors.. No one said anything, but everyone made no effort to hide their desire to avoid getting close to me. The modest crowd parted like the Red Sea around me as I made my way into the halls.

As soon as I'd left the room, I could hear a round of murmurs rise up behind me. It eerily reminded me of the toxic political climate of high school, in a way. So at the end of the day, I supposed it was nothing new. I wasn't sure where Bishop would be right now, but I'd already planned my first stop.

I stepped through a door and found myself in the Alfheim infirmary. The tranquil forest environment was truly a beautiful sight, and very relaxing. The mossy trees glowed with a mint-colored light. Beads of light floated through the air, appearing and disappearing every couple of seconds. I was so distracted by the hypnotic lights that I almost tripped on a stray root. The hospital beds worked into the landscape were on the far side of the "room", I made my way over to the one where Fachnan resided.

He was sitting up in bed, propped up by several pillows. They looked far more comfortable than the ones I'd rested my head on in the hospital. A pang of childish jealousy struck, but I ignored it. He was reading a book bound in dark leather. It wasn't until I was less than five feet away that he looked up from it, and looked at me with a critical eye. It wasn't quite a glare, there wasn't enough emotion in it for that.

"High Elder Fachnan." I said in greeting, making sure to put respect behind the words. After all my undeserved suspicion, he deserved at least a little bit of it.

"Ah, Tobias Leight." Fachnan spoke, his Irish accent moderate, as if it had been a couple of years since he'd actively lived in his homeland. "I was wondering when I'd be graced with your presence."

I detected a hint of sarcasm, or maybe it was resentment? But I wasn't going to let it bother me. I had a feeling it wasn't me he was angry with.

"I...came to check in on you, and I thought maybe we could talk." I said, trying to keep my tone as neutral as possible. I'd never liked the guy, and I had a feeling his poor attitude wasn't because of Kat's manipulation.

"How kind of you. I assure you, I'm quite alright." Fachnan said, almost dismissively. Then to my surprise, he asked, "How are you holding up? I imagine having a primordial being like the devil, a fallen angel, in your head isn't exactly easy on one's mind."

That's when I realized that Fachnan probably wasn't such a bad guy. Sure, he was an ass, but he wasn't evil or anything. We may never fully get along, but we were on the same side.

I knocked on the side of my head with my knuckles lightly. "I'm doing alright, if anything I think ol' Zazey knocked a few things back into place." Then I added, "How are you doing?"

His calm expression drooped into something sadder, shame maybe? "Our cerebromancers believe that Katherine has been planting seeds within my mind for years, so as to not make it obvious. She picked my brain for the knowledge needed to commune with Azazel and make her ritual a reality. There are gaps in my memory and knowledge, things I fear Katherine may use to wreak havoc on the magical world. It's...frustrating to know that the very thing I specialize in took advantage of me right under my nose."

I frowned. I tried to imagine what he must've been going through. Fachnan was an exceptionally powerful wizard. With that, I imagined, came a certain level of expectations, bordering on arrogance. I wasn't sure on all the details, but Kat had played Braun, Fachnan, and the rest of the Mystic Order for years in order to make her plan a reality.

"She was my age though, wasn't she?" I asked him. "Could she really have done that all on her own?"

Fachnan shook his head. "Unlikely. I suspect that she's only one agent of Azazel's followers. And she definitely didn't learn cerebromancy on her own. I'm sure there is someone behind the scenes even more dangerous who taught her what she needed to know in order to infiltrate our ranks so deeply."

"So she's just the tip of the iceberg then." I chewed on that thought.

Fachnan bobbed his head in an affirmative gesture. "While you may have thwarted her plans this time, I suspect this isn't the last time she and her allies will rear their ugly heads."

"When that time comes, I may need your help." I admitted. "I'm still learning, and I got lucky when I fought Azazel. He slipped up while he was still adjusting. You're an expert in the dark arts and demonology. Can I count on you to help me?"

Stroking his ego seemed to have worked, because his mouth curled upward into a smug smile. "Of course. You won't get lucky twice. When the time comes, you will know where to find me."

My mouth moved again before I could think. "What do you make of Braun?"

Fachnan looked surprised, like I'd just slapped him. "What do you mean?" He asked.

I sighed, choosing my words carefully. "See, initially, I picked you out as our big bad, the puppet master behind the scenes. But I have a hunch, and if I'm right, the real bad guy showed too much of his hand. The only person who knew I'd snuck in and out of the library was Braun. He saw me through my cloaking spell, but said nothing. He's not dumb either, he could hazard a guess what I was looking for in there. The tracking spell."

Fachnan took a moment, no doubt being careful about his choice of words as well. "I think that's a very interesting theory. A dangerous one. One you may want to keep to yourself for now."

I nodded in agreement. "Thank you."

I put my hand out, offering it to him. Hesitantly, he answered it with his own. We traded grips and nodded towards each other. As I did, Sylf the Ljósálfar noble emerged seamlessly from the trees. She was as beautiful as ever, literally glowing with a faint white light. Her long hair flowed through the air, despite what gravity had to say about it.

"Tobias Leight, I am glad to see you are well." Sylf smiled at me, though I noticed a hint of sadness behind it.

She had the look of someone looking upon a car crash victim. It was an expression full of pity, sorrow even. I'm not sure what she saw when she looked at me. I had a feeling she could see more of me than any normal person could. Did she see something in me left behind by Azazel? I wasn't sure if I'd ever find out.

Sylf guided me away from Fachnan, just out of earshot. He'd returned to his book, anyhow, so I doubted he was paying attention to what Sylf and I were doing.

"Is he going to be alright?" I asked her.

Sylf's beautiful face turned into something sad. "Mental manipulation is a dangerous thing, there's a reason that it is against the Wizard's Code to use cerebromancy to manipulate humans.. It damages and twists the mind. Naturally, our minds try to fight it, but this can lead to more, long-term damage. Manipulating a person, especially a wizard, can leave behind scars and side effects that can hamper their abilities for years, possibly for the rest of their lives. Fachnan is still very young for a wizard, especially for a High Elder. This makes his mind more susceptible to manipulation and the damage that comes with it. He probably won't be able to do anything more than studious work for a long time. His practical abilities will never be the same now that the chains placed on his psyche have been broken."

I frowned at that. It was sad that he'd been crippled that way. I didn't know the guy very well, and I wasn't particularly fond of him, but no one deserved that. I couldn't imagine what it was like to be manipulated that way. To be shaped into a tool for someone else. I suppose that I had been a tool in Azazel's grand design as well, and in a way, Fachnan and I had a lot in common.

"Please take care of him." I said. "I'll come back to visit him in a couple of days, see how he's doing."

Sylf nodded to me. "Of course, young wizard. I will do what I can to aid his recovery. After you've spoken you're your uncle and the remaining High Elders, you may want to come back and allow me to examine your mind for damage too."

The thought of Sylf poking around my mind was an uncomfortable one. I wasn't sure I wanted anyone inside my head anytime soon.

"I'll think about it." I told her, even though I had no plans to.

I tugged on Scout's leash and dismissed myself from the infirmary. Once I was back in the halls of Light Haven, I located a directory so I could find the gathering hall where I'd first met the High Elders. I found the room on the map and tapped it. A small pulse of power rang through the air as I did, and a path lit up for me on the floor. I followed it, and it wasn't long before I found myself at the large door with ornate golden carvings.

I took a deep breath, and approached the door. Just like the first time, it instantly responded to my presence. The golden carvings began to glow. With a low rumbling noise, the doors slowly swung open. I had been right in my assumption that Bishop was in the center of the large gathering hall, standing before the High Elders, who were sitting at their large desks that reminded me of a judge's podium. As the door opened, they all turned their attention to me.

Gulp.

Scout looked up at me, a quizzical look on his face. He looked at me as if to say, "Well, are you gonna go in or not?". I returned the look with a disapproving glare, and began to walk in. As I walked down the center aisle, I noticed the familiar face of Jacob sitting in one of the audience chairs. He looked a whole lot better than when I'd last seen him. His skin was strangely faded in some spots, like a bad sunburn that had begun to peel in places. That was weird to think about. He smiled at me and nodded to show his support.

I reached my uncle, who gave me a big hug. Damn, it felt like ages since I'd seen him. Though it had only been a couple of days. After a few moments, he released the hug and held me at arm's length.

"It's good to see you, son." Bishop said. "You've looked worse."

"And still better than you." I added.

I felt eight pairs of eyes staring down at me and turned my attention to the High Elders. I rubbed my fingers against my palms nervously as I stared up at them. Let me tell ya, it was nerve wracking. From what I understood, the High Elders were the most powerful wizards on the planet, and having their undivided attention made me rightfully nervous.

"Uh, hello." I said wittingly.

"Tobias Leight, it is good to see that you are in good health." Braun's booming voice echoed throughout the chamber. His German accent was showing a bit more than usual.

"Thank you, sir." I did an awkward half-bow. Don't ask me why. I was practically sweating bullets, okay?

Braun seemed amused by that, so I chalked it up as a point in the positive column. "Since Tobias has arrived, we may as well get on with our business."

To his immediate right sat a Hispanic woman, her black hair was in a neat bob cut, and it was streaked with grey. She wore a purple business suit with a white shirt underneath. She adjusted a pair of half-moon glasses before speaking.

"Tobias Leight, nephew of Bishop Leight, we are aware that you had an encounter with the fallen angel, Azazel, as well as several of his subjects." The woman spoke, her words tinged with a thick Spanish accent. "From Bishop's report, we understand that you were actually possessed by Azazel. Is this true?"

I looked to Bishop. His expression gave nothing away as he nodded to me. I swallowed nervously. "Erm, yes. But I fought him off."

"Even so, the nature of the entity who overtook your mind and body calls into question whether or not you've been compromised. For all we know, you could still be possessed by Azazel. It is my opinion that you should be destroyed, in order to avoid the risk of you destroying the Mystic Order from the inside out."

Braun frowned and spoke disapprovingly, "Elder De Leon, we have discussed this."

The woman, De Leon, sucked her teeth in annoyance. "Elder Braun, it would be naive to let the boy roam freely. If he is possessed by the devil, he could be scheming to destroy us right now."

"Answer me this, then." I spoke up. My mouth spat out the words before running it by my brain. "If I was truly still possessed by Azazel, would I even need to lie in wait before kicking the Order's collective ass? If he's as bad as you all make him out to be, I'm pretty sure he could tear this place apart, and there wouldn't be a damn thing you could do to stop him."

Silence. Oh boy, that was sure to win her favor. De Leon made a sound that sounded more irritated than anything else. Perhaps I'd made a good, albeit crude, point.

"Even so, I don't believe you should be allowed the freedom you've enjoyed around Light Haven so far. Disregarding the potential security risk of Azazel's chosen vessel being allowed to walk free, you've demonstrated a complete lack of respect for the rules, and us, considering your trip to the library reserved for only full members of the Mystic Order." De Leon lectured.

Oops, so Braun had told them about that. It weakened my suspicions about him, but not by much.

"What my colleague is trying to say," Braun said, taking the reins of the conversation. "Is that given the return to semi-normalcy, Azazel has been dispatched, the Grail having been safely returned to our vaults, and you all returning safe and sound, we believe that we should formally instate you as an apprentice of the Mystic Order."

"Huh?" I uttered intelligently.

"You will study under a veteran wizard, in this case, your uncle. Though we may have others step in when needed. Even for your uncle, you seem to be a lot to handle. You will be taught in the ways of the mystic arts, attend Order meetings as needed, and assist Bishop in defending his territory from any dark forces that may arise." Braun explained.

I cocked an eyebrow. "So, basically what I've already been doing?" I asked.

Braun smiled again. Even he appreciated the seeming redundancy of it. "Yes, but it will now be under an official capacity. There will be no rule breaking, you will learn and follow the Wizard's Code, and be under Bishop's tutelage until such a time that we can deem you a full wizard."

"And should you show signs of possession by Azazel, the Mystic Order will act to neutralize you." De Leon said in a tone of such finality, I felt my ass clench up on reflex. The thought of having to face even one of the High Elders in genuine combat made me nervous.

"Well, it's an honor to know that you all will be watching me so closely." I said, without even a hint of sarcasm. I swear.

Braun nodded. "If nothing else good came of this ordeal, it is a major victory to have recovered the Holy Grail. You did good work, being able to track it down as an amateur."

I remembered something, but decided not to bring it up. "Uh, yes. Thank you, High Elder. Though I wouldn't have been able to manage any of this, if it weren't for the help of my friend, Jacob."

Braun eyes lit up and he nodded approvingly towards where Jacob sat. "Yes, of course. You truly have excelled at your assignment of protecting the young wizard, golem."

Jacob's voice rose up behind me, from where he sat. "Thank you, sir. Serving the Mystic Order and protecting Tobias has been an honor."

"Well, your assignment is far from over. You have a long road ahead of you while Tobias' training continues." Braun said.

"I look forward to it." Jacob said. I could detect a hint of pride in his voice.

"Well, I believe that we've covered everything we had planned to today." Braun nodded. "You are all dismissed."

I followed Bishop back up the walkway, and Jacob fell in step with us as we passed the row of seats he'd occupied. We exited the chamber and the doors rumbled as they closed slowly behind us.

"Well, Tobias, your training as an apprentice begins today." Bishop said. "I hope you're ready."

"I am." I said. "I have so many questions though."

"Such as?" Bishop asked me.

"Well, if Kat didn't send that nagini after me, then who did? And if the Holy Grail was stolen from the Mystic Order's possession, who did it, and why stash it in a museum just so I could find it? Where's Kat now? And most importantly, what exactly happened to Azazel? No way in hell I destroyed him."

Bishop and Jacob exchanged a look of concern. Even after we'd won the day, there were still too many loose ends. Sure, we'd thwarted Kat's plans, but she was still out there somewhere.

"It seems like things are changing." Jacob said.

Bishop nodded in agreement. "And I suppose we'll find the answers to those questions soon enough. But until then, we have a lot of training to cover. With the current crisis at an end, we don't have to rush your training along any longer. There's a lot of gaps to fill in your knowledge."

"Oh, hell yeah!" I cheered, eager to learn even more new tricks and spells. Sure, I still had a lot of work to do to perfect the magic I'd already learned, but just thinking about all the new techniques Bishop would be showing me had me giddy, to say the least.

"Oh, here we go." Jacob let out a barking laugh.

"But, as a rule, maybe don't go charging head first into any deadly situations without me from now on, huh?" Bishop said.

"Yeah, yeah." I rolled my eyes.

I couldn't help but do a little dance in excitement as we walked through the halls. Scout trotted alongside me, his tail wagging as he panted excitedly. My training as a wizard was officially in full swing. I had a whole new world of magic and monsters ahead of me. There was so much to do and so much to learn.

I smiled as we approached the portal to Seattle once more. It wasn't just a portal to the city I knew and loved, but a door that led to the next adventure. There was a limitless number of possibilities ahead of me. Who knew what crazy monstrosity would try to kill me next? It was a simultaneously scary and exhilarating prospect.

My name is Tobias Caesar Leight, and that's my story.

Author's Note

Like many others across the world, the forbidden year of 2020 shook up the status quo of my life. I had no job, a shortage of responsibility, and no direction for what I wanted to do next with my life. In years past, I'd spun my wheels in the mud of college. I was never a strong academic, but I'd always had a love for reading and writing. Ever since I could pick up a pencil, I was writing. Whether it was original, half-baked comic books or derivative fanfiction, I loved to write. So, in October of 2020, I started work on this version of Tobias' first adventure. My interest and motivation waxed and waned over the following years, but eventually, the story you just read came into fruition. I hammered out the nitty gritty like a true pen monkey until I came up with a finished product, I can be happy with and proud of.

With this series, I aim to create a world that blends all facets of mythology together where they can exist in chaotic harmony. In the coming years, Tobias will face all manner of monsters and evil. I am truly excited to share Tobias' adventures with you.

First and foremost, I'd like to thank my family. They cultivated and encouraged my creative spark from a very young age. I was exposed to magnificent stories, whether it be through books, movies, or video games. To this day, I love experiencing new stories in those mediums, with no signs of slowing down.

A special shout out to my Uncle Neil, who was one of my first readers and provided a whole lot of honest and brutal feedback that helped shape this story.

Next, to my Discord friends. Makashu, Flare, Acheron, Iron, X, and all the rest of you guys. You were the first to learn of the blossoming world of Chronicles of Leight. Thank you for putting up with my constant rambling and the occasional @everyone to notify you guys of a major development in the story's growth.

To my girlfriend, Ashley. Without your encouragement and constant questions and curiosity, this story might never have been finished. You shaped and nurtured this story more than I could ever explain.

To my best friend, Ricky Martin (not to be confused with the famous singer). It has been awhile since I've had someone like you stick around for as long as you've had. Though distance may separate us, you will always be my best buddy. Even if you are incredibly annoying and infuriating at times.

And finally, to you, the readers, who took a chance on a brand new urban fantasy story. Without you, small indie authors such as myself would never have a chance to grow.

Thank you for reading *Fallen Son*. If you can, please leave a review. Books like this thrive off word of mouth and it only takes a sentence or two to help this book grow.

Scan the QR code below to find links to all my social media pages so you can stay updated on future projects!

Also consider signing up for my newsletter to receive a FREE exclusive ebook. *Gorgon's Blood* is a prequel story following Bishop Leight a hundred years before the main series.

If you enjoyed *Fallen Son*, consider checking out other books by the author!

<u>Chronicles of Leight Series</u>
Fallen Son (Book 1)
Fang Wars (Book 2)
Gorgon's Blood (Book 0.1)
Dreambound Fae (Book 3) *Coming Soon!*

<u>Tales of Leight Novellas Series</u>
Wizard Rising (Book 1)

Reading Order

Gorgon's Blood (Chronicles of Leight Book 0.1)

Fallen Son (Chronicles of Leight Book 1)

Fang Wars (Chronicles of Leight Book 2)

Wizard Rising (Tales of Leight Novellas Book 1)

Dreambound Fae (Chronicles of Leight Book 3) *Coming Soon!*